Diana Petre was born in 1912. She has written two novels, *Portrait of Mellie* (Bodley Head 1952) and *The Cruel Month* (Collins 1955). She went to four schools and the Royal Academy of Dramatic Art. When young she persistently refused to read books. In 1932 she married Louis Wilkinson who wrote novels under the name of Louis Marlow. She then started both reading and writing. She lives in London.

ALSO BY DIANA PETRE

Portrait of Mellie
The Cruel Month

The Secret Orchard of
Roger Ackerley

DIANA PETRE

PHŒNIX

A PHOENIX PAPERBACK

First Published in Great Britain by Hamish Hamilton Ltd
in 1975

Copyright © 1975 by Diana Petre

This paperback edition published in 1993 by
Orion Books Ltd, Orion House, 5 Upper St Martin's Lane,
London WC2H 9EA

ISBN 1 85799 016 1

Printed and bound in Great Britain by
The Guernsey Press Co. Ltd, Guernsey, Channel Islands.
British Library Cataloguing in Publication Data is available.

Illustrations

Foreword

AFTER THE death of my half-brother, J. R. Ackerley, his autobiography *My Father and Myself* was published in 1968. In it he tells of a letter which his father had left to be opened 'Only in the case of my death'. After a discussion of money matters this letter goes on: 'Now for the "secret orchard" part of my story. For many years I had a mistress and she presented me with twin girls ten years ago and another girl eight years ago . . .' The letter is dated 21 October, 1920.

This is the story of that 'secret orchard'. For many years I was obsessed by the mystery surrounding my mother. She hugged her secrets to her as though to have given them up would have threatened her life, and some of them she has taken with her to the grave. But in spite of the gaps it seemed to me that here there was still a vivid story to be told, the story of Joe Ackerley's father and my mother, and of us, their three daughters.

There are still people, especially of my own generation, who look on illegitimacy as shameful. I should be sorry to cause pain or embarrassment to anybody, and for this reason I have used fictitious names where I felt a degree of anonymity would be welcomed. It may be thought that I should have given the same protection to my mother, but I do not believe she would have wanted it. I could not have written this book in her lifetime, but now, if it were possible for her to know of it, I think she would be glad that her difficulties should at last be understood and made known. She was brought up in an age of intrigue and sexual secrecy and she never questioned the mores of her time. Her life was not a happy one; indeed, it was often almost too much for her, and the story I have tried to tell is a rather upsetting one. I have done my best to expose her secrets in the belief that her ineradicable shame was mistaken;

on the contrary, I see her courage and loyalty as matters for pride, and her long struggle with her own difficult nature as a story that deserves better than the modest oblivion with which she did all in her power to stifle it.

Chapter One

'IT WAS Uncle who was your father,' she said.

1 January 1930. We were in Vienna, just the two of us. We had arrived at midnight the night before, or rather, today. This was the eighteenth New Year's Day of my life. I was still seventeen and I was still rather desperately awaiting the start of a year in which my world as I knew it should be utterly changed.

My room was adjoining hers, and she'd called to me to say that she'd just rung down for our breakfast.

She was sitting up when I went in, looking quite at home in the strange hotel setting. She was always happier in bed than anywhere else, and a background of pillows suited her. She was the Kay Francis type, black and white. This morning she was wearing an apricot-coloured *crêpe-de-chine* nightdress with tiny pin tucks all over the top and creamy lace at the shoulders, and her nearly black hair was framed in the white square pillows.

A boy brought in the breakfast almost at once. There was China tea and croissants and some top-knotted rolls. She poured the tea.

The moment I had woken that morning I had gone over to the window—I was standing there when she called to me—and looked down at the first real snow I had ever seen. It was rich and thick like white fur, and the sunlight was unlike any sunlight I had seen before. The people in the street were different, too. You could see at once that no one down there had their head half screwed into their shoulders as they did in London against the cold. Here, heads, fur hatted, were up. I wanted to be out there, mixed up in it all, at once. I stood by the side of her bed looking at her.

'I want to go out,' I said.

'You don't want to go for a minute.' She patted the side of the bed. 'Just sit down here for a minute. It won't take long. And you want some breakfast.'

This was the first trip we had ever taken together—it was only the second time I had been out of England—and I had been terrified that she would be absolutely helpless as she was at home, and that I would be expected not only to look after her when she got ill—as of of course she would—but would also have to cope with our passports and tickets, getting out at the right station and finding our hotel. I knew I couldn't do these things.

But it hadn't turned out like that. I hadn't understood that she knew all about travelling. She, who was not inclined to enjoy things, was actually enjoying the finding and tipping of porters, the distribution of our luggage and the whole business of presenting the right tickets at the right moment. It was the competitive side of travelling which attracted her and which she clearly saw as a challenge entirely within her capacity. She rarely looked out of the window.

In no time at all after we got into the first-class, two-berth wagon-lits in Paris she had somehow turned it into our carriage and settled us down comfortably for the four-day journey across France and Germany and into Austria.

And she had been kind. I couldn't sleep in my top berth with the ceiling just above my face, and the shrieks of the express trains as they passed us in the dark. Every time this happened I thought my heart had burst into bits. Lately there had been any number of Continental train derailments; I could picture them only too easily, the train running straight on instead of rounding a corner. All through the night I knew that this was going to happen to us.

She had given me eau-de-Cologne to splash on my face, and when I couldn't stay up there any longer and climbed down and sat hunched and wretched on the floor, she wrapped me round with a blanket and laughed at me.

'You wouldn't have been much help in the war,' she said, teasing.

She was quite unlike her London self. She seemed to have no nerves at all.

This morning as I came through the door I had seen at once that she was still this new person. I went over to the side of her bed and stood there, mulish.

'But I want to go out now.'

'No, you don't,' she said, 'I've got something to tell you.'

I knew that nothing she would say would be of the smallest interest to me, and my face, without doubt, reflected my thoughts. Nevertheless, I grudgingly sat down. I said nothing.

She was looking at the sheet and making unnecessary movements over it with her long fingers. She was embarrassed.

I had saucer eyes and was often accused of staring. She was always saying, 'Someone stop that child staring at me!' I stared at her now and saw that she wasn't acting. I thought she was never going to begin.

'You must have sometimes wondered about your father,' she said.

I went on staring. We had been told ages ago, long before she came into our lives, that our father was dead; he was a tea planter in Ceylon and he had died there. He had seen the twins once as babies, when they were asleep, the legend went, but he had never seen me. When we were told this my first thought was: how dreadful for him never to have seen me, and after that I never gave him another thought. I never even asked his name, which was curious since I was an inquisitive child.

She was still looking down at the sheet, not seeing it, and I knew that she couldn't trust herself to look up. When she managed to speak she said it:

'It was Uncle who was your father.'

I felt as though a great ball of joy had been thrown at me, hitting me smack in the face. Every smallest aspect of my life clicked, upon the instant, into place. It was as though I had just this minute been born, but this time I was born complete, no longer the freakish issue of one parent. A voice seemed to be shouting at me: She's not your only parent after all!

Although I was seventeen I was still excessively childish. Being the youngest, and small, I had always been protected by the giant twins who treated me like some favourite toy, and my willing response to this rôle and the extraordinary loneliness of our lives had left me emotionally marooned. Just the same, if I had ever stopped to think about it—and I never did—even I would have known that everybody had a mother and a father. Only our case had always been different.

3

For the first ten years of my life—twelve for the twins—we'd had an unseen mother to whom we sometimes wrote letters, and a dead father who had never achieved any real substance in our minds and, for my part, having quitted the world without ever having laid eyes on me, had placed himself beyond the scope of my self-absorbed imagination. Occasionally, and guardedly, we were given news of our sole parent: first, she was away at the war, and later, when the war was over, she was too ill to return to us.

Then everything had dramatically changed. This unseen mother had incredibly turned into a flesh and blood person who had actually come to live with us—she had been with us now for seven years —and from that moment the worrying departments of my mind had been filled. There simply wasn't room for speculation about another parent.

We gave each other a long testing look. She had looked up and seen my face.

'Are you pleased?' she said.

'Yes.'

I got up and went over to the window because I couldn't tell her that the aspect of my joy which over-rode all others was the realization that the blood pumping through my veins and the various facets of my personality had not been transmitted to me solely by herself. I said carefully:

'Do the twins know?'

'Well, they seem to, but I asked them not to tell you. I wanted to tell you myself. Someone at the school seems to have found out and taken it upon themselves to tell them.' She gave a little poke at the pillows. 'Why people can't mind their own business I don't know!'

We had been to a number of schools in the last six years but, in spite of the changes, each one became and remained for her 'the school'. She had never set foot in any of them.

'Why didn't you tell me this before?'

'Oh, he wouldn't let me!' she cried at once. 'I begged and begged him. When he was dying and you were there it was such an opportunity. I wanted you to know before he was gone but he said, "Wait until afterwards." I think he was afraid it might spoil your feeling for him.'

4

My antipathy towards her was so unyielding at this time that a moment or two passed before I took in the full significance of what she had tried to do for me. Also, somewhere in the back of my mind I registered more clearly what she had just said about wanting to tell me herself. Since I believed her to be incapable of an act of generosity on my behalf these thoughts came as quite a shock. Now I was really staring. I saw that her whole face had softened.

'He was so devoted to you three, you know,' she murmured.

Uncle.

He had died only a few weeks ago at the Queen's Hotel in Southsea. She and I had been there, but only she had been with him at the moment of his death. We children had always known that he wasn't a real uncle. Ever since I could remember—when she was still unknown to us—he would descend upon us, out of the blue, two or three times a year. He was a fairy-tale person, a Father Christmas, a bringer of gifts, a giver of treats. We adored him.

He was the kindest man in the world, a man without faults. In seventeen years he had never been cross with me. I had never questioned this before, but now all I could see was the overwhelming sadness of it. I suddenly realized that I had never had a real relationship with him, nor he with me. And now it was too late. We had never met as father and daughter. We had never looked into each other's eyes *knowing*, and now we never would.

He had wanted it otherwise.

This last realization was so terrible that I closed my mind down on it. I went over to the bed and sat down and drank some tea. I never took my eyes off her, but now she no longer seemed to mind.

After she came to live with us he had taken to calling in almost every evening for a drink on his way home from the office. We had taken for granted that it was us, we children, whom he came to see, and not especially her. How could it be otherwise? They never talked over our heads or had asides, and they never held each other on greeting or parting, or even looked at each other as I imagined lovers to do. Never. From the moment of his arrival we totally monopolized him, and then, after a while of this, she would say:

'Uncle's tired now. Go into the next room all of you, and let him have his drink in peace. But mind you come back to say goodbye.'

When we went back they would be sitting just as we had left

them, and we knew she had been talking business with him. This meant explaining why she needed more money for us. She was a bad manager but she never asked for money for herself.

All this came to me as I looked at her and, suddenly, I could see quite distinctly that he had loved her much, much more than he had loved us. I felt no jealousy or resentment; I was simply stunned.

I stayed with her until I could see that she no longer needed me. She looked extraordinarily relaxed, almost happy, now that she had told me.

I went back into my room and dressed, my mind suspended. When I stood at the door again ready to go out, it suddenly came to me that everything about her, too, was different from what I had supposed. For her, too, as well as for me, it was not Uncle, the old family friend, who had recently died: it was her lover, the father of her children, her protector and supporter, her dearest and only friend, the one who knew all the secrets.

It was too much to take in all at once. I remember thinking: How can she lie there looking so serene when he's dead and he wasn't Uncle after all? And why are we staying in this rich hotel? Who's going to pay for it? Who's going to pay for everything from now on?

I said, 'I won't be long.'

She gave a little wave. 'Enjoy yourself!'

I walked about the city for a long while that morning, but I didn't see it. My eyes were steadfastly fixed upon myself. This New Year's Day had, indeed, totally changed my world. It would never be the same again. I had been handed a priceless gem, and although, in a way, this gem had been snatched, instantly and forever from my grasp, I knew that I had been enriched beyond my wildest dreams.

Although my head was reeling, I felt as though only now had I properly joined the human race. Absolutely nothing was as I had thought it was, and none of it could ever revert and be as it had been before.

This was exactly the sort of New Year's Day I had been craving ever since I could remember: an unimaginable shake-up. Now, at last, it had come.

Chapter Two

HER NAME was Muriel Haidée Perry and she was born on 5 March, 1890, or so I believed when I went to Somerset House to look up the registration of her birth. It wasn't there.

What I was really looking for—this was after she was dead and I had started to write about her—were the names of her parents. This was something that I had never been able to get her to tell me.

Soon after she came to live with us I asked her something or other about her mother and father—my grandparents—and she shut up like a sprung trap. I pricked my ears and asked more questions. She started to cry.

That was how it had all begun. As soon as I started to question her she was padlocked; her face changed at once—it became wooden, implacable—and in two seconds she was in tears.

Perhaps if she had been an ordinary sort of mother, with us from the beginning, I would not have wanted to collaborate with her youth, to know what she had been doing when she was my own age and what her thoughts were then; what her parents were like, and why, for heaven's sake, was she unable to remember anything at all that had happened to her before the war, which had started two years after I was born.

For the moment it is enough to know that everything about her origin and youth had been so abhorrent to her that she had, quite simply, rubbed it out. She wouldn't have it: it hadn't been.

It was always her way to act upon instinct; the more she felt remorse at something the more important it became to her to lock this something up in one of the dungeons in her memory and throw away the key. She was a liar on the most profound level; without the least regard for logic or the truth she would strike an attitude of mind-splintering stubbornness and hang on to it with all the

7

strength of her forceful nature. As a solution, of course, this couldn't and didn't work, but she clung to it just the same.

Anyone could tell she was full of secrets. You only had to look at her to feel the mysteriousness of her. She was a fascinator: one of those creatures who seem to come from nowhere and to be going nowhere, but who permeate the mind as a serum gets into the bloodstream.

In appearance she was tall—just over five foot ten—with masses of dark hair like Irish hair, and dark eyes, not large and of no especial colour, but wonderfully expressive. Her skin was dramatically white, and she had long arms and hands and straight legs, and a high un-English waist. Her voice was rather low and velvety. She was seldom angry, her nature was too melancholy for that, and even when she was angry she never really shouted.

We had gone to Vienna because the tickets were already paid for. They were the tickets which should have taken herself and Uncle to a spa to drink the waters. This was something they did once a year, usually at Bad Gastein in Austria, when we were back at school and she was free to go away. But this year Uncle had died, leaving the tickets in his wallet.

She hadn't cashed them in. She had kept them by her throughout the whole of the next school term, some weeks of which she had spent in a nursing home.

And she had another reason for keeping the tickets. She wanted to see Hanzi, to pour out her troubles, the loneliness and the fear of the future. Hanzi was a sophisticated little Viennese lady, one of the few people who knew the true situation. Hanzi had first met Muriel and Uncle together some years before when they were all at Bad Gastein, and subsequently Muriel often tried to coincide their yearly health trips. Hanzi was a woman of the world; she would have advice to offer. And finally, the tickets stood for escape. After Vienna would be the time to knuckle down and form a plan. Not before.

I don't remember ever hearing about Hanzi's husband, but she had a large sandy-haired daughter who wore an interesting brassiére with two holes in the cups through which her naked nipples thrust. I saw them one day in the changing room of an ice rink to which she had taken me. She peeled off a sweater and there they were,

8

rosy pink and deeply enviable. I was so thin at that time that no matter how much I jumped about it failed to cause the faintest wobble.

Muriel spent most of the time in Vienna in bed in the hotel, and Hanzi came to sit with her. They drank brandy together. Hanzi would arrive with her daughter, and then this girl and I would be told to go out and to stay out for a certain time. The daughter was rather older than me and I think she resented being fobbed off in this way. Sometimes we walked about the city and sometimes we went to the ice rink, but whatever we did we each failed to stimulate the other. In the evenings I went to the opera alone and sat in the gallery throbbing with nerves and excitement.

One day when I got back to the hotel Muriel was sitting up in bed brushing her hair. She had made up her face and seemed brighter.

'Hanzi says there's no earthly reason why I shouldn't marry again,' she said. 'On the Continent men prefer women of a certain age. Hanzi says I should leave England altogether. She says I'd have a much better chance living abroad. It could be quite nice living abroad . . . don't you think?'

She said this last almost pleading, halfway recalled from the fantasy. Marry again? It was this slippery escape from reality which always worked on me like a cold douche. I felt my practical mind jumping in all directions.

'Living where abroad?'

'Oh, I don't know, does it matter? Anywhere, really . . .'

We stared blankly at each other. I had punctured the dream.

Uncle had gone to the Queen's Hotel in Southsea straight from a nursing home in Richmond. He'd had cancer of the tongue, and for several weeks he'd been treated with radium needles. He was said to be cured. At Southsea it was hoped that the sea air would set him up again, and when the summer holidays were over and she was free again they would set off together for Austria.

It is necessary at this point to explain how matters stood at that time in our home. In 1927, when I was fifteen, Uncle had installed us all in a house in Castelnau, Barnes. He had bought it in Muriel's name.

She had taken great trouble with it and done it up charmingly. In the drawing-room, which was a clear apple green and gold, she had had a large bow-window built out over the garden, and there were always flowers there in a deep porcelain bowl. She loved porcelain and had picked up some pretty pieces here and there which gave her great pleasure. It was a room of some elegance and it was large enough not to be dwarfed by a grand piano. She had a flair for making a room attractive; the overall effect was not original, but it had a certain delicacy, and she had a pleasant sense of colour. The bedrooms were surprisingly dull; it was in the drawing-room and the dining-room that she had taken the most trouble.

Altogether, it was a pleasant house set back from the road with a little drive. She must have had high hopes when Uncle bought it for her. Now, at last, everything would be different, everything would start to go right. It would be a new beginning for us all. She had not been happy in the house in which she had joined us in 1922, but that was now in the past and could be forgotten. The new house should be the rightful beginning. And it was directly on the route which Uncle took every day from his office in Bow Street to his home in Richmond. He made this journey in the same car with the same driver, Morland, every working day of his life. Nothing could be simpler for him than to make a call at our house on his way home in the evenings.

But in all these calculations for a new and better life—a life that should redeem in full the disappointments which had tumbled upon her like an avalanche since the day she had made the decision to take up her rôle as our mother—in all her calculations for the real beginning she had left out something. There was a flaw to these plans, and at that time this flaw was still known only to herself.

She had become a secret drinker.

We had hardly ever seen her have a drink, and never two. When Uncle came she gave him a whisky and soda and seldom had one herself. Occasionally, when she was going out—this in itself was a rarity—she would say, 'I'd better have a little drink to pick me up. I don't want it, but it'll do me good . . .' And she would make a face as she took the first sip as though it were a vile-tasting medicine. But we knew—it had come to us gradually but very distinctly—that she was two people instead of one. And we knew, after the first few months in the new house, that one of these people was in danger of disappearing altogether.

When she was all right she was a charming, *soignée*, lazy and loving woman who stayed in bed until lunchtime and sent us on errands about the house, gently laughing at us in a flirty sort of way. When she was in this mood her favourite pastime was changing the furniture around. Like everything else, she did this upon impulse.

'I'm going to change my room round today,' she would suddenly say, 'I'm sick of looking straight ahead. We'll start with the chest of drawers. I think I'll have it over there . . . If two of you take one side and one the other . . . Oh, what a fuss you make . . . None of my workers in the war made such heavy weather about shifting a little furniture. You should have seen some of the things we did . . . We'd go into a barn—just a rough old barn—and in no time we'd have got it nice and comfortable for the men to sleep in . . . you always see to your men first . . . Go on, all of you . . . push . . . anyone would think you were made of jelly. I don't know what the youth of today's coming to. You'd never have won the war!'

These were the happier days. Like a general she directed operations and was pleased with results.

On the other days, when she was the other person, we hardly saw her in the daytime. Her bedroom door would be shut and she would stay, silently, behind it. We had a daily woman called Mrs. Kemp with an enormous stomach like permanent pregnancy who did the cleaning and most of the cooking. On those days Mrs. Kemp brought us word that Madam was ill and would not be coming downstairs. We had come to know that ill didn't mean 'flu or anything needing a doctor.

It was at night that she would emerge. At night she would wander about the house from room to room, never turning on the lights, like a lost soul, with tears, which she never raised a hand to wipe away, running perpetually down her face. She would be in a nightdress, an open dressing-gown, and no slippers, but on her feet there was always a pair of silk stockings, half on and half off, as though on each foot she had started to put a stocking, toe first, the foot folded inside, and then, having drawn the stocking up just beyond the ankle—stopped, leaving the thigh part still in front of the foot. As she shuffled up and down the unlit stairs and in and out of the rooms, the stocking ends trailed upon the floor behind her. She never tripped.

Nor did she stagger in the way that most drunk people do—if she had we might have understood sooner what was going on—and whether her speech was slurred or not I never knew because when she was like this she never spoke. If you said something she seemed not to hear it. She was like some poor demented sleep walker, or a ghost or Lady Macbeth. She was always weeping; her face was never dry.

These night prowls had started soon after we moved into the house in Castelnau. With all her secrets still hugged to herself we had no idea why she was so unhappy. We were unhappy too, in the ruthless, uncomprehending, leaden way of children. The move itself had left her in a state of collapse. The smallest extra pressure, domestic or emotional, always knocked her right over, and yet this was the woman with the magnificent war record. It was very confusing.

We knew that she had been immensely brave and selfless in the war. She had come back from abroad with any number of medals and citations for bravery. We knew this. She sometimes talked to us about her war experiences, and then her face and her voice changed and she was lost in a passion of nostalgia for the life that was now gone. We knew, without being told, that this was the period of her greatest happiness and fulfilment; she would have given anything to be back in the war again.

It was when we contrasted this war heroine with our mother that confusion set in. The woman of endless resources—even of some humour—compassion and tirelessness was simply not to be seen. Everything was too much for our mother, molehills were mountains, and the notion of her actually enjoying our company never entered anyone's head. It was as though she lived alone, isolated, inside a bottle, and we three lived collectively inside another bottle. There was no means of communication.

Women with an intuitive understanding of the needs of men are seldom any good with children. Muriel was as deeply possessive and maternal as any primitive in the jungle, but faced with three young *people* and their urgent needs she was lost. She had no idea what to do with us, the very sight of us was enough to make her ill with apprehension. She felt herself abandoned without knowing why, and this, together with all her secret bogies, had driven her to despair.

My bedroom at Castelnau was beside hers with a communicating door; the twins slept on the other side of the landing. One night I was fast asleep and woke, instantly and totally, as though from an electric shock, to find her face no more than six inches from my own. The communicating door was open and the light from her room shafted into mine. She was gazing down into my face as though she had never seen me. She looked like a mad woman. Wrapped in the night silence, neither of us spoke. I'd stopped breathing. It seemed that she went on staring like that for ever, and then, without a word, still bent over, witch-like, she padded from the room in her grotesquely stockinged feet.

This was not the only night visit she made into my room. I awoke in the same way on other occasions to find her face nearly touching my own. Neither of us ever spoke, and I never knew what it was that prompted this demented scrutiny of my sleeping face. She never did it to the twins.

We had been living like this for some time when she made a rare visit to the hairdresser one afternoon and left us alone in the house. As soon as she was gone the younger twin, Stella, the brave and vivid one, said:

'I think I know what it is. She drinks. I'm sure of it. She can't be back for hours now so this is our chance. We're going to search the house.'

We were in the drawing-room when she made this statement and she didn't wait for an answer. She simply left the room and walked purposefully up the stairs and into Muriel's bedroom. Helen, the other twin, followed and I followed her.

'We'll start with the wardrobe,' Stella said.

She opened the doors and we all stood back and stared. The floor of the cupboard was crammed with empty gin bottles, some upright, some fallen over in heaps, the skirts of the long evening dresses tangled up in the mess.

'I told you so,' said Stella, 'I knew it. Now for the drawers.'

It was the same story. Pushed to the back and concealed among the sweet smelling silks there were empties in every drawer.

At first we didn't touch them. One of us stood on a chair to reach the top of the wardrobe, and of course there were bottles up there; there were more in the bedside commode, and the greatest concentration of all was under the skirts of the bed. At last, with every drawer and door pulled wide, we stood silently grouped together in the middle of the room. There was a ringing noise in my ears. I think we all knew that what lay exposed around us like an accusation was the measure of her loneliness. Then Stella broke the silence.

'We'll get all this lot cleared out,' she said briskly, 'and then we'll go down to the dining-room. There's some wine in the cupboard. We're going to empty it all in the sink and put the bottles in the dustbin, and I'm going to tell Uncle. He mustn't send her any more. The next time he comes you two must keep her away somewhere to give me time to speak to him alone. When he knows about this he won't allow any more drink to come into the house.'

The force of Stella's resolution took my breath away. She had always been fearless. A little earlier arrangements had been made for the twins to go to a finishing school in Paris ('They're such hooligans'). From the start Stella had said that nothing would persuade her to go. She simply wouldn't go, she said. Nevertheless, clothes had been bought for both of them and the fees paid for the first term. At Victoria Station Stella refused to get on to the train. Helen, already in it, went to Paris alone. I had been dumbfounded by this display of willpower. Stella had a will that was inexorable, and every time I saw it demonstrated I was overcome with admiration. Whenever I said I wouldn't do something I found myself doing it within the hour.

On that dreadful afternoon of discovery I knew that we were trying to recover our mother, that for some reason she was unable to save herself, but all I could truly feel was terror at the thought of her return. Might it not be literally unbearable to have so terrible a secret laid bare—and by your own children?

In the dining-room there was wine and brandy and liqueurs. The twins pulled corks, emptied bottles down the sink in the kitchen, and threw the empties into the dustbin. I did nothing but follow them from place to place. I couldn't go away and leave them to it, and I couldn't take part in this plunder; nor did they expect me to. They knew I was a coward, always fearful of trouble, so much so that lately they had sometimes excluded me from plots. 'She'll only tell if someone insists.'

When the deed was finally done there was not a drop of drink in the house.

Her return is sponged from my mind; nor do I remember how long we waited for it. I think she shut herself up in her room and simply telephoned from there for fresh supplies, but I'm guessing. Nor do I remember how and where Stella's private talk with Uncle took place. But it did take place. When we asked her what he'd said she replied that he'd looked startled, almost stunned, and said nothing at all. But he acted. The next morning several cases of wines and spirits were delivered to the house. All was as before.

We'd been living in Castelnau for less than two years when the twins ran away. They were eighteen and, being illegitimate, had now attained their majority. I didn't know then that illegitimate children came of age at eighteen, and nor did Muriel, but she found it out just as the twins had. She couldn't tell me about this without telling me more, so she simply said that 'sometimes' children of eighteen could not be recovered by law.

We both knew they would never come back.

We each received this blow in our different ways. I felt as though my limbs had been cut off, and Muriel could no longer bear to sleep alone at night, so I pulled my mattress into her room and slept on the floor at her side.

Without the twins in the house the tension was greatly reduced and Muriel and I lived side by side with our separate thoughts. Now, more than ever, there was nothing to do all day long.

At the end of the holidays, instead of going back to my old school I was sent to a new one in Essex, my sixth change, and Muriel was left alone in the house. Inevitably she started to drink heavily and after a while she went into a nursing home.

It was at the end of my second term at the new school, in late June, that Uncle came to the end of his treatment in the nursing home in Richmond and went to Southsea. He went alone, but he didn't pick up in the way that they had hoped for, and Muriel wrote to tell me she was going down to keep him company.

When the term broke up in mid-July they were both still there. She wrote again to say that I was to join them.

This was a big relief. I'd been dreading the long summer holiday in the house in Castelnau without my sisters. I'd always been hopeless at amusing myself, and although I seldom wanted to do whatever the twins were doing—they both had a passion, unshared by me, for out-of-doors—I tagged along rather than be left alone. I never read. Somehow I couldn't bring myself to do this. I meant to start reading one day, but in the meanwhile nothing would persuade me that in books I should find an escape from the paralysing boredom in which I seemed to be locked. It was a vicious circle and I couldn't get out of it.

So I was glad to be going to Southsea. It must be better than Castelnau, I told myself. Just the same, I was nervous.

I loved Uncle dearly, but I was in awe of him. For such a sweet man he was remarkably unapproachable. He was big and slow moving and majestic and old. And now he was ill as well. I had never grown used to the terrible spasms of pain which wracked him at increasingly short intervals as the years went by. It was his neuritis, Muriel said, and the pain stemmed from the little finger of his left hand, causing him to judder for a second or two as it shot through him. I'd always been terrified that one of these convulsions would seize him while I was in his arms at greeting or parting. It had never happened yet, but it might.

I'd already stayed in a hotel with them once when I was younger. That time, too, was in the summer holidays when the twins were away staying with school friends. Instead of going to Bad Gastein that year she and Uncle had gone to Harrogate because they had to take me with them, although at the time this didn't occur to me.

We'd stayed at the Majestic Hotel. It was still afternoon when we arrived and Muriel said she was tired after the journey and was going to rest. She told me to go out for a walk and explore the town and not to disturb her until dinnertime.

When I went along to join her at the arranged time she was just coming out of her room and about to close the door behind her when Uncle emerged from his room which was the next one along. He took the key from her and locked first her door and then his own and then they both turned to greet me.

I'd never before seen either of them in evening dress, although I often fingered her clothes in the wardrobe at home. This dress was new and, as Uncle soon declared, mighty swish: it was long and black and *décolleté*—all her dresses were cut very low in front—with the slenderest of straps over the shoulders, and the back in a low V exposing a lot of her straight spine. We knew she was proud of her back; it had been much admired, she'd told us, a straight back being a rarity. Tonight she looked radiant. And so did Uncle. He was very handsome, with a ruddy complexion and silver-white hair, and he was holding himself within his well-cut clothes—at any rate in the hotel corridor—like the guardsman he'd once been.

I had no clothes for evening. This was a considered policy on her part and I don't think she meant to be unkind. I was too young for it to matter, she said, but I think the real reason was that having missed our infancy and childhood she now wanted to stop the clock and keep us childish for as long as possible. 'Don't you ever dare grow up!' she would sometimes fondly say. And there was another reason. We were all rather pretty children, and this alarmed her. She held the lowest possible view of human nature—except for Uncle who was on a pinnacle by himself—and she meant to keep us in ignorance of the wicked ways of the world for as long as possible. 'Children should keep their illusions,' was a favourite phrase, and she meant to see to it that we kept ours. It therefore followed that any kind of dressing-up would make us more conspicuous and could only end badly. We were, in any case, not easy to pass over. The twins were six foot tall by the time they were thirteen, and so alike that no one could tell them apart—always a cause for comment—while I was comparatively tiny and so bone thin as to seem permanently convalescent. All in all 'clothes' were a bad idea.

So now, beside these glorious creatures, rested, bathed and scented, in this big de-luxe hotel, I, in my ugly day dress, felt a stone inside me as we went down the stairs to dinner. I was outside the magic circle. But there was worse to come.

It was not until we were seated at our table with, it seemed, every waiter in the room in attendance upon us—Uncle used to tip in advance as well as afterwards—that Muriel raised an arm to shake out her napkin and I saw, horror of horrors, that she hadn't shaved her armpits. Had she forgotten? Whatever the reason for this unbelievable lapse, my rigid English sensibilities were outraged. I might have recovered from the humiliation of my shabby appearance, but this was too much. I sulked all the way through dinner.

She, on the other hand, was in the best of spirits—her afternoon rest had done her good. I had never seen her so lively. She kept gesticulating with her long white arms in a way that I knew she never did at home where it wouldn't have mattered. They drank champagne and I wondered why they were so festive and happy.

Later, in her room, she asked me what was the matter.

'Don't you like it here?' she said. 'This is the best hotel in Harrogate. You might show a little gratitude to Uncle for bringing you. You hardly spoke a word at dinner.'

I glared at her. 'You haven't shaved your armpits,' I said.

She laughed. 'Oh, you silly child. Don't you like it? On the Continent women never do.'

'We're not on the Continent.'

'No,' she said mildly, 'we're not. But we might be . . .'

I have sometimes wondered what would have been my feelings if she had told me then and there that Uncle was her lover and that she hadn't shaved her armpits because he preferred her with them unshaved.

At Southsea I found that she and I were staying at the Royal Pier Hotel and not with Uncle at the Queen's. She said the Pier was cheaper and I accepted this as a sensible explanation. It was more or less round the corner from the Queen's.

In no time I felt as though I had been living there for months. It was better than Castelnau, but not much. I missed my sisters. It was always they who decided what we should do and I was lost without them. I was their private clown, and now I had no audience. I couldn't think what to do with myself.

There were two focal points to our days, lunch and dinner, which we ate in the restaurant at the Queen's with Uncle. His mornings were taken up with visits from the barber, a masseur and the local doctor, and sometimes a specialist came down from London for a check-up. In the afternoons he rested.

This daily routine was unchanged except that sometimes, suddenly, in a flurry, Muriel would say that we wouldn't be joining Uncle today because his son was coming down, or his son and daughter were coming down. On those days we stayed away.

I knew quite a lot about Joe and Nancy. Once, thrillingly, we had run into them by mistake at Frascati's in Oxford Street. This was before Muriel had come back into our lives. Our housekeeper whom we called Auntie—pronounced Antie, she was a Scot—had taken us into London one morning to Frascati's to meet Uncle for lunch. He was already there when we arrived and we were all making our way up the central aisle to our table when a young man and woman of spectacular good looks bore down upon us from the opposite end of the room. They had finished their lunch and were leaving. At the sight of them Antie and Uncle suddenly stopped. We stopped as well. The atmosphere had become electric. The golden couple approaching us were talking together, smiling, sharing some joke. It was only at the last moment, at the point of collision, that they found themselves face to face with their father and his party. What a surprise!

Introductions were made, and from that moment Joe became my idol. He had a charming voice that seemed to come through a filter of gauze, and a mocking smile, and he was wonderfully graceful in his movements. I noticed that he really looked at each of us in turn instead of passing over us like a paint brush. Nancy was brilliantly pretty and smart, but I barely saw her. It was Joe who enslaved me.

They didn't stay. It was the briefest of meetings, over in minutes, and this handsome couple continued their progress between the tables.

Eventually, seated at our own, behind menus, it was a little while before normal breathing was regained, although, I fancy, Uncle had recovered at once. But we took our cue from Antie, and we could see that she was rattled. Something forbidden had just happened. We knew we were not allowed to meet Joe and Nancy but I, for one, had never questioned why this should be.

At Southsea it was the same. If Joe and Nancy were coming down it followed that Muriel and I would stay away. Naturally. It was part of the familiar pattern. But Muriel couldn't altogether stop herself from talking about them. It appeared that Joe had a friend, a deep-sea diver called Albert, who lived in or near to Southsea. Joe would be coming to see his friend as well as his father.

'He wouldn't make the effort otherwise,' she said bitterly.

She was jealous of Joe. She knew that his father loved him and was proud to have a son who was an artist, even though he, his father, didn't understand his son's work. Joe was a writer and an intellectual. He was literary editor of *The Listener* and he had an office at the B.B.C. Muriel thought it rubbish that his father should regard him as intellectually superior to himself and indulge him in the matter of his working-class friends. She told me that he'd once taken a policeman home to dinner at Richmond and now there was this deep-sea diver. Joe was selfish. He never considered his father's feelings in the way that his father considered his.

'He's just a fancy boy,' she said.

In a woolly sort of way I knew that Joe was a homosexual although she had never actually used the word. It would have made little difference if she had. Homosexuality meant two men instead of a man and a woman, but I had no idea what any of them, men with men or a man with a woman, did. Simply, it meant that Joe was even further removed from me than he might otherwise have been, thus greatly adding to his desirability. He was now in his early thirties and he was still my idol. Nancy was less interesting to me. It seemed she was spoilt and difficult. She had married two years before and had a son, Uncle's first grandchild, and for some reason she and the child had gone back to live in the family home in Richmond. The husband, who was American, had also gone back to his home. Uncle's wife was seldom mentioned and never by name; she was simply Uncle's wife, an over-timid lady who never went out and had crises in her room. She, certainly, wouldn't be coming to Southsea to see him.

At the beginning I had felt sympathy with Uncle's wife because I, too, was afraid. There had never been anyone ill in my life. Would he look different now, and might he fall down or do something else dreadful in front of us?

I need not have worried. He didn't seem so very ill; he was heavier, slower, more stooped, a little more remote, perhaps, but the charm and the manners and the kindness were unchanged.

Since the move into the Castelnau house we'd seen him far more frequently than ever before. As I've said, he often called in on his way home from the office, drank a weak whisky and soda, floating a large white capsule in it to soften the outside—this was to ease his neuritis—and about half an hour later Morland drove him on to Richmond. He never stayed long, and in this way there had never been time or opportunity for talk.

In Southsea, I thought, it would be different, and it was this that made me nervous. To be left absolutely alone with him, even for five minutes, was unimaginable. What would happen? In a simple, visual way, children gave him pleasure, he often said so. He liked animals too, in much the same way. But he didn't like anyone to answer back; he didn't much enjoy contrary opinions. You somehow felt this without being told. He was not a man with whom people easily took liberties; there was an air of keep-your-distance about him. Once, ages ago, I'd become over-excited when he hadn't understood me, and I'd cried out shrilly:

'You're a silly old *fool*!'

It was a dreadful moment. He didn't say anything, but the shock of surprise on his face and my own shock at the sound of my own voice coming out with such words was paralysing. Muriel had rounded on me at once.

'Don't you dare talk to Uncle like that!'

I've sometimes wondered what it was that made me shout at him like that. It was a kind of rudeness that was out of character for me. Was I, perhaps, unconsciously trying to break through his protective barrier? And why did he feel the need for this permanent armoury? Was it because, in truth, he was a rather shy man? Whatever the reason, it was inhibiting. And now, at Southsea, there was the further inhibition of his being ill.

All in all, those two daily meals were an ordeal. In the five or six weeks in which they took place—the last weeks of his life—I don't recall a single conversation between him and me. I doubt there ever was one. I was often pert and opinionated, but at that time I'd have cut my tongue out rather than say something uncomfortable. All I remember is the weight of him in his chair at the table—would he ever be able to rise from it?—and his unfailing good manners. And oddly, I can still hear the sound of his voice in my ears, deep and slow and never raised—but it isn't saying anything.

Muriel wasn't drinking at this time and I'd more or less forgotten that she ever had. She didn't change from one person into another any more; she was the same every day, not the best of companions, but unalarming. I don't think she realized at this stage that Uncle was dying. She seemed content enough with our life at the hotel. She enjoyed getting up late and resting in the afternoons, and she never seemed to feel the need of mental activity. It was I who sighed and complained of boredom and spent hours slumped in a chair in her room.

'Why don't you go for a walk?' she would say.

So I mooched about the town, and once I went for a ride on a speedboat. Before I arrived she'd met a couple in the bar who ran a speedboat from the end of the pier. They were friendly and gave me a free trip and told me to come back any time I liked, but I was morbidly shy of seeming to sponge, so I stayed away.

And then, one day, something happened. Another glorious mistake, even better than the one at Frascati's, took place.

Uncle and Muriel and I had been lunching as usual. We came out of the restaurant and up the little staircase into the entrance hall and paused there before separating, Uncle to take his afternoon rest in his room and we to return to the pier.

We were standing like that in the centre of the hall when the street doors went back and, lo and behold, Joe and Nancy, unheralded, were suddenly in front of us, side by side, as though placed in position for a curtain call.

Once again there was controlled confusion. Nancy's eyes were the colour of harebells and she was wearing a navy blue dress with white collar and cuffs, and Joe's silky fair hair was ruffled by the wind. As they stood there you could see they were used to admiring looks.

They had driven down in Joe's open car having decided on coming at the last moment, they said, the weather being so good, and lunched on the way. They were very gay and chattery. How was Dad feeling today? They'd had a splendid drive down, very little traffic, sun all the way. How good it was to smell the sea.

They did all the talking and we stood there. Then Joe left us to take their bags out of the car.

They had brought in with them a heady atmosphere of freedom and sophistication. I wanted to stay with them for ever, but almost at once Muriel said it was time for Uncle to rest. We left before Joe had come back.

It was always easy to pick up Muriel's mood. As we made our way in silence to our own hotel, our minds thrumming from the recent encounter, there was a certain sympathy between us. Never articulate, Muriel was acutely sensitive to atmosphere, and she too had been caught up in the attraction, and had brought away with her, just as I had, the essence of the meeting, so that for once she and I were actually sharing something. I remember feeling this quite distinctly and with pleasure, even though it was she who had dragged me away.

Many years later I learnt that the impact of this second meeting was, in its different way, almost as full of interest to Joe and Nancy as it had been to me. Joe had already run into Muriel at the Queen's before I arrived, so that she was no longer new to him. But he and Nancy had both clean forgotten the twins and me at Frascati's, so that when they made their dramatic entrance at Uncle's hotel and saw, as well as Muriel, a thin, fair-haired girl standing beside their father, they were seeing her as though for the first time. It seems that they were both, upon the instant, struck by the singular resemblance of this girl to their father and to each of themselves, particularly to Nancy. Yet oddly, at this point, neither of them followed this remarkable coincidence through to its logical conclusion.

The following morning Muriel asked me, as a favour to herself, to go for a walk that afternoon and not to come back until four. She didn't offer an explanation and I didn't ask for one.

When I got back she was different. She was mooning about the room, idly trailing her long fingers over things, not seeing them. She wasn't lying down as she usually was, but she wasn't agitated. There was contentment in her wandering, a kind of softness that hadn't been there when I left her. She said that Nancy had been to see her and that they'd spent an agreeable hour in the bedroom talking. When I asked her what they'd talked about she was too dreamy to answer.

It was Nancy who told me many years later. They'd talked about nothing in particular. Nothing direct had been said. But they'd liked each other. It was only when Nancy saw the large photograph of the twins on the bedside table that she knew and felt sure that Muriel knew she knew.

Joe and Nancy had had a brother, Peter, who was killed fighting

23

in the war in 1917. Unlike them Peter was dark; the twins were dark. When Nancy looked at the photograph of the twins, what she saw was her brother Peter, whom she'd loved. The resemblance was unmistakable, as strong as it was between Joe and Nancy and me. In other words, in their family there had been one dark and two fair children, and in ours there were two dark and one fair. It seemed that the dark ones and the fair ones of the two families particularly favoured each other, although between all of Uncle's children there was a family likeness.

After this of course the game was up. Joe and Nancy pooled their findings; we were clearly his children and Muriel was his mistress. They were amazed and amused, but not unduly ruffled. They were both intelligent and generous minded, accustomed to amatory surprises of one sort or another, and they didn't take this one too seriously. After all, it barely fringed—or so they mistakenly believed —upon their own lives. They agreed to keep it from their mother and then, both in their different ways, ceased to dwell upon it.

In the meantime appearances were upheld. Muriel would have told Uncle about Nancy's visit and they would have realized that it no longer mattered who ran into whom. Perhaps, quite simply, Uncle was now too tired to go on juggling. Anyway, the ban on meetings was now lifted. Nancy went back to Richmond and the next time that Joe came down to Southsea Muriel announced that he and his deep-sea diver friend would be joining us all for lunch.

Things were looking up.

She didn't discuss the change in attitude; she simply said that they would be there, and when we got to the hotel there they were, waiting for us. We all went down the stairs and into the restaurant.

Uncle sat at the head of the table and put Joe and Albert on one side and Muriel and me on the other. Joe was beside his father and I was opposite Albert. There was nothing very remarkable about him. He was quiet, though not, I felt on our account; he was a quiet sort of man. I somehow knew that Joe was in love with him although nothing in their behaviour gave the least hint of it, only, I thought, had their relationship been more casual Joe would have taken pains to bring him into the conversation, such as it was. He didn't do this.

It was a sticky lunch; only Joe and Uncle were up to it. They politely chatted rather than talked, but I remember nothing of what was said. I, as always under stress, was struck dumb and Muriel was not much better. She was no longer used to being with strangers, or indeed, to the most modest social occasions. The last six years of her life had been spent exclusively alone with us or alone with Uncle—this last far more often than I then realized—and since she had no outside interests or even read newspapers, let alone books, general conversation was not easy for her. We all separated immediately after lunch.

I was shrivelled with remorse at my own behaviour, and I wandered fretfully about the town that afternoon chewing on the bitter taste of my lost opportunity. Joe was my first intellectual. I passionately wanted someone like him to be interested in me. But how could Joe be interested if I wasn't interesting? How did one become interesting? And was it possible for two people to achieve a sympathy between them if one was clever and the other not? That day I'd had a unique opportunity lasting through all those rich courses at lunch—and I'd thrown it away. I told myself that it was the presence of the others which had held me back. If only I'd been alone with Joe it would have been a different story . . .

I was to have my wish.

I can't think how it came about that he and I should have found ourselves alone in the hall of the Queen's one morning, but we did, with no one in sight to interfere with us. It was my dream come true. I suppose we greeted one another with some surprise and no doubt the leap of joy inside me was written all over my face. I only remember the last thing he said, and it was better than any of the fantasy talks I'd been dreaming up lately.

'I've got my car outside,' he said, 'why don't we go off somewhere and have a drink by ourselves?'

I felt as though Zeus himself had reached down a hand and scooped me up.

It was a low open sports car with the two seats crushed together. I climbed over the side and slotted myself in. He did the same on the other side and drove off. I couldn't believe it was happening.

'Where shall we go?' he shouted.

Luckily he didn't seem to expect an answer. He was a very bad

25

driver—rushes forward, sudden stops, screeching of brakes—but there was no doubt in my mind that this was what good driving was. The town was transformed. I'd thought it colourless and dead and the people in it the same. That morning it was sparkling with life and every face that I caught as we flashed by had a story behind it. We pulled up at a pub on the edge of the town and climbed out.

I'd never been inside a pub. It was crowded and noisy, a sailor's pub, quite small, and there were hardly any women. I followed in his wake to the bar and he turned to look at me. His eyes weren't harebell blue like Nancy's, but they were very blue, lighter than my own, and they looked right into you.

'What are you going to have?' he said.

Once again he didn't wait for an answer. He said we should have a Little Brickey. It was, he said, a particular kind of local beer, good and very strong. He turned away from me to order the drinks and then went on talking easily and happily to the barman, consciously throwing the net of his charm around him, giving, as it were, a little tweak here and there to the net according to the barman's responses.

I was watching this little play with interest. I wasn't thinking with my head but with my feelings, and now my feelings told me that Joe found the exercising of his own charm irresistible; he played people.

This discovery was a little chilling, and it was quickly followed by another discovery that was even more chilling. It came to me as vividly as though I was reading it in a book that Joe's interest in me was minimal; he had asked me out solely as an alternative to drinking alone.

The disappointment made my head spin. There were only seconds to go before he'd face round and hand me my drink and after that it would be up to me to entertain him and prove myself. And I knew, still not in my head but in my feelings, that I couldn't do this; he wasn't going to find me in the least entertaining.

He turned round laughing and gave me my drink. He went on smiling. It was a social smile and I tried to match it. He asked me one or two questions about myself—none serious—and I answered Yes and No. He asked me more, but it was impossible. I couldn't

26

talk to him. I was blinded with hero-worship. I could hardly swallow. He offered me a cigarette and I shook my head.

'No,' he said, mock solemn, 'I suppose that would be going too far.'

I'd been smoking for nearly two years but I knew my hand would shake as I took the cigarette and that he'd see it.

He stopped trying quite soon, and then he changed his position and looked round the bar and caught an eye here and there and generally merged with the others. He was quite at home in here. This is where he comes with Albert, I thought, and I wished he were there to help me.

When we had drunk the beer—it was bitter and vile and I seemed to have swallowed it upwards into my head instead of down into my stomach—he took hold of my arm and we made for the door. Outside he turned me round to look into my face.

'Now let's see,' he said, 'are you drunk?'

I wasn't only drunk, I was in real danger of throwing up, but I wouldn't admit it. I shook my head meaning No.

'Oh, what a pity,' he said lightly, 'that was the whole idea.'

He hadn't been serious with me for a moment.

We got into the car and drove back in the same erratic style to the hotel. Neither of us spoke. I think he'd already forgotten I was still there. I couldn't know that over twenty years would go by before I'd be with him again and that when I was, at last, we'd instantly and easily start to be friends in the way that I'd dreamed of for so long. When this did eventually take place he had no recollection whatever of having once taken me out for a drink in Southsea.

Uncle collapsed quite suddenly. He became ill one night and never came downstairs again. Nurses were brought in, day and night, and Muriel and I at once moved into the Queen's so that she could help them.

All through August he'd held a sort of daily court in his room with the barber, the physiotherapist and the local doctor, and sometimes his Richmond doctor came down with a London specialist. Then there were the visits from Joe and Nancy. It had all helped to pass the time. He was seldom alone for long.

Now, after his collapse, the place was more like a hospital than a

27

hotel. In the corridors you ran into nurses, men with oxygen cylinders and electrical equipment, errand boys who'd suddenly been sent out for something, and endless specialists—heart, cancer, urinary and so on—abruptly summoned from London. The hotel manager was distraught; the holiday season was not yet over and he dreaded a death on the premises.

I wasn't allowed to see Uncle. Muriel's room was nearer to his than mine was, so I sat in there on the bed, waiting for her to come back with news. I knew that something very serious was happening —death never crossed my mind—and I wanted to stay as near to it as possible.

'I don't mind you being in my room if you want to,' she said, 'but if you really wanted to help you'd go out for a walk.'

She was with him almost all the time, and whenever she came back to her room I was there, stupefied with hunger, lack of sleep and boredom. We had stopped going down to the restaurant for meals. Once she had sandwiches sent up, but neither of us could eat them. I knew she didn't want to be alone at this time any more than I did, and although she was always urging me to get some fresh air I knew she was glad to find me waiting in her room. I wanted to ask the nurses what was going on in his room, but I never found the courage to speak to them. I began to feel invisible. At night, when Muriel felt him to be safe for a while, she lay on her bed in her clothes, and when the night was nearly over she sent me back to my room and we both tried to get some sleep until daylight.

Several days passed in this way and she never once cried or broke down, nor did she seem to be straining against tears. I wasn't entirely surprised. I already knew that all that was best in her nature responded with instinctive joy to the tending of the sick. I knew this from the way she talked about her war experiences in France and Italy. We had been an unrewarding audience, barely polite, but she'd had no other and she needed to talk, to give affirmation to this intensely personal period of her life. I didn't always listen, and when I did I said discomforting things.

'You enjoy war.'

'Oh, you silly child, you don't understand a thing.'

'Tell me, then.'

But she couldn't.

In a way, she was enjoying nursing him in his dying; it was the channel through which she projected her love. I, too, wanted to help in some way, to be involved; I envied her having so much to do.

'Couldn't I go in for just a second? I wouldn't stay or speak.'

'He can't see anybody,' she said firmly.

I think he died in the early part of the night. She knew it was coming and she made me go to bed as she wouldn't be leaving him. It was early morning when she came to tell me.

'It's all over,' she said, 'he went quite peacefully. If you like to get up now I'll take you along to see him.'

His room was large and light with two big windows overlooking the gardens. Both of these windows were wide open, but the sickly smell of drugs still clung inside the room and made my heart thump.

If you didn't look at the bed, or at some oxygen cylinders stacked tidily in a corner, you'd have thought the room was ready for re-letting. It was immaculate; every trace of his having lived there for several weeks and just died there had been removed. There wasn't even a suitcase in sight. All was bleak and after-the-event, and in spite of the reek of formaldehyde you felt that nothing had ever happened in here.

One of the nurses was in the bathroom doing something; I could see her through the door. Perhaps his things were in there. I'd stopped for a moment at the door and now I went forward and over to the bed.

He was my first dead person.

I didn't know that dead people went yellow. I was surprised but not offended by the tight yellow skin that no longer looked like skin. Nor did this noble, diminished face look like a man's face. It was a dead person's face. It wasn't really very interesting. He was lying there like some carved figure on a tomb, his large, beautifully shaped hands folded over his chest. There were no more rucks in his face; it was smooth and yet far less arresting than the live face had been. Above all, it was cold. You didn't have to touch it to know that. I had thought I was going to see Uncle, changed, of course—for one thing without his spectacles—but Uncle just the same. But I was wrong. Uncle simply wasn't there. He'd always been standing or sitting down, never lying flat like that, and his face had been heavy and warm and old; this head was much smaller, the waxen skin

29

stretched tightly over the skull. It was not alarming and I felt no emotion at all. Beneath his hands there was a faded snapshot which she must have placed there. I could see enough of it to know that it was unfamiliar to me. It would be a snap of his family and I felt it would be unseemly to examine it. I wasn't surprised to see it there; it was a gesture on her part which fitted her. His family had always come first.

I don't think either of us said anything. She was quite at home in this drug-drenched room. She had been up all night and she still had the absorbed air of someone engaged in a job not yet finished. It was she who had done all the ritual laying out after he died, using the nurse as her assistant rather than the other way round.

We both stood for a while, one on either side of the bed, looking down at him. I wanted to do the right thing and I hoped she wouldn't do something awful like falling on her knees and praying. She didn't. She didn't even urge me to say anything. We started to leave quite easily—there seemed to be nothing more to do in the emptiness of the room—and I had just got to the door ahead of Muriel when, quite suddenly, I fainted.

I felt a hand at the base of my neck and realized that I was on the floor looking up into the unfamiliar face of the nurse.

'If you ask me,' she said crossly, 'what this child needs is a square meal.'

She took me down to the restaurant and the two of us ate an enormous breakfast of eggs and bacon and toast and marmalade.

During all this time Muriel had only me, difficult, withdrawn, and still in the dark about Uncle, for comfort and support. Early that morning she'd sent a telegram to Joe at the B.B.C. He came down later in the day to sign forms and take away his father's things. Then he went back to London. I didn't see him. She and I were to leave the next day in a hired car behind the hearse; we would proceed thus at marching pace all the way from Southsea until the hearse branched off to Richmond, and then our car would go at normal speed into London and home.

'I'm not going to have him going off all alone as though nobody cared,' she'd said.

In the afternoon, when we were packing, she showed me the

30

tickets to Vienna because she couldn't stop talking about them. Taking them from his wallet had upset her.

'After all, they're mine. They're nothing to do with anyone else. And I've taken most of the money, too,' she said defiantly. 'I don't care what they say. I know he'd have wanted me to have it. I hope you're not going to be difficult about it.'

'Of course I'm not,' I said. 'Of course he'd have wanted you to have it.'

'God knows I need it,' she went on, 'I suppose I've got about sixty pounds in the bank. I don't know what we're going to do. If only he'd managed to put back the money he took out for Nancy's wedding. I begged and begged him, but once it was out I knew I hadn't a hope.'

I'd heard this story before. She was always trying to get him to settle some money on us children, and after years of going on at him she'd succeeded. He'd done it. But when Nancy got engaged in 1925 it was this money that he'd released to give her a slap-up wedding. He'd never managed to put it back.

On the afternoon of the day he died we were both in that state of numbed anguish that comes after a dreaded event has drawn to its close; sleep and hunger have lost their meaning and so has activity. I was stifled with inertia. I heard what she was saying as I took things out of the chest of drawers and passed them to her to put in the suitcase, but the words didn't mean anything.

And then I did an extraordinary thing.

'Can I have some money, please?' I said. 'I'm going on the speedboat.'

She was folding up a nightdress and she suddenly stopped, the nightdress wound round her two hands like a silk muff. She was aghast.

'You're not thinking of going on the speedboat today?'

'They're waiting for me,' I lied, 'I told them I'd be down.'

Her eyes contracted. 'On the very day that Uncle's died you can think of going on a speedboat? Have you no heart? Have you no feelings at all?'

'They're waiting for me,' I said.

She threw the nightdress, anyhow, into the suitcase. She was staring at me, trying to bore into my mind.

'You're so hard, I don't know where you get it from. With the poor old boy not cold yet. Have you no shame?' She spread her arms. 'Well, I suppose if that's how you feel you'd better go.'

She picked up her bag and opened it and brought out some coins. I took them from her and left.

I've often wondered why I did it.

You could say that the main policy of our upbringing had been to keep us as wholly removed as was possible from the rest of the world and everybody in it: nothing must be allowed to happen in our world. And nothing did. No births, deaths or marriages ever occurred to sweep us up into ecstasies of involvement. We never even caught other people's colds. We were friendless and germ free. Now, for the first time, a death had occurred along the corridor, the death of that sweet man Uncle—or so I believed—and from first to last I'd been excluded. I'd simply been in the way.

I wasn't aware of these feelings at the time but I think they must have been there and that I seized upon the speedboat as a gesture of revenge.

As I made my way down to the end of the pier I kept trying to feel Uncle's death, but it was like trying to reach the other side of a bolted door; no matter how much I hammered upon it with my fists I couldn't open it. I didn't know then about delayed shock. I didn't know that several weeks would still have to pass before I'd find myself, at last, face to face with the realization that I should never see him again.

This happened to me some time after I was back at school again. I woke abruptly in the middle of the night in the dormitory, and there it was, piercing into me. Until this moment I hadn't known how much I'd loved him. I thought I'd forgotten him.

I was used to being unhappy, it was like a part of my everyday clothing, but this was something I'd never before experienced: for the first time I was suffering a loss. We'd been brought up never to cry or show that we were hurt—brave little girls don't cry—and we didn't cry, any of us. But no one had taught me how to contain something of this magnitude. I felt grief welling up inside me, straining at my ribs. I thought my heart would break.

I pulled the clothes up over my head, and the tears poured out of my eyes into the pillow.

*

On 7 September, 1929, the following obituary appeared in *The Times*:

Mr. Alfred Roger Ackerley, of Blenheim House, Richmond Hill, who died at Southsea on Tuesday at the age of 66, was one of the founders of Elders & Fyffes Limited. He was known throughout the country as a benefactor of all charities, especially hospitals. It was his custom to give a christening cup to each child born to members of his staff, and he always called them his godchildren. When a young man he served in the Royal Horse Guards (Blues) during the Egyptian campaign, and was a rider in point-to-point races. He entered the fruit business in 1892. With Mr. A. Stockley he founded Elders & Fyffes, and saw the firm's import of bananas from the West Indies grow from 50,000 bunches a month to 2,500,000. The business was formed into a limited company in 1901. Mr. Ackerley was a man of sterling personality, and was highly esteemed by all who knew him. He leaves a widow and a son and daughter.

Nearly a thousand business men from all over the British Isles as well as from the Continent attended the funeral at Richmond Cemetery yesterday, and the wreaths were so numerous that four men were specially engaged to load and unload them. The procession of mourners reached the length of the largest part of the cemetery, and two police officers experienced difficulty in regulating the long stream of private motor-cars. The small chapel in the cemetery, where a brief service was held, was totally inadequate for the occasion, and quite two-thirds of the mourners were unable to enter.

33

Chapter Three

HOW AND where they met, even when, is far from clear.

In Vienna I had learned that Uncle was my father. On top of that Joe was my half-brother and Nancy my half-sister. It was all barely imaginable. I had looked on Joe and Nancy as Olympian figures, far beyond my reach; now, it seemed, I was related to them by blood. It was a dizzying thought, and the more I dwelt upon it the more clearly I saw that this was only a fraction of the wonders that were being kept from me. There was more, much more, and I was determined to get to know every smallest part of it. I must be told everything, and the only person who could open the doors to the Holy Grail was Muriel herself. I saw her as someone possessing information which I passionately longed to share; I saw it as part of my inheritance: her parents were my grandparents; her early life had formed her into the woman who had become my mother. I must be accorded my rightful place in this tapestry.

Before Vienna my interest in her early life had been spasmodic. After Vienna it became an obsession. I could think of nothing else. I went on and on at her and by a process of merciless persecution I managed to squeeze out of her a little story, a mere skeleton, about her childhood which, having once related, she trotted out time after time without the smallest deviation or embellishment.

As a story it was so profoundly unsatisfactory that I felt as though the top of my head was coming off. The first time I heard it I couldn't stop myself from interrupting, but she didn't listen. As the gaps in her story gobbled up the statements I kept on interrupting, and every time I did this she simply went deaf. I started to shrill at her, and she started to cry.

This pattern was to be repeated many, many times. Like an answering service she'd give me the same set phrases again and again and again. Nothing would budge her; nothing would make her change or expand upon a word of this tantalizing and novelettish tale.

Without interruptions it went like this:

'I was brought up in Clifton. I never knew my parents. My mother died when I was born. I was brought up by my step-brother and his wife. They had two little girls of their own. The wife didn't like me and nor did the two little girls, but my step-brother was kind to me. He was an artist. I used to sit in a corner of the studio and read all the time, and he often used to paint me. I never went to school. He knew all the famous artists and writers of the day and they used to come to the studio to see him.'

This was all.

I coaxed, bullied, wheedled, took her by surprise, pleaded with all my heart, but nothing would persuade her to tell me properly, to expand, explain, elaborate. She was like someone on the other side of a tiny eye-hole grid: we could just see each other through it, but she wouldn't keep her face still for me to see her truly. And she wouldn't let me in.

I never believed this story, if only because of the resistant way in which she told it, but at the same time I felt that somewhere in it there was a grain of truth which, if only I could seize upon it, might lead me to the rest. She knew nothing about pictures or painting, or the way painters talk about pictures; even the evocative smell of turpentine meant nothing to her. It was impossible to believe that she had spent much time in a painter's studio.

I'd come in at an angle. For instance, I'd never seen her read a book or even a newspaper beyond the headlines.

'What did you read in a corner of the studio?'

'Macaulay.'

'What else?'

'Oh, I can't remember. There were such a lot of books.'

'What famous writers and artists came to the studio?'

'Conrad.'

'Who else?'

'Oh, don't go on! You're so cruel! I've told you again and again. Why do you have to go on?'

It was always the same, always Macaulay, always Conrad. They

35

seemed to be the only names she knew. She never told me the names of her parents, the stepbrother, his wife or the two little girls.

'Oh, I don't know, it's so long ago!' she would cry.

But I went on with the questions.

'What kind of paintings did your stepbrother do? Did he ever sell any? What happened to the two little girls? How did you come to leave this house? At what age? Where did you go? Since you never went to school who taught you to read and write? Did you share a bedroom with the girls or did you sleep on sacks by the stove? *I must know these things.*'

But I never did. She squirmed, evaded and broke down, always, into tears. I never spared her. It never crossed my mind that she was ashamed of some element in her early life. I saw her, quite simply, as denying me information which was mine by right. I could see nothing beyond this.

Once I said, 'Why were you called Haidée?'

She made a face. She didn't know, she said, but it was a nasty name, and as soon as she was old enough she'd dropped it and was known thereafter as Muriel Perry.

'I think it's Muriel that's nasty,' I said with habitual candour. 'I'd have dropped the Muriel and kept the Haidée.'

She must have been named after Byron's Haidée in *Don Juan*, the beautiful daughter of a Greek pirate. Haidée went mad and died for love. I should like to know who it was—poet or sea lover?—who gave her this romantic name. I think the reason she disliked it was a fear of mispronouncing it. She could never be persuaded to attempt the simplest unEnglish word.

Once, when I was asking her for the hundredth time why and how she'd left Clifton, she made a rare slip. I was saying how old was she when she came to London? How much money did she have? How had she come, in what sort of vehicle? Where had she spent the first night, and what had prompted her to spend it there, wherever it was?

She started to answer. She said she'd had to leave Clifton after she'd been seen in a box at the theatre with Uncle. Her face became quite savage when she said this, and as soon as she'd said it she knew she'd gone too far. She became confused. I quickly pressed on, skipping the journey. After she got to London, I said, what on earth

36

did she do? She'd recovered herself quickly, and now she was looking very, very wary.

'I got a job,' she said carefully.

'What sort of job?'

'I got a job in an office,' she said, looking me straight in the eyes, daring me to disbelieve her.

This was the sort of calculated insult that always finished me. I shouted at her.

'Doing typing and shorthand and double-entry book-keeping, I suppose!'

Whenever I attacked her she simply fell to pieces. She never shouted back or attacked me for bullying. Instead, as now, her hands flew up to her face and she rocked backwards and forwards, weeping.

'Oh, what does it all matter now? It's all over and done with. Why do you want to know? Why can't you leave me alone?'

But I couldn't give way and neither could she and, as time went on, this battle became the very cornerstone of our relationship with each other. It was a hopeless situation, and it turned each of us into the enemy of the other.

There was another story, totally different, about her early days with Uncle, but she didn't tell me this one until she was seventy and dying.

We hadn't seen each other for many years, but when I knew she was dying I'd come back to sit with her for the last six months of her life. I'd done this not only for her sake but for my own as well. I knew that if I didn't seize this opportunity to make peace with her before it was too late I should never be freed from the echo of our battles.

On this particular day I'd been reading aloud. It was very quiet and peaceful and near the end. Lying there among the pillows she suddenly gave me one of the old sly looks from the sides of her eyes.

'I expect you've heard about the Tavistock,' she said.

Now, this was the sort of invitation that I'd dreamed about back in the old fighting days. But it had never come. Until this moment she had never offered me, as it were, a slice of the forbidden cake.

I must explain that some years before this my half-brother had told me that he and Nancy always supposed that when their father

37

first came to know Muriel she was working in the bar at the Tavistock Hotel in Covent Garden. Joe had told me this during a period when I'd given up my quest for her mysterious past. She'd beaten me and I no longer cared, or so I believed. But I had seized upon this story with renewed interest.

So that was it. Muriel had been a barmaid, and it was a simple matter of snobbery that had set off the paranoiac secrecy.

But this was too simple an explanation. For one thing, Muriel was remarkably lacking in snobbery, that is to say, she was never a social climber. In an age of the most rigid class distinctions she accepted the well born as a fact of life, but she never tried to pass herself off as one of them, and she never, as a true snob would have done, looked down on anybody. Abstract matters of this sort didn't interest her: some people were well born, others weren't, and for herself . . . well, when she was a young girl a gipsy once told her she was the natural daughter of a foreign princess. She could see it in her hand, the gipsy said. This was a story that Muriel liked to tell us adding, a little shamefacedly, that of course it was nonsense really.

When Joe suggested to me that she had been a barmaid I found I couldn't believe in it. Try as I might, I couldn't bring to life an image of her as a working-class girl with rough hands and ways, banging down glasses and dealing with rough men. Every time I tried to see her in this rôle, fitting comfortably into the rumbustiousness and vivid coarseness of Covent Garden, the picture went blank. Nor could I believe that in 1909 a large and famous pub like the Tavistock would put a girl like Muriel—a younger version of the Muriel I knew—behind a busy bar; a girl without a trace of an accent and with the soft appearance of someone brought up in a cultivated manner.

I had dismissed the barmaid story as improbable. I had forgotten it. So when she lay dying and mentioned the Tavistock I thought I was hearing the name for the first time.

'I expect you've heard about the Tavistock.'

'No,' I said, 'tell me.'

She shifted a little in the bed.

'I used to keep the books,' she said.

This was too much, but I didn't shout at her as I had in the old days. I said mildly: 'You, who can't add one and three?'

'I did, I did!' She plucked at the sheet. 'I used to stand behind the desk at night—there was a little desk just inside the door—and tick off the ones who were staying, when they came in late at night.'

She looked at me, uncertain if I would play along or argue, and when I did neither she looked relieved and seemed to doze off.

To bring her back I said: 'Tell me about Uncle in those days.'

She was awake at once. She pulled herself up a little in the bed. 'There were these two men,' she said, as though I knew all about the Tavistock and what she was doing there, 'they were friends and they always came in together.' It was the handsome fair one who used to tease her, the other one hardly spoke to her.

'He was always looking at me and teasing, and I wasn't going to have that.' She gave a little twitch to the sheet. 'I used to get as far away from him as I could. He could tell I didn't like being teased and that made him do it all the more. He kept looking at me and calling out things. I thought he was horrid.'

She went on talking, her voice weak and flutey, a little smile on her wasted face. She was telling herself one of her favourite tales. It may have been a true one and just as easily it may have been one of her established fantasies.

She said that on nights before and after business trips to Rotterdam he stayed at the Tavistock. Richmond, where he lived, was a long way from Tilbury where he caught the boat. She told me that one of her duties was to see that the coal scuttles were well filled at night in the bedrooms. On one of the pre-Rotterdam nights she'd gone upstairs to make sure that the teaser had plenty of coal for his fire. He was already in his bedroom. She had knocked and opened the door. His coal scuttle was full and the fire burning well.

'You look cold standing there in the doorway,' he'd said. 'Come in and get warm.'

Roger Ackerley was born on April Fool's Day in 1863.

In 1909—this is the latest year in which they could have met—Muriel was nineteen and he forty-six. He was, by then, a rich man, well established in his business, a middle-aged cosmopolitan who'd travelled a great deal and was used to enjoying himself and being liked.

Not only was he exceptionally handsome, with great charm and

39

authority of manner, he was also a man with much experience of sexual conquest. With his good nature and his jokes and his ardent sexuality he must have knocked all Muriel's ideas about men sideways.

When she was dying she said: 'He was father, lover and friend all rolled into one. You always felt so *safe* with him.'

And she was not the only one to have had implicit faith in Roger. All his life people had trusted him; steadfastness and niceness were threaded into his charm. Nevertheless, right at the start he told Muriel one thumping lie.

He said he was married.

He *had* been married to a Swiss girl, Louise Burckhart, but she'd been dead for sixteen years and he hadn't married again. He had, however, a few months after the death of his wife, found another partner, a young woman called Netta Aylward, whom he'd picked up on a Channel packet crossing to France. But he hadn't married her, although by 1909 she'd borne him three children, two boys and a girl. He lived with them all in perfect amity in a high house in Richmond Hill. He told Muriel that Netta was his wife; he also stated categorically that he disapproved of divorce.

Roger was the seventh of eight children, five girls and three boys. He was brought up in a little village in the country not far from Liverpool, and although later he became a London man he never looked quite right inside buildings: he never entirely lost an invisible background of tweed and dogs and a co-existence with the elements. He always noticed and commented on the weather; it mattered to him, like the health of an old friend.

His mother died when he was only two, and when he was thirteen his father lost his money on the Stock Exchange and Roger was forced to leave school and go to work as a clerk in a firm of auctioneers in Liverpool. At the same time this large family moved into a smaller house, a mere cottage, at Rainhill, a village outside Liverpool.

This was not a very promising start for a high-spirited lad, and it wasn't long before he broke loose. When he was sixteen he was discovered in bed with a girl, and this caused such a rumpus in the family that he ran away to London and joined the army, falsifying his age. He was already nearly six foot tall, and later became six foot two.

He loved horses, and enjoyed his life in the army, serving as a trooper first with the Royal Horse Guards and later with the Second Life Guards.

In 1889, no longer in the army, he met and married Louise Burckhart, the only child of wealthy parents who were captivated by their handsome son-in-law. They gave him an allowance of £2,000 a year.

For the first time in his life Roger was financially secure. He was also happily married. The young couple travelled extensively, as the fancy took them, over Europe. But it was not to last. By 1892 Louise was dead. She suffered with her nerves, so Roger took her to Paris to undergo the cold water treatment. This meant having a hose of cold water trained on to the small of the back. As a result of this drastic treatment Louise caught pneumonia and died, and for the rest of his life Roger carried her photograph in his wallet. When the time came that he had a daughter he named her Nancy Louise.

Roger's father-in-law continued the allowance. He'd made it clear that he meant to remember Roger in his will, but only a few months after Louise's death he, too, died. And he died intestate.

Roger came back to England a penniless widower. During the soldiering years he'd made friends with a young man called Arthur Stockley who was now establishing in London the firm which was to become Elders & Fyffes. Roger joined his friend and from now on he never looked back. He'd found his niche. He was an adventurer with an instinct for the moment, and in commerce he'd found a channel through which his large personality and flair for negotiation could flourish.

In 1909, when he was calling in at the Tavistock with Stockley, he was one of the firm's directors and already known as the Banana King. He was also living in the Richmond house with Netta Aylward, known as Mrs. Ackerley, and their three children who were all registered under their father's name. He had still not remarried.

The Tavistock Hotel was a famous old pub. This whole area of Long Acre was dotted with pubs, but the Tavistock was Roger's favourite and he used it frequently, dropping in there with Stockley for a breather from the office and to pick up racing tips. He placed at least one bet every day of the season and claimed to break about even at the end of the year.

The Elders & Fyffes offices were at 31 Bow Street, a mere stone's throw from the Tavistock, which was situated on the north face of Covent Garden market, almost in the middle. Roger's office was next door to the police station and opposite the Royal Opera House and the beautiful italianate Floral Hall.

When we were still very young we sometimes made a rare expedition into the west-end with our nurse, and then we'd call for Roger at his office and he'd take us into the market. His room at Elders & Fyffes was on the ground floor on the right. I remember it as dark and gloomy and ugly, not a room to be at ease in. He'd be seated at an immense roll-top desk when we were shown in, and we'd crowd around him and finger his paper-weights and any curios he'd recently picked up, and he'd patiently tell us their history; he liked snuff-boxes, enamel and silver. In this gloomy setting he was like a stranger to us, only the heavy scent of cigar smoke linking him with our Uncle.

After a while we'd leave the office and he'd take us into the market. This was the crowning moment. Towering above the crowd, with his cigar and his grey Edward VI homburg with the curled brim, he'd make a slow progress like some royal personage.

Writing in *The Grower*, R. E. Delefield describes the people of Covent Garden:

> They are members of a tribe that has somehow wandered away from the rest of us and built a strictly private fortress in the streets between the Strand and Holborn. Here they have always lived, speaking their own language and practising their own customs. One can be *with* them but never *of* them. One is either born into their midst or remains outside it, stupefied and amazed at their application to a calling that is almost a cult ...

Ever since he joined with Stockley these people had been Roger's daily familiars; they were an integral part of his business life. He had a particular affection for the costermongers, the men with the barrows who, on fête days, wore their Pearly King and Queen regalia. Every year at the Richmond Horse Show he presented a donkey and cart to the best costermonger turnout, and afterwards he'd be photographed with the winners, resplendent in their black velvet and plumes and pearly buttons. Roger would be hardly less

42

resplendent in a dove grey cutaway coat, pepper and salt trousers and a grey top hat, a large cigar in his hand. He was godfather to any number of costermonger children and gave a silver mug and spoon to each one when they were christened.

In those days the market porters still carried pyramids of baskets balanced on their heads; you could stare your eyes nearly out of their sockets, willing a topple, but the baskets never moved; they seemed to be glued to the tops of the porters' heads as they picked their way between the barrows and the carts, the horses, and the children about their feet. There was always a lot of noise; shouting, and horse noises, snuffling into feed bags, harness shaking, stamping of metal shoes on the cobblestones.

Roger loved the market. He seemed to know everyone. Like royalty bestowing favours he'd stop for a word here and there before passing on; he'd compliment a man on his display of fruit or vegetables, and he'd watch the children playing barefoot on the dirty cobblestones and slip a coin into a grimy hand. Sometimes, he'd simply stand, proprietorial, a little smile showing beneath his moustache, surveying with deep satisfaction the teeming ant-hill of order and disorder around him.

In Muriel's day the whole area was still steeped in its own louche history. Thick with prostitutes and exotic characters, villains and beggars, it was a quarter in which energetic trading took place in the daytime, and excesses of every description throughout the night. Artists—Conrad must surely have spent London nights there— foreign visitors and the aristocracy drank and gambled and indulged their secret tastes, and in the House of Commons motions were frequently tabled seeking to clean it up both morally and physically.

By the time that Roger first took us to the market—probably about 1918—it was a paler version of itself, more law-abiding around the clock, particularly at night, since its earlier habitués were now either killed or away at the war. Nevertheless, the inimical atmosphere still clung; nothing could diminish the stabbing colours of the fruit and vegetables on the barrows and the flowers in the Floral Hall.

We had no reason to know it then, but the bar of the Tavistock ran parallel to the market. It was a long bar with steps down to ground level; in good weather the doors were always open. As we passed it we never gave it so much as a glance, but what must Roger's thoughts have been as he steered his little group of three unacknowledged daughters past the doors of this familiar bar where only a few years earlier their mother, his mistress, had been employed?

I've sometimes wondered if it was Roger himself who placed her there, so handy to his office round the corner; if he found her somewhere—in Clifton—unhappy and in trouble, and asked the landlord at the Tavistock, as an expedient, to take her on to help where necessary.

There is a teasing constancy about Clifton in this elusive tale. In his autobiography Joe Ackerley writes about his maternal grandmother who, as well as her two sisters, was illegitimate:

I remember my grandmother as a very beautiful old lady, but she was said to have looked quite plain beside her sisters in childhood. However, there were to be no opportunities for later comparison, for as soon as the latter were old enough to comprehend the shame of their existence they decided to hide it for ever from the world and took the veil in the convent in *Clifton* where all three had been put to school.

Clifton is a suburb of Bristol and Roger was often in Bristol on Elders & Fyffes business. The banana boats left from there for Jamaica. If he didn't meet Muriel in Clifton or Bristol the coincidence of her coming south and ending up almost on his doorstep in Covent Garden is even greater.

But this is conjecture. What is indisputable is that the whole of Muriel's young life was spent within a framework which she loathed and of which she was traumatically ashamed, and that the final chapter of this life that she was so determined to keep from us took place in Covent Garden. Whether she was a true working-class girl or not she was, at least at this time, living the life of one. There is her own account when she was dying, and the fact that at home in Richmond Roger often referred to her as 'Muriel at the Tavistock', and then, later on, as 'Muriel—who used to be at the Tavistock'.

Some years after Muriel's death a bundle of letters came to light.

They were wrapped in an envelope and tied with a strip of faded blue celanese, a relic from an old nightdress; the days of the beautiful *crêpe-de-chine* nightdresses with pin tucks and real lace were long over. On the outside of the envelope Muriel had written: Uncle's letters.

Only three of these letters belong to this early time and two are undated. In spite of being a business man Roger rarely dated his private letters, he merely put the day of the week. In the following letter he signs himself Chug, and he went on signing letters to her in this way until he died.

It was a nickname we had never heard. With us she called him Uncle, sometimes Roger, never Chug. Chug belonged strictly to their secret orchard.

Saturday   31 Bow Street
                                                        W.C.

Darling of my heart,

What a nice letter I read in the crowded Strand yesterday. Why wouldn't you let me read it in Gatti's? Were you ashamed of having written it or had you changed your mind & found you did not love me any longer. Dear child, one thing is plain & that is that I am the disturbing element in your life. How can I make up for this to my lonely sweetheart that I am so fond of. Why did you ever meet me you must ask yourself & with good reason. Against this darling put the fact that I am a nice man, & a man who really loves you. I have never given a thought to another woman since I first kissed you & your hold on me is stronger now than it ever was. These are facts & not mere love letter writing. You know I love you & you ought to know how I long to be with you always & how sad I am at your loneliness. You know how happy I am when we are together & it is a test of real affection dear, when one is as happy with a girl in the daytime, as one is at night. We have had one or two good times together, altho they have been horribly short & we may have some more equally good. You eat, drink, sleep well when I am with you & I am like a boy again in your arms. Let us love each other sweetheart & let things slide a bit longer.

I am going to take four kids & two grown ups to the Oxford

matinee this afternoon. Next to being with you seeing children jolly and happy is my greatest pleasure.

What a funny day, wind, & rain & sunshine. It is like your life for the last few months, not as much sunshine as one would like. Dear Heart, consider yourself strained in my arms, with your dear sweet body nestling close to me & our mouths waking passions in each other.

Your own,
Chug

There is nothing in this letter to show where Muriel was now living, but the theme of her loneliness was one which was to recur again and again. Since knowing Roger it had been highlighted—'we have had one or two good times together'. But he wasn't always there. When she was alone she was alone.

Friendship is never easy for someone who has created an alienation of the self. I have sometimes wondered if Muriel was brought up in an orphanage. It could be said that orphanages are like mental hospitals, that the machinery to run either is intrinsically the same. The reason for Muriel's total suppression of her early life is open to speculation; what is beyond doubt is that by wiping it out, by refusing to accept memories that were unbearable to her, she was performing upon herself the most extreme psychological surgery. I stress the importance of this violation because nothing that she did and became makes sense unless it is understood that the whole of her life was built not so much on lies—although of course there were lies, and liars create their own punishment—as on a vast vacuum of silence and evasion, of interior nothingness, which was all that was left to her after the wholesale denials.

This is a piteous condition of life, with its own irreversible absolute: as the years go by the truth becomes more and more agitated; the energies that go into the maintenance of the fortress are herculean: the guns must be manned night and day. It embodies the very root of paradox, and Muriel's case was no exception: she was brave and timid, true and false.

Roger almost certainly knew the whole truth about her, but I doubt that anyone else ever did. I don't imagine he would have had much difficulty in getting her to tell her story. He was kindness itself and exceptionally tolerant for a man of any age, let alone his own. I think the opportunity of Pygmalion-like improvisation must have pleased him; her waif's history would have touched him where he was most vulnerable. He liked neurotic women. The three principal women in his life, Louise, Netta and Muriel, were all neurotic. He hadn't in any real sense, a social conscience, but he had a generous heart. He was known as a champion of the underdog, a good touch, and if he lent a sum of money instead of giving it he was ingenuously proud when it was paid back.

He liked re-planting people, scooping up unfortunates and giving them a chance. There were always one or two of his protégés on the pay-roll at Elders & Fyffes; they came and went. The one we knew best was a Spaniard called Manuel, an ingratiating, rather sinister man, whom Roger used as errand boy. He'd call at our house in Castelnau with parcels and messages, and sometimes he did commissions for Muriel. When Roger died he was instantly sacked—and so were all the other protégés—and some months later turned up on our doorstep, drunk and menacing, a tramp again—Roger had found him on the Embankment—muttering threats. Muriel gave him money and told him not to come back, but for some time afterwards we were startled whenever the doorbell rang. We never saw him again.

There was nothing common in Muriel's appearance or manner, but in some ways she thought like the very poor. She had a deep distrust of everybody, especially of men, although the presence of a man in the room affected her like champagne. She was pessimistic, suspicious and touchy, but perhaps these are simply qualities of the emotionally deprived. Only Roger was set apart.

'He was always such a gentleman,' she would say mistily.

In those days he bowled her over in a way that no other man was ever to do. She put him on a pedestal and kept him there. Other men existed to be made sport of; they'd let you down quick as look at you. In time she would instruct her daughters:

'Never let a man know you care,' adding, with a gesture from her long hand, 'keep him dangling . . . '

But she didn't keep Roger dangling. In no time she was pregnant.

Their first child was stillborn, a boy. This can only have come as a huge relief to Roger; the last thing he wanted was a second family. But Muriel was heartbroken. She'd hoped for a son. Through the long months of pregnancy she'd dreamed of herself with her baby and what it would mean to her to have a son. Babies were adorable creatures and, like many rootless women, she was possessive: a child would be something of her own; it would ease her loneliness. She may have felt, too, that it would bind Roger more closely to her, although I doubt she ever really felt the need of an extra tie. Right from the start she knew in her bones that he would never desert her. And she was right: he never did. He was a man who, once committed, stuck to his word. This was how he ran his business. And he loved her: he had made her believe that she belonged to him, totally and for ever, and he to her, and that all the other facets of their lives were irrelevances.

The following letter was written for Muriel's twentieth birthday. She was now six months pregnant for the second time.

4.3.10   31 Bow Street, W.C.
Dearest and best,

These are my best wishes for your birthday. May we continue to love one another for all the birthdays there are to come & may you be happy all the time. I went to Fortnum & Mason just now & bought you some peppermints, two kinds. I hope they will be strong enough. On my way west I bought you a photo of your Chug out with his banana barrow. This is my birthday greeting. I wish I could give you a motor car instead of a mere barrow. I have sent £10 to your bank so that you won't be absolutely broke before I see you on Wednesday.

Mind you write to the Imperial Hydro at Blackpool also to the Docks at Manchester. Saturday & Monday morning will find me at the former & Tuesday morning at the latter place. I am so glad the weather is keeping nice, the wind is easterly today at last but the sun is shining. Take care of yourself sweetheart. Everything is paid for at Herbert's, so you have nothing to do but get your key. I will arrange about the parrot when you feel settled.

I had a rotten game of cards last night, two women who talked babies all the time. See that your sheets are well aired before you sleep in the flat.

    Bless you my beloved,
        Your
          Chug

She gave birth to twin girls. They were both enormous and she nearly died.

Once more Muriel was denied a son, but this time she did her best to make up for it. She pretended that one of the twins was a boy. She seems to have hit on this whimsical fancy right from the start and, curiously, it was the second child, Stella—there were twenty minutes between the births—whom she cast in this rôle, the child who, chosen by chance or instinct, would prove to be her truest daughter, the one with many of her own traits of character. To Muriel Stella was 'my son Sam'. She would not be dressed in boy's clothes or in any outward sense be presented as a boy, but for years to come Muriel would fantasize about her and write letters to My Son, and get letters back signed Your loving son Sam. Roger also indulged in this fantasy and wrote to My dearest Nephew.

It was Roger who registered the births. Where it said Name of Father he wrote: George Perry.

They were beautiful babies, good as gold. But gold has not the same value for everyone, and Roger saw this new little family as an unmitigated nuisance. When he came to see Muriel, fitting in his visits between the demands of his office and his home, it must surely have been with the principal intention of taking her to bed. And how was this to be comfortably achieved with two tiny children and a nursemaid in close proximity in the next room? The flat was very small.

There were rows. She could no longer join him on trips to Rotterdam and Paris, the nursemaid was too young to be left in charge. Muriel was always tired and she talked of little but babies. Roger was a father to her as well as a lover and it wouldn't be surprising if this was the rôle she wanted him to play now, at least for a while. The dangers of making love were only too apparent.

Once, when he came with a bunch of flowers, she opened a

window on to the street as he left and hurled the flowers down on top of his head. She was never docile.

And then, to bring everything to a head, thirteen months after the birth of the twins, she was pregnant again. This was the last straw and Roger was furious.

Muriel was at a crossroads. Something would have to be done, but what? Roger had urged her to 'let things slide a little longer'. Since then things had, indeed, slid. She was ill throughout all her pregnancies, worried almost beyond endurance, deeply ashamed, sick and perpetually tired. The longed-for escape from her past that Roger had brought about had simply landed her in a prison of domesticity that every fibre of her being cried out was wrong for her. Instinct told her that she wasn't meant for this. Before she found Roger she had been fortified in the belief that one day 'something' would happen to save her. And something had happened. But instead of walking out into a paradise of freedom she'd walked straight into a trap. She might just as well have gone into a prison cell and closed the door behind her.

All that was best in her complex nature, compassion and a hither-to undreamed-of capacity for organization, would find an outlet three years later in the war, but she wasn't to know this then. All she knew now was that she couldn't go on like this. And nor could Roger. Sometimes when he came to see her he wouldn't even go into the babies' room to look at them. He was sick to death of babies and pregnancies.

Among Muriel's advisers—who were they?—someone must surely have pointed out that if she didn't make herself more available to Roger and stop drowning herself in nappies and motherhood she might well lose him altogether—and then where would she and her children be?

The strain of living in a manner that was totally against her deepest nature must finally have forced the issue. The instinct for survival, which was to save her so many times in later years, came to her rescue now. Their big decision, the most serious decision that Muriel had ever had to face, must have been made before the birth of their third child. It was carried out soon after. The three children would be brought up apart from Muriel, with Roger as their legal guardian. Everything would be done for their care and happiness, but Muriel would make her life elsewhere. The separation would be absolute. There would be no visiting.

During her third pregnancy Muriel moved, with the twins and the nursemaid, into a flat near Sloane Square, a surprisingly long way from Bow Street. She suffered tortures of shame at her condition and was so fearful of being seen that she only went out for exercise after dark. She used to say that her third child never had a chance because during the whole of the nine months of pregnancy she was lifting the heavy twins in and out of the bath.

I don't think she ever considered adoption. She was too loyal for that, and too possessive, and it may be that something in her own history made it particularly unacceptable. We were her children, and would remain so, brought up by somebody else.

During the waiting months an old Scottish crony of Roger's, a Dr. Coutts, died rather suddenly. He left a spinster sister aged sixty-six who'd kept house for him for many years first in Glasgow and then in London. He'd left her penniless except for his effects, furniture and the like.

When Roger mentioned Miss Coutts and her furniture it seemed providential. Muriel had absolute faith in Roger's judgement; after all, he'd had years of experience in employing people. And he knew how to get things done. As the sister of a doctor Miss Coutts was obviously a suitable person to entrust with children. Roger must now arrange for someone to find a house for Miss Coutts and her furniture and make all the other arrangements. In a little while Muriel would be well again and better able to cope with her life. Lately everything had somehow got out of hand; the problems had snowballed and made her ill. She hadn't meant things to work out like this. The children wouldn't suffer, she'd see to that, but for herself there must be a stop. At least for a while.

A house was found near Barnes Common, Miss Coutts's furniture moved into it, and a household set up to look after the children. This was made up of Miss Coutts herself as housekeeper and cook, responsible to Roger, a trained children's nurse called Frances, Ellen, an under-nurse, and a cleaning woman.

I was born in the Sloane Square flat on 7 April, 1912, around midnight. It was a Saturday night and Muriel's doctor had confidently gone to the country for the weekend. The baby was not due for at least another week, and the monthly nurse who had been engaged had not yet come. Roger was away on a business trip.

When labour started the nursemaid ran all the way to the doctor's house for help, leaving Muriel alone in the flat with the twins, and eventually returned, in the nick of time, with a stranger, a young locum on weekend duty. Once again Muriel gave birth with the greatest difficulty. All her confinements were terrible ordeals; she was so ill after the birth of the twins that a fortnight went by before she saw them. This time it was much the same but, unlike the twins who had been so good, I cried and cried from the start.

The monthly nurse moved in and Roger came back from abroad, but it can hardly have been a time for rejoicing; indeed, the distress and confusion in the flat was such that my birth was never registered. Muriel was torn in a hundred ways: she was proud of her beautiful twins and loved them; she loved Roger; she loved all new-born creatures. She wanted to do the right thing, the best thing for everyone. And she had to save herself.

As soon as she was well enough to move the twins and I were taken away to start a new life in our new home and Muriel left the Sloane Square flat. But before these two events took place the twins and I were photographed with our nurse, all seated in a studio boat. On the back of this photograph Muriel wrote: 'Nurse had this taken—thought you'd like to see.'

Chapter Four

THERE IS no proof that the separation took place as early as this, but legend and common sense come out strongly in support of it.

There was the legend that our next door neighbour in Barnes, Major O'Connor, fell in love with me at first sight when I was placed in his arms over the garden fence, and the point of this joke was that at the time I was a baby in long clothes. There was no legend that Muriel had ever come to the house, let alone lived in it or, indeed, that she had ever met Antie Coutts, Frances or Ellen. On the contrary, there was a strong feeling that she was unknown to them all, certainly to Frances and Ellen.

In 1912 the twins were only two, but in 1914 they were four. Had they moved to Barnes when they were four they would surely have had some dim recollection of earlier surroundings. Neither of them did. It can, however, be argued that they both had a strong unconscious memory of a mother with whom they had been in closest contact for the first two years of their lives, but I shall return to this in a later chapter.

In 1912, when Muriel found herself the mother of a third child, there was one problem above all others that could no longer be ignored. Her status. She was still called Miss Perry. She only went out after dark. This was a situation that couldn't go on. If she kept us with her now she would have to do it openly, as a permanent statement. She would have to call herself Mrs. Perry—as she was to do ten years later—and she would have to leave the Sloane Square flat and move into a house with nurses and staff and set herself up there as a widow or divorcee. If we were to stay with her no other course was open. There was never a word to suggest that any of this took place.

She couldn't bring herself to do it. It was too final. She had a horror of being pinned down. 'You're always trying to pin me down,' she would say. It was like that now. She couldn't commit herself to a life of conventional motherhood; everything in her shrank from it, and certainly this was not what Roger wanted her to do. It was true that he liked to see children 'jolly and happy' at the theatre, but babies were not children, and you can't take babies to the theatre. Later, whenever Muriel mentioned Roger's antipathy to us children she always added, loyally and apologetically:

'Of course that was just at the beginning. When you were older and he got to know you he was so devoted to you all . . . '

If Muriel had been with us between 1912 and 1914, when she was at once swallowed up in the war, she would have talked about it later on. She talked willingly enough about the first two years with the twins, her face lighting up with a fond little smile of recollection. 'They were such lovely babies, and so demanding. You'd no sooner finished feeding them than it was time to start again.' But, after the details of my birth, my story abruptly ended, and it ended because she was no longer there to know it. She had no memories at all of me as a child of up to two years old, when the war started, nor did she ever speak of the twins as toddlers of three and four years old.

As time went on I think she came to feel guilty about those two years before the war and persuaded herself that they had never been. Like her own early life she wiped them out. She could never bear to be seen at fault or in any way in the wrong, and I think that later she couldn't bring herself to admit that when she found she was going to have another child she simply lost her head and allowed herself to be persuaded into flight at the earliest possible date. I don't believe she ever quite managed to square this flight with her own conscience. She felt guilty, and in order to ease this guilt she slightly shuffled the cards of her memory. It was the war, she told herself, that had separated her from her children, as it had so many other mothers.

It was never difficult for Muriel to make these slight adjustments in her mind. Once, when I was myself married, I suggested to her that she and Roger had been singularly careless about contraception.

'It wasn't *my* fault,' she said at once, affronted. 'I didn't know what was happening.'

Roger hadn't wanted more children; he had wanted a mistress. He was increasingly enraged each time that Muriel became pregnant, and since she was a woman who crooned over all small things he was no doubt jealous and demanding. His principal aim in 1912 must have been to get her well again, rational, and available once more to himself. He had said, 'Let us let things slide a little longer.' Now, perhaps, it was she who urged this same course. For herself. Roger should make all the arrangements for their children's future, but Muriel must be allowed to get away for a while, even from Roger, particularly from Roger, to find quiet and peace before deciding how to straighten out her life. She lived by instinct and emotion, not by rational thought. Did some voice now whisper that if she could drift a little longer—as it turned out for two years—all these decisions would be taken out of her hands?

Roger probably took her abroad and left her in a hotel somewhere and joined her whenever he could. Something like this must have happened. It seems likely that during these two floating years she never lived anywhere for long but moved about. This would have suited her admirably, and no doubt after the first agonizing break had been made and all her most pressing problems had been left on the other side of the Channel, she recovered her strength quickly enough. This in itself, in hindsight, may well have added to her feelings of guilt.

She liked hotels. In a hotel she could change her clothes several times a day, and she could flirt a little with the husbands of other women under their very noses and know herself safe within the international code of transients. She liked lying in bed and pressing the bell and gossiping with the chambermaids about the other guests. She gave them lives and remarked on their clothes and their eating habits. It was a way of not being alone without involvement. She liked to watch the daily development of amorous intrigues on the beach, smiling to herself beneath her parasol. She was always vaguely malicious about other people's romances, a heritage, perhaps, from her early days. She quickly established her own nest out of the most impersonal hotel bedrooms. By draping her pretty clothes here and there, and wandering about, lavishly splashing the room from the huge bottle of Gherlain's Jicky with which Roger kept her supplied, the transformation only took a few moments. Roger must have bought these enormous bottles of scent in twos because Netta, also, was never without her Jicky.

I think that Muriel had no real home at this time and that when she was not abroad she stayed with friends in London. For she had friends.

We came to know two or three of them, all women, after she moved in with us in 1922. We never liked any of them, and Muriel's relations with them were wary, based, it seemed, on ties of long association rather than affection. They were her confidantes, or partially so. They were all of the same type, rather beautiful, unmarried and childless, idle and lonely, disillusioned with life, solitary drinkers when we knew them, and they all seemed to live on money left them by mysterious men.

Of these women Irene was the most striking, with her classic profile and porcelain skin. She lived in a flat off Baker Street and Muriel sometimes took us with her to lunch there. In the dining-room there was a small round looking glass hung in the most curious place, right up in the cornice; and it was hung at an abrupt angle, trained down like a camera on to the chair at the head of the table. Here sat Irene. When she was talking to Muriel she faced this little mirror in the ceiling, watching herself, and when Muriel was talking to her Irene was still gazing upwards, her lips drawn forward a little, as though for a kiss. She couldn't take her eyes off herself. Sometimes she would turn her head to one side as far as was possible while still maintaining her gaze in the mirror, but of course here in the dining-room the beloved profile was denied to her.

I found this performance enthralling, and after our first visit I said so going home on the bus. I mimicked Irene, widening my eyes and making a *moue* with my mouth. Muriel smiled indulgently.

'I suppose she is a little vain,' she said, 'but you shouldn't have stared like that. I was quite ashamed of you.'

In 1912, then, at the time of her flight, Muriel was a beautiful young woman, attractive to men. After a hated childhood and adolescence she had found passion and comparative security with a father-lover; she had become an accidental mother; she had been rescued and re-planted, if not on solid ground at least on fragrant and well tended sand. But she still had no idea of her potentialities, even of what she wanted to do with her life. In spite of Roger, whom she loved, and her children and the mercy of release from the old life, her instincts and feelings were still in an agony of frustration.

The following undated letter seems to belong to this uncertain time. It is written on Roger's office paper, and Muriel has cut out the address, 31 Bow Street, W.C., against prying eyes, thus destroying three lines on the back of the first page.

Sweetheart mine,

Don't tease me about going away without even letting me know where you go. You know you can't. Surely you know that I love you. Not merely your *body*, dearly as I love that, but *you* yourself. Remember that I am yours & you are mine. We *must* love each other or the whole thing would be a ghastly affair. Love purifies it all. I can't *say* these things to you but I can write them. I mean them too. If it ruined me in the long run you must stand by me. I am miserable without you. Not being a demonstrative man, given to paying you compliments, you may doubt me at times, but I assure you I am all yours sweetheart. I have never written love letters dearest, but I always try to tell the truth to pals. You and I are pals, we are lovers too, altho' I don't deserve it, but I am more to you than any other man is, or can be, as you & I know. Don't let any silly ideas get into your dear head about me except that I am an old fool who loves you.

I don't care what you *think* about other men, you must always put me first.

Sweetheart I must arrange matters for you, and you must tell me frankly what you want to do & it must be arranged to suit you as far as possible. Don't do anything [3 lines missing] everything easy. I am going to eat, but I shall be thinking of my sweetheart. Everything I have you can command & if you don't know it & feel it by this time, you ought to.

Your own
Roger

Somehow two years went by, and in August 1914 Muriel was back in London, excited, fearful, drugged, like everyone else, by rumours of war.

57

Chapter Five

IT COULD be said that the whole of Muriel's life until now had been spent in a search for her own identity. She had no real conception of herself; she had already played several rôles and none of them had been right for her. Now, with the condition of war, the whole of her difficult nature collected itself together and responded with a passion of gratitude.

There are some natures that only in times of crisis inhale their native oxygen: only in disaster and collective suffering do they achieve their own psychic balance. Muriel was one of these. Only by losing herself in service was her deepest nature freed. She was without religion, but in every other way she accepted the conventional mores of her times. She was patriotic: the sight of the Union Jack made her heart beat faster: she was a royalist, a true believer in the British caste system, the general supremacy of the British race, and the inevitability of war. War was glorious. In other words, she shared with the general public a collective mind, and when war was declared she found herself, for the first time in her life, at one with the masses in their pride of heart.

She never told us how it came about that she, along with a handful of other enthusiastic women, came to be pushing hand trolleys stacked with buns and tea on the platforms at Victoria Station, and generally giving cheer to the troops as they entrained for the coast and the ships to France. But she was a founder member of this modest scheme.

I was never able to picture Muriel as a barmaid in Covent Garden, but I can see her vividly on the platforms at Victoria Station in her Kay Francis rôle, pouring tea, handing mugs, concern and kindness in her expressive eyes, and with every movement proclaiming her awareness that soldiers are also men; I can hear her voice, soft and musical, and the way she laughs at their jokes, quietly, more like a low chuckle, not exposing her teeth; and I can see her hand laid lightly on a khaki sleeve in a spontaneous gesture of farewell and encouragement.

This is not a derisive picture. It was only when Muriel was lost in a sympathetic rôle that her rigid defence mechanisms slackened, and when this happened she wore the rôle like an overcoat and made it her own. At these times she was irresistible; she soothed merely by her presence and the unmistakable current of her concern. Like many fatherless children she had looked up to men, and they had failed her; always excepting Roger, men were coarse and treacherous. She now discovered that soldiers were different; soldiers were superior beings, not to be judged by class and rank and accent. Her first contact with the troops had a deep and lasting effect upon her. Her admiration for the Tommy never changed, nor did her feeling of privilege in being among them. She, who had always tended to think ill of people, was now to witness the courage and fortitude of ordinary men, and to discover in herself strengths that she had never dreamed of.

In the beginning the trains, packed with troops, were all rolling out to the coast on the first leg of the war. But the Germans had marched through Belgium almost unimpeded and the Belgians had fled; furthermore, by mid-September, with the battle of the Marne, trench warfare had begun. The scene at Victoria Station had been chaotic since the outbreak of war; now it was doubly chaotic. As well as troop trains pulling out, there were now, at all hours of the day and night, trains rumbling into the dimly lit station packed with Belgian refugees and weary soldiers from the battlefields in France.

'They just fell out when the doors were opened,' Muriel would say, 'they were filthy and dead tired and some of them were wounded. And yet when they saw you with a cup of tea in your hands . . . you can't imagine what it did to them . . . the change that came over them. You never heard a word of complaint. *They* wanted to help *you*.'

The hand trolleys were swamped. Not only were there not enough of them, money and supplies were also hopelessly inadequate. Organization on a totally different scale was now essential, and a

59

journalist who happened to be at the station one day advised an appeal through the daily newspapers. *The Times* took up the cause. A letter headed 'On leave, cold and hungry', triggered off an avalanche of funds—Elders & Fyffes were one of the firms to respond—and another paper printed a photograph of troops at the station above the caption 'Can you spare a pound of tea or sugar?' The response from the nation was immediate and overwhelming and, once started, continued in a steady stream.

5 January, *Daily Graphic*: '. . . A rough buffet had been set up on (the platform), and held an array of tin mugs, certain steaming pitchers of fragrant coffee, and piles of bread and butter and sandwiches. In Victoria as everywhere else the lamps are darkened, and decreased in number, and the damp mist of the evening mingling with the steam of the engines . . . was a luminous haze in the uncertain lamplight.'

The Red Cross had taken over, and on 15 February The Soldiers & Sailors Free Buffet was formally opened, with Muriel as Quartermaster.

Her job was now one of organization. Exceptional circumstances bring out exceptional qualities in people, and Muriel was now seen to be a brilliant and ruthless fund raiser, a wartime Robin Hood whose demands were not easy to resist. She was proud of her promotion to Quartermaster, but she missed being down on the platforms among the men. Their incredible gratitude for her small services to them had been an inspiration to her. Nothing, she felt, that she or anyone else could do to help them could be enough, and she threw herself with a full heart into her new assignment. No ardent missionary ever pitted her wits more cunningly against hard-headed business men than Muriel now did to raise money and supplies. She was tireless and unrelenting. 'Not many of them got past me once I'd made my mind up,' she would say, a sparkle in her eye. Elders & Fyffes were prominent with regular contributions, both from the firm itself and from Roger's own pocket. He was proud of her work, and may well have had a hand in placing her at the station in the beginning. The newspapers went on with their backing.

16 September, *Daily Sketch*: '. . . Those people, and there must be many, who don't visit Victoria Station in the small hours, can have little idea of the magnitude of the work carried on there by the Red Cross Buffet. No form of woman's work could be more useful and more splendidly patriotic. I came away, after a few minutes talk the other day with Miss Muriel Perry with some insight into what womanly energy and self-sacrifice can amount to in times of stress. It may sound a tolerably simple matter to provide refreshments for the brave boys who arrive at the station, tired and hungry, at the most ungodly hours, but I assure you it is not.'

The Buffet was now in full swing, with no lack of voluntary helpers. When Muriel talked to us about those days she never mentioned any of her co-workers by name, but she would say, 'It was never the same after it got so big. A lot of society women came into it.'

18 October, *Daily Graphic*: '. . . On tables on the platform are piles of fresh cut sandwiches, steaming urns of tea and coffee. The buffet is a bright oasis in the wilderness that is still before Tommy's eye, and Mrs. Matthews, who overlooks it, is enthusiastic over the heart that her hundred or so helpers put into their work . . . With so numerous a staff it is possible to have four shifts of six hours . . . "It is indeed quite wonderful in its way," she added in a smiling aside, "to find how gladly they all buckle to the work, and women, remember, who would never dream of entering their own kitchen . . .".'

The Buffet had been running for nearly a year when a special war correspondent for the *Daily Telegraph* in Belgium was brought home and appointed Transport Officer Eastern Command. He was put in charge of Victoria Station. This was Captain Patrick de Bathe, a handsome, moustachioed figure, born in 1876 and now thirty-nine. He had been in the Consular Service and was honorary attaché at St. Petersburg and then at Berlin between 1899–1905. He had been married and had a son, now ten years old.

Pat de Bathe was a man with a jealous disposition and a high temper. Muriel never gave us the details of their first meeting, but

61

no doubt the duties of the Transport Officer and the Quartermaster of the Buffet often overlapped. They got to know each other, and Pat de Bathe fell in love with her. He gave her a ring.

Muriel had always lived her emotional life on an island of dreams, and she made no exception now. She was a flirt through and through; it was a game that she found irresistible. She told him nothing about Roger and her children, but she accepted the ring and wore it.

Oddly enough, she never minded talking about this dubious episode. Once, aghast, I said, 'You mean you didn't tell Pat about Uncle and us?' and she answered, 'How could I? It would have ruined Uncle . . .'

Nevertheless, she must have been careless. After a while Pat de Bathe became suspicious. Somehow he found out where we children lived in Barnes and came, one day, to seek us out. He didn't stay long and when he got back to London he went at Muriel in a towering rage. He seized her hand to remove the misgiven ring and in doing so broke her finger. This dramatic little scene took place at Victoria Station among onlookers. There was a scandal.

'He never forgave me,' Muriel would say, a note of pride in her voice. 'He married again later on—I don't know who—but he wasn't at all happy with her.'

No doubt it was Muriel's duplicity that had so enflamed the jealous Pat de Bathe, but there was another reason why the discovery of her secret may have touched him in a delicate area. His own family could justly be described as riddled with illegitimacy.

He was the youngest child of General Sir Henry Percivale de Bathe, 4th Bart., K.C.B., J.P. Born in 1823, Sir Henry had married Charlotte, daughter of William Clare in 1870, but before this marriage took place Charlotte and Sir Henry, both unmarried, had produced four children, three girls and a boy. After the marriage they had two more boys. It seems almost incredible that a man of Sir Henry's standing should have openly conducted his life in this irregular fashion, but so it was. Legend has it that the obstacle to their marriage was class: Charlotte, the fruitful mother of his children, was not of his class. However that may be, when Pat de Bathe gave Muriel the ring in 1915, the situation was this: Sir Henry was dead; of his three sons, Maximillian, Hugo and Patrick, only the last two were born after the marriage in 1870, thus causing the baronetcy to pass over Maximillian in favour of Hugo. The three daughters, now Lady Burnham, Lady Somerleyton and Mrs. Harry McCalmont were, like their eldest brother Maximillian, all born out of wedlock and consequently outside the possibility of inheritance. It was not until much later, after the Legitimacy Act 1926, that they were able to present a joint petition to regularize their positions. This made no change to the succession of the baronetcy—the Act specifically precludes the inheritance of titles—but it meant that the four petitioners and their issue would now be in a position to take their proper places, after any future family death, in the sharing of properties and monies.

When this petition was eventually filed in 1928 all the claimants were extremely elderly. Since theirs was a case of such a delicate nature they assumed it would be heard in camera and that no one outside the family would ever get to hear of it. It was heard in open court and, although Lord Burnham, whose father was the founder of the *Daily Telegraph*, managed to suppress the more gossipy newspapers, he was unable to prevent a brief summary from appearing on the legal page of *The Times*. On 21 February, 1928, in half a dozen lines, the facts were there for all to see.

It was Lady Burnham who felt this exposure the most keenly. She was a deeply religious lady, always involved in good works, indeed, she was widely known as an almost saintly character. In the ensuing burst of gossip she suffered agonies of shame.

But this was far in the future, and if Muriel ever saw the report in *The Times* she kept it to herself. It seems unlikely that Pat de Bathe had told her of the skeletons in his cupboard, but Mrs. McCalmont may have done so after Muriel's own decortication.

Mouse McCalmont was the most intelligent and emancipated of the three sisters, the only one who had become friendly with Muriel before the rift with Pat. She lived in a house in South Audley Street, and Pat had often taken Muriel there to see his favourite sister. She was quite unlike Muriel's other women friends who were all voluptuous and empty headed; indeed, this was a curious friendship, on Muriel's part unique, in that it was based on respect. Mouse McCalmont was worldly and extremely rich; now a vivacious widow, she had been married long before to a millionaire racehorse owner.

After the war, when Muriel was with us at Barnes, Mouse McCalmont came several times, and later still she came to Castelnau. I remember her as a small, erect, aristocratic little figure with a cool assessing look. She hardly spoke to us children, but she looked us over, top to toe, as she must have done her husband's racehorses in earlier days. You knew she wouldn't miss much. And she was outspoken. The rift with Pat made no difference to her friendship with Muriel.

As so often in this tale of Muriel's activities accuracy is impossible. After the drama of the ring she was forced to leave the Buffet—to us she explained it, 'A lot of them were after my job, they were jealous of me'—but there is no way of knowing exactly when this came about. The last report of her presence at the station appeared in *The Tatler* on 15 August, 1917, under a full page photograph.

> Miss Muriel Perry is the capable Quartermaster of the Soldiers' and Sailors' Free Buffet at Victoria Station, where 200,000 men a month are fed at a cost of one penny per head. They are given meat sandwiches, cake, tea, and fruit. Miss Perry has been working the buffet ever since the war began; first in a small way for Belgian refugees, and later on, after The Times letter, 'On leave, cold and hungry', permission was obtained to feed the soldiers from the front and travelling from one camp to another. This buffet costs about £1,000 per month, and is entirely supported by voluntary subscriptions and has no paid labour whatever . . .

She had worked at the Buffet for three long years, a remarkable achievement for a young woman not hitherto noted for an orderly mind and physical endurance; she must have astonished herself with her resilience to privations. The finger-breaking incident would have taken place at the end of this time. But before this, at some time in 1916, the year of Verdun with its catastrophic casualties, Muriel had written a letter to Roger. It was an emotional last testament, and she didn't send it. She kept the first part of it and, as with all her papers, at some later time cut away a too-revealing passage from the second page and destroyed the rest. It bears no address and is simply headed: Monday morning—12.30. Above this, to give it a more authoritative air, she has later added—1916.

Dearest of Men,

Take care of my babies when I am gone. I leave them to *yr sole care*, to do as you think best, but I want you to see them from time to time, and as their guardian you can do that. They will only have *you* if I go. Don't leave them with their present nurse, only until you can arrange something else. I do not know what to suggest about Miss C—I am afraid it would not answer. Do not bind yourself to anything. My one prayer since their birth has been that they shall grow up to be good women. Tell them this when they are older . . .

Muriel must have wanted her daughters, eventually, to read this part of her letter—the rest would have been for Roger alone—or she would not have kept it. By 'gone' she means dead; she was not to go away until 1918. The reference to 'their present nurse' and 'Miss C' is baffling; we didn't change nurses in 1916 and Miss Coutts was with us from the start and stayed for eleven years. When I first read this letter I smiled when I came to the part about 'good women': Muriel was bored to death with good women.

As early as 1915 she had obtained a passport with a visa for the Italian Red Cross in Italy. She never told us why she had chosen Italy, but clearly it had been in her mind from the first.

When the war started Italy was theoretically an ally of Germany and Austria-Hungary. Throughout the first year of the war she had been courted, with promises of rich rewards if she would come in on their side, by Germany and the Austrian-Hungarian Government separately, and by the Allies. In April 1915 she secretly signed with Great Britain and France, and a month later declared war on Austria-Hungary only. It was not until more than a year later that she declared war on Germany.

It seems unlikely that Muriel knew of these diplomatic machinations. She never read newspapers and, in any case, a rigorous censorship forbade all military news. Why, then, had she planned to go to Italy as early as 1915? One or two X-ray units, run by British and American women, were there already, and she may have heard of these and hoped to join them. Certainly she wanted to be at the front in the fighting. Her initial work among the soldiers on the station platforms at Victoria Station had made a deep impression on her and she wanted, above all, to find some way of getting back into their midst. She had been proud of her job as Quartermaster and founder member of the Buffet, but now it was too big and impersonal. She felt cramped; she never liked working with a lot of people, especially not with women, and she didn't like being told what to do, what she called 'toeing the line'. 'I'm not going to toe the line,' she would say. She fretted for danger, and also for work that was more individual to herself.

A word must be said about Muriel's passport. An affair of fourteen sections, it opens out like a map, and here, too, she has been at work with the scissors. In later, sadder, years she would sometimes get out what papers still remained with her, her medals, photographs and wartime passport, and try to recapture the lost times. And when she did this she would snip out with a pair of scissors a portion of a letter, the address on Roger's office writing paper, and anything else which, at the moment, she saw as a threat to exposure. She has dealt in this way with three sections of her passport; three sections are missing, notably those giving details such as Place of Birth of Holder, Name and Occupation of Parents, and so on. Here, as everywhere else, she has destroyed the path that would have led to her origin. Only the self-created Muriel Perry remains.

She turned to Mouse McCalmont for advice, and together they formed a plan. Mrs. McCalmont would present a Motor Kitchen to the Italian Red Cross through their headquarters in London, and Muriel would take it out to the front in Italy. If this venture proved a success they meant to follow it up with other Motor Kitchens. Muriel renewed her visa.

When she talked to us children about those days she gave the impression that it was she, alone, who had taken the Motor Kitchen to Italy, indeed, we had always believed her to have driven it as well, until one day it turned out that she couldn't drive. In fact, she had a soldier driver with her and a Red Cross co-worker. In all the photographs of the first Motor Kitchen Muriel is standing alongside it with a co-worker—the same one each time—a short, plump little lady in Red Cross uniform. But Muriel never spoke of her, just as she never named any of her co-workers at the Buffet.

This was partly from feline exclusivity and also because the force of her own involvement with her work was so great as to preclude the help of others. Muriel's early history had ruled out sharing; whatever she did she did as though she was doing it alone, even when this was not really the case.

Before finally leaving for Italy they took the Motor Kitchen to France on several short campaigns, but of this no record remains. When Muriel went to Italy she went as a private person attached to the Italian Red Cross and her movements are recorded in her passport. In France she needed no formal passport, but went over as part of a specific military campaign.

She was plunged into the fighting for the first time, but I don't recall her ever speaking of it. Her war stories tended to revolve round personalities; they were never about places and rarely about situations. For instance, she told us that before she left for Italy she had more than once come into contact with Sir John French. He had been impressed by her singleness of purpose, and he told her that if, when the war was over, she wanted to go on working, he would do all that he could to help her.

She left London for Italy on 4 May, 1918. Her passport reads: London to Milan via Havre, Modane, to report to Brit. Consul on arrival at Milan and proceed to Mouselice as directed.

I wish, now, that I had paid more attention to Muriel's stories about Italy and the Duke. One or two of these stories were favourites, often told, but the sort of details that I would now like to know are lost for ever.

The Duke—Muriel never called him by his name, he was always 'the Duke'—was Emmanuele Filiberto, Duke of Aosta. Born into the ancient and illustrious House of Savoy in 1869, he had entered the Military Academy in Turin when he was sixteen and made the army his career. Immensely tall and handsome, he was a very titan of a man; a superb horseman, seated on his horse he looked, for all the world, like a bronze statue rather than mortal man. And it was not only in his physique that his majesty lay: he was supremely royal, steeped in his own ancestral glory. He made his cousin, King Victor Emmanuel III, look like a pipsqueak.

The Duke was now in command of the Third Army. When

Muriel left England the forces under his command had been fighting for the past two years along the Karstic ranges dividing the north-east of Italy from Austria, successfully defending this frontier in eleven battles of the Isonzo. The Duke took a patrician pride in his soldiers, and in these long drawn out battles gave them the motto *fina alla meta* (until the goal is reached). They had conquered Gorizia and reached the foot of Hermanda, less than twenty kilometres from Trieste, and they had repeatedly held the Isonzo line. It was only when German relief forces were added to the invading Austrians at the battle of Caporetto—the twelfth battle of the Isonzo—on 24 October, 1917, that the Italians were defeated and the great withdrawal began. The Duke successfully disengaged his forces and, through the hard winter months and on right through the spring, led them across central Italy to the banks of the Piave. Here he disposed his forces from Montello to the sea. In the following June the Austrians attacked and met with insuperable resistance. In this vital battle of the Piave the Duke displayed his tactical powers: the forces under his command held out and finally conquered. The battle was won, and as a consequence of his conduct in this action the Duke was later promoted to the rank of General of the Army.

Throughout the Piave campaign in June Muriel was at the front with her Motor Kitchen. She was now where she had wanted for so long to be, in Italy, in the thick of the battle among the fighting and the wounded. She was a born nurse, gentle, selfless—no terrible sight was ever too much for her—and untiring. Such a fastidious woman that she couldn't put her hand down the side of a chair for fear of what her fingers might meet with, she seemed unaware of danger. It meant nothing to her. Her job was to tend and comfort fighting men, and this is what she did. The fact that she spoke no word of Italian, either then or later, nor any language but English, never worried her.

'You don't need languages to look after people,' she would say.

Muriel had already come upon the Duke before the battle of the Piave. On a day when he was reviewing troops she and her co-worker, the only two women on the spot, had been presented to him. When Muriel talked about this first meeting she did so in such a way that we took for granted that she had made another instant conquest, and we may have been right; it was, after all, her way.

The presentation over, Muriel soon had occasion to write to the Duke and, not knowing how to begin a letter to a royal military commander, she put: Dear Man. The Duke was so charmed with this novel form of address that thereafter he often signed his photographs and gifts to her with the initials D.M.

In July, after the decisive battle of the Piave, the King visited the front to distribute medals. Muriel was awarded the silver medal, Il Valore Militare: on the back of this medal, on a blue riband with silver star, is inscribed Piave, and, enclosed in laurel leaves, the name Perry Muriel, above the dates 13–23–VI–1918. Of all her decorations—finally eight—this was the one that meant most to her, and she kept a translated account of the ceremony at which she received it.

15 July 1918, *Tribuna*: 'During the summer call for Decorations for bravery, amongst rewards, there were two English ladies. Miss Muriel Perry of the British Motor Kitchen, was presented with the Silver Medal. At the call for the presentation, one free figure with judgement stepped forward, the figure of comfort to our combatants, with charitable face of a sister, always in the first line of trenches, always indefatigably with the example and courageous words, helping the transport for the wounded, contemptuous of the danger on the days of battle. When called Miss Perry took her place like a soldier, before the Italian King, bowed aristocratically, without smile, without touch, when she received the prize for valour. The King pinned the medal, shook hands giving her fervid words of admiration. Miss Perry without a move replied in monosyllables, bowed and disappeared.'

Muriel had been raised in an era when women were expected to engage in flirtatious intrigue; coquetry was as natural to her as the blood running through her veins. Now, as well as the personal fulfilment which came to her through her work, she had captured the interest of the Duke. She never gave a thought to his vast wealth, his palaces in Naples and Madrid and their fabulous treasures and works of art—she was not interested in art—but she responded joyfully to his attentions. He was a brilliant feather in her cap.

In July she received a letter from the Italian Red Cross HQ in London which starts, 'Dear Miss Perry, I apologize for not having sooner answered to your letter without date . . .' Not only did Muriel seldom date a letter, she often failed to seal the envelope. She would push it to one side to delay as long as possible the nasty business of licking the flap, and then forget it. This letter goes on to compliment her on the great success of her Motor Kitchen and her own personal bravery, and urges her to return to London as soon as possible to organize more Motor Kitchens to be taken out to Italy. The writer says he has heard from de Bathe that she is willing to do this.

In August she was back in London. These dangerous wartime journeys across the sea never worried her. In peacetime she was an appalling sailor, always sick, but during the war even this disability seems to have been over-ridden by her dedication to duty. 'In war-time you don't think about yourself, you do what has to be done,' she would say. Once I asked her, 'Weren't you ever frightened?' and she answered, as though to a foolish question, 'There wasn't time to be frightened.' Neither of these statements can have been strictly true, but Muriel believed them to be, and I think her imagination functioned in a particular way that made them truer than they might have been coming from most other people.

In London she saw Roger, Pat de Bathe and Mouse McCalmont. The result of this mission was entirely successful and on 21 August she returned to Italy as Commandant of a unit comprising another Motor Kitchen and three ambulances, donated conjointly by the Italian Red Cross, Mrs. McCalmont and Elders & Fyffes.

The Duke was delighted. Her reputation for fund raising and organization, let alone for bravery on the battlefields, was now so well established that he devised a new scheme to raise money for his beloved soldiers. He suggested to Muriel that she set off on a fund-raising mission to New York, and she agreed to go. Pamphlets were printed and hundreds of photographs of the Duke, to be distributed in interested quarters; a visa was obtained and the date of her sailing set for September. But this assignment never got off the ground. Muriel became ill.

She always claimed that it was the Duke who now saved her life. Later, when the war was over, he, in his turn, became ill and returned the compliment: he said it was her constant presence by his bedside that had saved his life, thus binding them together in equal indebtedness. But that was still to come. Muriel was now gravely ill with dysentery.

The Duke arranged for her to be taken to a convent known to him in Trieste and she was operated on at once. It was a big intestinal operation and her life hung in the balance.

'They carried me in on a stretcher,' she would say, 'but I didn't really know what was happening. I was crying, and the Mother Superior bent over me and took my hand. I can see her face now . . . it was rather a wonderful face . . . She said, "You are crying now, and you will cry again when you leave—but then it will be because you are leaving us!"'

When Muriel first described this affecting scene I could picture it clearly: her dark hair splashed around her head on the stretcher, her tragic eyes full of tears, and the holy nun in her habit smiling down at her. I hoped she had cried when she left.

'And did you?'

'I certainly did not,' she retorted.

The Duke always met with personal devotion wherever he went; his dramatic roman-coin looks, his lineage and, above all, his passion for his country and his soldiers, made him a born leader; the rest followed as a matter of simple inevitability. He had married Princess Elena of Orleans who was deeply religious, and between them they held considerable power. Muriel was the Duke's special responsibility in the convent, and the nuns, no less susceptible than anyone else, nursed her with a dedication that she had never before encountered. Like many people of harsh upbringing she was always amazed by goodness—she never changed in this attitude—and this was her first experience of practical religion. She was deeply impressed. She was herself a good nurse, and on the battlefields she had witnessed countless unforgettable scenes of heart-rending devotion among the men, but this was something altogether different. She could never equate the radiance on the faces of the nuns with the poverty of their lives and the suffering all around them.

She was ill in the convent for months. The Duke brought her a little crystal and silver crucifix for her bedside and a beautiful ancient icon to hang on her wall. He came with flowers and special foods. And he talked: he talked to her about his plans for the glorification of the Italian Army, his vision of the part that Italy should play in the post-war world—he embraced fascism from the start—and the ever-pressing need to raise money from outside. Unaware that she was not interested in history he talked history at her, pacing about the room, adroit in his movements, as large men often are.

'I'm afraid I didn't always listen,' she once said, smiling, 'he used to go on so. I think he had his country on the brain.'

One day he brought with him a letter he had received from England. He read it to her. The writer said he felt impelled to inform the Duke that unbeknown to him he was harbouring in the ranks of the Red Cross an English spy called Muriel Perry. The letter went on to say that the Duke, as a military man, would know the customary punishment for spies. The letter was from Pat de Bathe. Muriel had been less than tactful when she saw him in London.

'And what *are* you going to do?' she said.

For answer the Duke tore the letter in two and threw the pieces on the fire. 'I think he is a very jealous man,' he said.

Muriel was fond of the Duke and grateful and flattered by his attentions. He was twenty-two years older than she, six years younger than Roger. She happily played the part of inexperienced naïveté and enjoyed being reprimanded by a man who was old enough to be her father. During her convalescence a notable Italian figure died. The Duke arranged for Muriel to be at the cathedral for the elaborate burial service. She arrived wearing a scarlet and white check dress and coat. Shocked, the Duke sent her back to change into something more suitable.

'How was I to know?' she said, shrugging, her eyes alight with fun.

When she finally left the convent—dry-eyed—the Mother Superior gave her an ebony and silver crucifix, the kind worn by nuns on a chain from the waist. They would always remember her in their prayers, she said. Muriel kept all these holy gifts, but religion was never within her scope; her tightly defensive interior controls could never accept intrusion on such a scale. Nevertheless, the nuns, and particularly the Mother Superior, had affected her more deeply than she realized at the time.

In January 1919 Muriel was back in London for repatriation. The war was over, but she had no intention of giving up her work. At last she had found a way of life that uniquely suited her special gifts; with the support of the Duke she had tailored it to suit herself. She spent two months in London and then left for Belgium. Still attached to the Italian Red Cross, she organized a rehabilitation centre, raised more money, and then went back to Italy, where she remained from April to December.

The Duke gave her commemorative presents: a charming little Winged Victory in gold on an ivory plinth with a silver plaque inscribed in English 'To Muriel Perry on the 1st Anniversary of the great victory in appreciation of her heroic work with my brave soldiers'; this is signed E. Fidi Savoix. There is a silver cigarette case with his monogram in diamonds surmounted by a coronet with chip rubies to represent the crimson velvet within; the case is opened by a sapphire stud, and on the back is written 'Battaglia del Piave' 29–VI–1918 M.P. from D.M. And there is another silver cigarette case with a strip of blue enamel and a silver star in the middle of it, to commemorate her medal, and the inscription 'Muriel Perry Commandant British Ambulance—Nel triste giorno della fine della terza armata—con gratitudine—per quanto compi per la sua gloria . . . Emanuele Filiberto di Savoix—Trieste 22.VII.1919'.

All the Duke's gifts are engraved with his own facsimile handwriting. Muriel treasured them and, as the years went by, more and more poignantly they came to symbolize the glorious life that was gone for ever.

There are two more entries in her wartime passport. On 1 December she left London for Vienna to report there to the British Military Mission—this was for the organization of another rehabilitation centre—and then on 17 December there is a visa at Paris for Prague via Switzerland. This is the last entry. She kept this passport as a relic of her precious war life, and also, perhaps, because it was the last of the old type passports; from now on they came in a different form.

For the next two years, 1920 and 1921, we children were told that she was still recuperating in Italy, not fully recovered from her big operation, moving from place to place in search of sun and rest. This may have been so. She sent us letters from different hotels to say she was getting stronger or feeling rather weak, and our letters to her were full of concern about her health.

But she was not in Italy for the whole of this time. Roger was not forgotten. She was now conducting her own life with a minimum of controls. She worked spasmodically when the Duke sent her off on a specific mission, but her health was still delicate, and she had long periods in between these missions when she rested and enjoyed herself. In this way it was a simple matter for her to join Roger in Paris or some other capital city where Elders & Fyffes business had taken him abroad. With the war over the firm had once again taken up the threads of foreign commerce, and Roger had always been the director to undertake this side of their affairs; he had a flair with foreigners and he enjoyed travelling. He was hugely extravagant on these trips abroad, but so far he had managed to waive all serious trouble with his fellow directors. This was to come later.

These reunions in foreign hotels must have been rapturous. Nothing keeps lovers at white heat more surely than prolonged absence; that is, if they are well suited. After Roger was dead I often used to wonder what he and Muriel were like in bed together. That he was her first satisfactory lover there can be little doubt, nevertheless her attitude to sex remained ambivalent. She once said to me, 'You don't do that sort of thing any more once you've had children.' Joe Ackerley's Aunt Bunny—Netta's sister—used to say that Roger had a coarse side to his nature, and she may have been right. He was emotionally inarticulate—'I can't *say* these things to you . . . not being a demonstrative man . . .' but he may well have been a powerful performer, uninhibited except in speech. And he was her haven, what home is to people who have a home. Muriel had never had a home, nor parents, nor ever been for anybody the person who came first. Roger embodied the nearest she would ever come to all these things. When she was with him he must have made her feel that in his heart, if not openly in his life, she was, for him, the one who came first. It would be afterwards, when she was away from him, when the compelling force of his sexuality was only a memory, that her Victorian attitude took over. She had always despised men; in her mind sex was something that worked against women, it was something that women had to put up with. She had a deep ambivalence about sex which, as the years went by with no outlet for her violent feelings, drove her inevitably to discontent and drink.

But this was still to come. Those early post-war years were still an extension of the golden age that had started for her at Victoria Station in 1914. They were never to be equalled. What is not clear is why it all came to an end. By 1922 the Italian idyll was over. But why? There must have been plenty of work of the same sort to do, and she never talked as though her association with the Duke had soured. They parted with affection, and some years later she told us that he had flown over to London to take her to lunch at the Ritz and then flown back again. 'Just to see you?' I asked, incredulous, and she answered, 'Of course!'

It may be that Roger urged her return; perhaps, too, she was tired of living in a country whose language she still didn't speak, or perhaps she was simply ready for a change. When she came back to England in 1922 it was not with the idea of an idle life ahead of her. The unproved Muriel Perry of 1914 was now a confident young woman with a shining personal war record—she had been decorated seven times for her war work, three times by the Italians, once by the Belgians, and three times by the British, including the O.B.E. The delicate problem now facing her was to find exactly the right channel through which to offer her services.

Chapter Six

WHOEVER IT was who found the house in Barnes could hardly have done better. It was a well-built little house in Woodlands Road, semi-detached, the right size, and it was just off the route between Uncle's home and his office. With the lush and charming common at the end of the road it was almost like being in the country.

Woodlands Road is a pleasant little blind-end street with a trickle of a stream running across the end. Our house was number 18, one from the end—the blind end—with a flowering chestnut tree at the gate. We had a small garden in the front and a larger one at the back which stopped at the railway line. The house slightly rocked whenever a train went by and we'd boast to strangers that *we* no longer noticed the tremble.

Two pictures have stayed in my mind from when I was three or four, and they are both to do with the twins' calipers. This was during the war when food was short and we all had rickets. To keep the weight off their legs the twins wore irons attached to a harness that strapped around the waist, and they had a surgical pram like an open coffin in which they sat, face to face, their stiff legs stretched out side by side. I see them sitting there, trapped and unprotesting, in that box on wheels, while I jog about in my own pram, unconsciously proving that my legs aren't fixed. And I also see them seated on chamber pots placed side by side in the middle of the night nursery. Because of the calipers they couldn't get off these pots without assistance, so I used to prance around them, pulling faces and generally displaying my freedom of movement.

The twins were docile creatures in those days, totally dependent on our nurses, so lacking in will power as to be almost doll-like, while I was constantly on the move, trying to provoke them into action. Later, as soon as they could get about freely our rôles were reversed: it was they who led and I who followed.

On our outings in the prams—Frances took the coffin pram, Ellen mine—we attracted some attention. For one thing, the twins were like peas, identical; only I could tell them apart and I could never understand how anyone could mistake one for the other. To me there were a hundred differences, admittedly slight, but differences just the same. We made a striking little party: there was the twin-ness and the curious pram; there was elegant Frances dressed in a long dark blue cloak and a charming little bonnet of dark blue velvet and straw which tied under the chin with a velvet ribbon—it was like an inverted little basket for bird's eggs—and bringing up the rear there was Ellen, with me in my own smart pram. And this was not all. When people stopped to stare at us Stella would give one of her wonderful smiles and gazing strangers would go 'Ah!' She had a smile of the purest radiance, and when she was thirteen, soon after Muriel joined us, it vanished never to return.

Ellen stayed with us until the twins stopped wearing calipers, and then she left. She was a strong rosy-faced country girl and we liked her, but Frances must have missed her even more than we did. She used to chase Ellen round the table in the day nursery and Ellen used to squeal until she was caught, and then the apple cheeks got redder.

Frances was strict. She had carroty hair and a temper and we were slightly frightened of her. She slept in a little room off the night nursery and always left the door open. When we talked instead of going to sleep she used to pin the sheet over our heads with a large safety pin clamped into each pillow case. It was terrifying, but it must have worked because when I woke up the sheet was under my chin again.

We didn't hate Frances but we didn't love her. She never played with us, and when she was drying us after a bath she'd rub very hard between the legs. If one of us cried out 'You're hurting!' she'd retort 'No, I'm not', and rub all the harder. I don't remember her ever laughing except for when she was chasing Ellen round the table.

She may have been fond of us but if she was she didn't show it. She never fondled us or told us that she loved us or did anything

77

endearing. She was immaculate, never a crease in her aprons nor a hair blown loose. She took a fancy to the signal-box man on Barnes Common. Up there in his box overlooking the line he pulled a lever to release the gates. She used to organize our walks so that we called in at his box. If a train was not due he'd come down and take a little stroll with us and hold my hand all the way. I used to look forward to this but Frances put a stop to it. I must not hold hands with men, she said, and it was up to me, the ignorant signal-box man knowing no better, to see that my hand wasn't there to hold.

She stayed with us for several years after Ellen left. I've sometimes wondered why. She didn't seem attached to us, and almost any household would have been more enjoyable. She had every other Sunday off and in those slender hours of freedom she must have found romance because she left us, eventually, to be married. We never saw her or heard from her again, and if she did get married we were not invited to the wedding.

Frances and Ellen hated Antie Coutts, and so did all the governesses who came after them.

In appearance Antie was squat, hardy and ruddy faced—she must have been a buxom lass—with wispy white hair caught up in a little round on top. Dressed always in black there was something formidable about her; she had a way of standing which might, you felt, have buckled a tank, feet astride, the weight well back on the heels. She dressed in layer upon layer of strongly smelling black skirts and petticoats and a tight black bodice. Her large wide breasts, pushed up by a whalebone corset, used to fascinate me. I'd press them with the palms of my hands, rubbing, in a circular movement. She always told me to stop at once, but I could tell that she liked it.

Round her waist, under some of the skirts, she wore a chain which had a black bible attached to it hanging at knee length. She never read her bible openly, but when you came upon her unawares she would be sitting, knees well apart, emitting a stronger than usual pissy smell, the bible open in her lap. When she saw you she'd drop the bible forward with a sudden movement, the chain clanging a little, and flip the concealing skirts over it. Nothing would be said, but there was always a moment of electric embarrassment as the finder and the found recomposed themselves into a semblance of normality. Antie was a God-ridden Scottish Presbyterian.

She was a woman of strong feelings who had spent her life trying to subdue those feelings. She loved us, especially me, and she put a strict control upon herself. She never kissed us or caressed us, not even at bedtime. She *said* Goodnight. We were taught that if you were hurt you didn't cry and you certainly didn't expect to be taken into somebody's arms and comforted. The most dire punishment she ever inflicted on us was a negative one: she would stand in front of the offender, arms akimbo across her broad chest, the whole force of her heavy personality beamed on to the culprit before her.

'You had better not say your prayers tonight,' she would say, and then she would leave the room.

It was always a dramatic little scene, full of pain. The loss of Antie's regard quite swamped any terrors that removal from God might have held. It seems a curious punishment coming from a Christian, and it had a strong effect. You had betrayed her trust in you and only time would heal the wound. It was her conviction, often repeated, that no child ever lies, which again seems curious in a woman who had spent so much of her life among the poor.

Together with her obsession with sin Antie had another characteristic. She was a miser. When her brother died she was penniless: when she died eleven years later it was discovered that she had bought a substantial annuity for herself just a few months earlier. In the meantime, throughout her life with us, she made a weekly journey to Barnes, taking us with her, across the common to the bank and straight back again, having cashed a cheque for the weekly expenditure. But she only drew out a fraction of the money that Roger had paid in. No matter how much money she'd had to draw on she would have done the same. With her enclosed nature, sin-ridden and stoical, she was thrifty through and through; it was her first principle of life. She had an abhorrence of show in any form, so we were dressed in institution-like serge because this was good for us. Had there been no food shortage during the war we'd surely have had rickets just the same. Antie couldn't bring herself to spend.

There was never enough to eat. When Frances and Ellen complained of hunger Antie gave them bananas. Roger had arranged for a crate of bananas to be delivered to us every week by Carter Paterson. But a crate of bananas is a lot of bananas in a small household and most of them lay black and stinking in the locked store cupboard to which only Antie had the key.

Nobody ever liked Antie except us. No doubt she treated Frances and Ellen and the others badly. She was a dour and eccentric old peasant woman who rarely laughed, and when she did it was slightly shocking because her false teeth were a deep yellow. She was never cross, never showed favouritism, although we all knew that I was the object of her adoration, and in spite of her being weird and smelly we were not afraid of her. She was ours. She would have gone to the stake for us.

Dr. Coutts's furniture was like Antie herself, ancient, stuffy and bad smelling. Hideous, too. The two downstairs rooms, front and back, were furnished with her things, and so was her bedroom. Every piece was chipped or broken; there wasn't a chair which sported four healthy castors, and the round table in the front-room had a broken leg which had to be placed just so. These rooms were perpetually dark, with heavy musty old curtains shutting out the light. Nothing was ever mended or changed and, except for the gleaming black grates which were Antie's especial pride, nothing was cleaned. Windows were kept firmly shut against draughts.

Antie's bedroom, at the head of the stairs, was forbidden to the cleaning woman. Its door was always ajar, day and night, emitting a constant whiff of mould. We hardly ever went into this room. It was Antie's private lair and deeply alarming. But the other two rooms on the first floor, the day and night nurseries, with Frances's little room off the night nursery, were a different story. These rooms were light and airy and had been specially prepared for us with white beds and furniture and pretty floral wallpaper. The day nursery overlooked the garden. Ellen slept in one of the three rooms on the top floor.

Mr. Woodhouse, a bachelor, lived next door to us in the end house. Antie said he was a retired school master and very learned. Occasionally, he would lean against a silver birch at the end of the garden and chat with Antie over the fence, but the moment we joined them he'd move off. Antie said he was shy with little girls. We were never asked into his house.

On our other side were the O'Connors. Major O'Connor was

serving with his regiment in India and rarely came home on leave. His wife was a tall, reserved, rather stately woman with smooth grey hair. There were two sons, Patrick and Dennis, who were only at home for school holidays. Patrick was handsome in a Brylcreem sort of way, and Dennis had freckles. The O'Connors took little notice of us until the Major came home, and then almost at once he'd be out in the garden and calling over the fence.

'Where's my sweetheart? I want to see my little sweetheart!'

He had crinkly white hair and a wide face and very blue eyes, and he was stocky and muscular. The fantasy of his being in love with me was fostered whenever he came home on leave. One day, when I was about ten and he was alone and, he said, lonely, he invited me into his house, sat me on his knee and undid all my clothes.

'What—*another* vest? Let's see what's underneath, shall we?'

It was said he was a ladies man and that Mrs. O'Connor was an unsuitable wife for him. Soon after the unbuttoning incident he retired and they all went to live somewhere else.

On the opposite side of the street there was an Irish family of nine children and their parents. We often saw them in the street but never spoke. Antie said they were disgraceful. For one thing there were too many of them—in itself a disgrace—and they were allowed to run wild, she said. Certainly they played in the street. The bearded father was a professor at a university and had once, outside his own house, been mistaken for the coal delivery man—the ultimate disgrace. I used to gaze at them from the other side of the street but I never thought of crossing over. Now I wonder what they thought of us and why they, so uninhibited and casual, never broke down the barrier between us.

The other personage in our small world was Uncle. He'd arrive, out of the blue, two or three times a year, always in the same car with the same driver, Morland, and we'd rush out to help bring in the parcels that had overflowed from the seat on to the floor. When he arrived like this, almost buried under presents, he announced himself as William Whiteley, the Universal Provider, and we gave shrieks of joy. We'd drag him into the house, all shouting at once, and scramble to sit on his lap. We weren't allowed to sit on laps so this was our ultimate aim when someone—anyone—came in from outside. We'd be scolded afterwards, but not while the visitor was still in the house. It was worth a scolding.

We knew that Uncle was not our uncle, just as Antie was not our aunt, but we never discussed these things among ourselves, just as we never discussed the remarkable fact that we, unlike everyone else, had no friends.

Uncle never stayed long on these visits, and as soon as he'd left Antie would sweep up the presents into her capacious arms and carry them off to her bedroom—another temptation combated—to add to her ever-mounting hoard.

Sometimes the post would bring us a foreign parcel from Muriel; party dresses, woolly caps and gloves, all sorts of things. We were allowed to undo the parcel, taking care not to cut the string, and gaze for a while at the treasures within. Then Antie would scoop them up, distaste written all over her face, and stomp with them out of the room. Sweets, crystallized fruits, toys and clothes were all condemned as 'too good to eat—play with—wear'. All such gifts found their way into Antie's secret hiding place in her dark and musty bedroom.

She was a crank, mistaken in almost everything she did, but her motives were selfless; everything she did, always, was done with our good in mind. Pretty clothes might have made us vain, so day after day we wore prickly serge. But there was one sop to vanity that she fostered. The twins had strong brown hair and mine was fair and silky. We were all as proud of my blonde hair as though it were something that we'd collectively won at a fair. So it had to be brushed and brushed, and at night it was knotted up in unyielding rags. This wasn't done every night, just often. We all wore a side parting and a fringe, and my hair, being so precious, was the longest. Later, Muriel would say:

'If you ever go dark I'll murder you!'

In the summer Uncle sometimes arrived in the car and then sent Morland away and went home to Richmond by train. When this happened we'd decorate his grey homburg with flowers and small branches, slipping the stalks behind the ribbon in a frenzy of care. 'Look out, you'll make a mark!' We must have made many marks on the pale grey felt but he never seemed to mind. He'd given us each a miniature set of gardening tools—this was a present that

82

Antie approved of—and she'd marked out three separate little strips of border where we could each grow what we liked. When Uncle was going home on the train we plundered our small allotments to decorate him, and when he left, his garlanded hat upon his head, we set off with him across the common dancing round him like a carnival. When we got to the station we'd leave him at once and race home to take up our stand at the bottom of the garden to wait for his train to come by.

I can still feel the thrill as we picked up the first throb of the train in the distance. One held one's breath as it approached, nearer and nearer, louder, clearer. If we missed him! But we never did, and the climax only lasted an instant, a flash across the eyes.

He'd have pulled the window down and be leaning right outside the train. And his flowered hat would still be on his head. We waved and leaped about in an ecstasy of joy, but he was gone in a flash, unbearably gone, and now the rhythmical noise of the receding train, taking him from us, was like a mocking dream when the goal is snatched from the grasp. We never knew when he'd come back.

We never questioned the isolation of our lives. We had no friends at all, neither children nor grown-ups, and we weren't allowed to go to public places, not even to church, particularly not to church, since how could there be a place for such as us in the house of God? Old and ignorant as she was, Antie must have put two and two together and seen our situation as fishy, to put it mildly: the young and absent mother, the banker's order from Uncle who was no uncle, not to mention the remarkable resemblance between him and all of us. I think it was her aim to prepare us as rigorously as possible for a life of atonement for the wickedness of our birth. She saw us as children born of sin and wickedness—no doubt she'd had plenty of experience of illegitimate children in the slums of Glasgow— and since she loved us her first principle in our upbringing was to keep us as rigidly removed from the world as she could manage. No doubt this fitted quite comfortably with her instructions. If we mixed with people they might talk to us, asking questions. Furthermore, we might catch something.

Once a year, for our health, Antie took us for a month to a house by the sea that Uncle had rented for us at Ramsgate, Margate,

Bridlington or Teignmouth, and we paddled and bathed in the icy sea and ate jam sandwiches on the beach and climbed rocks and shrimped. We picked wild flowers and made daisy chains and sand-castles and ran after butterflies with our nets; we had donkey rides on the sands and watched the Punch and Judy Show. We did all these things like other children, but we did them all alone. Even on the crowded beaches and in the sea, where parents and children paddled and swam and splashed each other, our isolation from the human race persisted. We didn't know how to be sociable—we knew we mustn't be—and no one ever approached us.

We must have made an uneasy picture: three solemn, emaciated children and their old and formidable guardian. Solitude communicates itself, and maybe parents kept their children from us as rigorously as Antie kept us from them for fear of catching something. Certainly we returned from every summer holiday as friend-less as we were before. And hardly any healthier. What we were all suffering from was boredom, the monotonous erosion of the ego. We enjoyed the sea and the beautiful pale sand between our toes and the search for wild flowers, but the deeper need, the loneliness and longing for physical contact was still as urgent as it always was in Barnes. Each of us would have willingly exchanged the whole of the seaside holiday for one emotional scene, a pistol shot, a torrent of tears, a threat of suicide—anything of this nature that included us.

Stella, Muriel's 'son', was a thumper. In spite of cries of 'Stop it, she'll get cancer if you hit her *there*,' she was always thumping Helen. Once she tried to throw her out of a window. She was our savage. It was she who bit a piece out of a tumbler so that for years afterwards we were made to drink out of enamel mugs. She was a tomboy sort of girl who hated indoors. She had a passion for animals, but we weren't allowed to keep animals. We had a tortoise—it some-how wandered in one day and never left—called Blimey, and a frog in the little pond at the bottom of the garden. And there was Bobby, the robin who nested every year in the ivy on the wall dividing us from the O'Connors'. One year Bobby's mate was so tame that she allowed us to feed her with milk-soaked biscuit proffered on the tip of a finger when she was sitting on the nest, and Bobby himself used to land on the nursery window sill and sit there, cocking his head from side to side. Once he flew in and perched on a thimble on the mantelpiece.

My sisters had their special twin relationship but I never felt left out, and I never got thumped, possibly because I was always ailing. I couldn't keep food down; I was always vomiting and having headaches and temperatures.

This weakness couldn't be ignored, and nor could Stella's violent and inexorable will. It was only Helen who never found a way to draw attention to herself. She sometimes leant on primogeniture, but it always failed. There was a paleness, a lack of firm outline, to her personality. She somehow lacked a true identity. She was left-handed and forced to use the right. In Stella and myself there was clearly a life force of extraordinary tenacity which kept bursting out like lava with claims for recognition. Had there been someone to speak for Helen, to cherish and foster her individuality, she might have found a more rewarding rôle to play than merely that of Stella's twin, but there was no one to do this and, sadly, there never was in her later life either.

We were all excessively childish. We lived from day to day in a state of head-splitting boredom and anxiety, and we all grizzled.

'I don't know what to do.'

'Well, go into the garden and play.'

'I don't want to.'

'Well, you can't stay fugging in the house all day. Go on, all of you, out into the garden, and don't come in again till teatime.'

I hated being put outside. I hated out-of-doors. I'd stand there, leaden, as though I'd just been thrown into a cell facing a life sentence. How could one pass the hours till teatime? Sometimes, in a despairing effort to make contact with some living thing, I'd dig up worms from the borders and lay them in a line on the lawn and kiss them one by one.

In winter the highlight of our week was dancing class in Barnes. Frances took us. It was held in a hall at the back of the cinema in the High Street. To reach this hall you had to pass behind a black curtain which hung down at the back of the stalls. The curtain was divided in the middle and you could pause for exquisite seconds at the point of division and watch the madly flickering screen. It was like being gently stabbed by a thousand needles. There was always a rowdy audience, catcalls, stamping feet, whistles and cries of encouragement greeting love scenes and galloping cowboys alike, while the piano in the orchestra pit fought it out with the sten-gun crackle from the screen. I was a film addict from the first. A gigantic close-up of Lupe Velez, her Indian ink-black lips writhing in a love agony, made me feel I was drowning in some magical embracing substance, and later, in dancing class, I would float a length of chiffon about and roll my eyes and pant as openly as I dared.

When we came out the High Street would be dark and stinging cold, perhaps with snow on the ground. We'd be tired and a bit giddy from the nervous excitement. The homeward walk across the common was endless, and in the dark it was spooky, too. There was a lunatic asylum at the end of Priory Lane, just a hundred yards from our road. Some wag, offering his protection, once told Frances and Ellen that the loonies were always escaping and hiding in the bushes on the common, waiting to pounce on innocent passers-by. Frances was just as fearful as I was—her voice turned snappy and she bunched her cloak about her—but the twins were never alarmed by the dark.

Antie would be waiting for us. She'd come clumping down the stairs to answer the door-knocker, and then she'd follow behind us up again, puffing, her face scarlet. The fire would be blazing in the day nursery, the table laid for a tea of boiled eggs, and a pile of bread would be set by the fire ready for toasting. We always had boiled eggs after dancing class. Antie would stay with us, watching the yellow fingers of buttered toast as we dipped them into the yolk.

She would want to hear every detail about the dancing class, and she looked to me to act it out for her. She hung on my words, her bright little eyes, all blue without whites, glistening as I spoke. Usually I played up, glad of an audience, but sometimes the burden of her love seemed to choke me, and I'd punish her with silence. When this happened it was called sulking.

'Shrimpy's got the sulks again. Well, we'll just have to do without Shrimpy, won't we?'

It was Uncle who called me the Shrimp. He had a dye made of a little scarlet shrimp for my dove-grey writing paper, and there was always a sugar icing shrimp on my birthday cake. Uncle liked to stamp our names on things. Even our gardening tools had our names on them: Helen, Sam, Shrimp. Only Helen, to her distress, was always called by her proper name. When she was thirteen she wrote pleadingly to Muriel: 'I don't like the name of Helen at all. Do find me another one. Do find me a boy's name or a nickname.' She signed this letter Plain Helen.

I remember Frances leaving but not which year it was; I fancy I was six or seven. There were no tears or last-minute hugs. She left briskly, her pretty bonnet tied beneath her chin, the flaming hair smooth and orderly. We never saw her out of uniform except in a long concealing nightgown.

After she had gone we had governesses who came and left in quick succession. They were poor creatures, timid, no longer young, whom life had already defeated. Often there were tears; not one of them had the smallest gift for teaching or even the spirit to stand up to us. As always it was Stella who was the ringleader. Enormously tall, she went for them; she threw things at them, stabbed at them with her pencil and then banged out of the nursery—which Antie said should now be called the schoolroom—refusing to do lessons. Nothing would persuade her to come back until the governess had left, at least for the day.

No one had ever had more than the flimsiest control over Stella. 'She's her own worst enemy' had become a sort of litany that Antie and Frances chanted in unison. Looking back there were not so many acts of real violence; it was the potential of her will power that impressed itself upon us all. I was never in the least afraid of her— I knew she would never turn on me—but, living as she did, precariously balanced on the brink of a personal disaster in which Helen and I would also, when it came about, be sure to go tumbling down as well, she generated a tension, a feeling of foreboding, that kept one permanently in a state of unease.

There was something wild in her nature, some atavistic element less cushioned than is usual. She was like an elephant standing in a forest of trees, its head merely leaning to the tree trunk in its path, hardly seeming to move, so that the sound of ripping roots and the crash of the fallen tree seem to be happening in a context unassociated with the animal's progress. She was slapdash and inarticulate and would stand bewildered and uncomprehending among evidence of wreckage.

'Why don't you think before you act? What do you suppose will become of you if you go on like this? You're your own worst enemy, that's what you are, your own worst enemy. And you always have been.'

She was a vital child with a restless and energetic spirit which demanded action; inactive she suffered a kind of perplexity, like someone who'd been hit on the head or was psychologically handcuffed. She couldn't adapt.

There were three yearly treats in our calendar, the Christmas pantomime at Drury Lane, Bertram Mills's Circus at Olympia and the Richmond Horse Show. Every year as the date for the Horse Show drew near Uncle would say that, alas, he'd failed to get us seats for his day, the day when he presented the donkey and cart, but he'd got them for the day after and he'd be thinking of us, he said. The difficulty was that on his day he always took Netta and his first family, and after the presentation he introduced them to his friends and colleagues.

We had learnt to ride when I was six, and the memory of those afternoons in Richmond Park are the happiest of my childhood— like dancing class when we were younger they were followed by boiled eggs for tea—but even here there was a shadow. Helen was terrified. Somehow she couldn't do it; somehow her over-long limbs totally failed to communicate with a horse. As fear went flooding through her the horse was instantly aware of it and ran away with her. She could never look at us when we caught up with her, and we tried not to look at her as she sat there hunched with rage and humiliation, her face livid with unshed tears.

She wouldn't give in. I don't believe she ever asked to be let off this twice-weekly nightmare. It was Stella and I who pleaded with Antie privately.

'She doesn't like it. Does she have to do it?'

'Of course she does,' said Antie, who had never sat on a horse in her life.

'But it isn't fair. She's frightened . . .'

'Fiddlesticks. She'll soon grow out of it, you'll see.'

88

Muriel.

Diana, Helen and Stella in Richmond Park during the War. The photograph was taken to send to Muriel.

Helen and Diana bathing.

Diana aged 15.

Diana, Stella and Helen in fancy dress.

Joe, Nancy, Peter and Netta.

Muriel, 1914.

Muriel.

The Duke of Aosta.

Awaiting decoration, July 6th, 1921.

Muriel.

Roger Ackerley.

Roger and Muriel touring in Austria.
The man on the left was probably an agent.

Muriel in the Church Army, 1948.

But she didn't grow out of it, and the memory of her masochistic courage haunts me still.

At the Drury Lane pantomime we always sat in the royal box, with tea and chamber pots in the interval awaiting us in the ante-room. Uncle sent Morland to take us in his car, but he never came himself, from his office round the corner, to see us 'jolly and happy'. Perhaps we always went on a Saturday when he was at home.

A treat of a different sort was an air raid at night. I would be wrapped in a rug and carried—a pleasure in itself—downstairs. The twins came down by themselves; being so tall they were difficult to carry and Stella had once squirmed out of Frances's arms and somehow landed on the front door handle, making a deep gash in her forehead. While the raid was on we sat bunched together downstairs and Antie gave us warm milk and biscuits. On the day after we'd look for shrapnel on the common to add to our collection. Once, on a summer's afternoon, we stood in the garden transfixed as a zeppelin in flames floated by in its appalling beauty so slowly that it seemed to be fixed in the sky.

If Antie took a newspaper we never saw it. Frances had a mysterious grapevine of information about murders and scandals unconnected with the war, and the cleaning woman came daily with her own sources of catastrophic nourishment.

As the war went on Frances took us for walks up to the top of Roehampton Lane where wounded soldiers from the Star and Garter limb hospital were to be seen on benches taking the air. They wore bright blue suits and scarlet ties, and sometimes they whistled at Frances. When they did this she became very hoity-toity.

'Take no notice,' she'd say, 'the cheeky beggars . . .'

To us the war meant separation from our mother, or so we were told, and when it was over and she still stayed away and our life went on at Barnes without the smallest change, we simply forgot or ceased to wonder why she wasn't with us.

Chapter Seven

IT WAS on a spring afternoon in 1922, when I was ten and the twins were twelve, that we heard a knock at the door. This was still something of an event in our house and we raced to open it. I was the first to get there, the twins close behind me and Antie waddling up behind them. I opened the door.

On our doorstep was a tall vision wearing a large hat with a long, rust-coloured veil falling loosely over it. Beyond, at the gate, was a motor car, its chauffeur on the pavement looking carefully away. This transcended anything we could have hoped for. Speechless, we stood and stared. The vision spoke.

'Well . . . haven't you something to say to me? Surely you know your own mother . . . ?'

The voice matched with the rest.

We were not the only ones to stare. Muriel, too, could hardly believe her eyes. Throughout the intervening years, whenever she was lonely or ill or miserable she had comforted herself with the thought: One day I'll get back to my babies . . . Encapsulated in her memory as though it were yesterday she had a picture of the baby twins she had last seen ten years ago. In all her letters to Antie she had begged for snapshots of us, but Antie had turned a blind eye to these pleas. When Muriel drove out to see us that day she knew, of course, that we were no longer babies, we were children now, but she had lived on her memories for so long that they had superseded common sense. She was totally unprepared for the sight of two giraffe-like creatures and a spindly small one, all freak-thin and poor looking, who stood gazing at her when the door went back. At the sight of us she felt her world collapsing about her.

After the first shock on the doorstep she followed us into the house, into our home, and looked around in mounting disbelief:

everywhere her eyes met with ugliness. It was not only the house that was dirty; we were dirty, too, and so were our dreadful clothes, serge tunics with white blouses that were black with dirt round the neck; we were white faced and nervy and, horror of horrors, we all spoke with an accent. She remembered the clothes she had sent us from France and Italy. Where were they? Why were we all so twitchy? We looked uncared for, almost like slum children. How could it all have come about? Why had no one told her? It was like a nightmare.

To get Antie out of the room—she was hovering about like some dusty black panther protecting her young—Muriel asked for a cup of tea. She wanted to be alone with us, to feel our presence, to ask for an explanation, to touch us, grimy as we were, but in the short time that Antie was in the kitchen she couldn't find a word to say. It never crossed our minds that she was too upset to speak. Then Antie came back and poured her a brew such as servants drink, and it came in an old brown tea pot with a rubber on the spout. There was no tea service.

It would be difficult to say who received the biggest shock that afternoon, Muriel, Antie, the twins or I, because the reasons for shock were different for each. Antie must have had her own night-mare in the kitchen as she waited for the kettle to boil. What did this visitation mean? After all this time was it the end of the old life? As well as a threat to her own future what unwelcome effects would it have on the children?

The twins were thrown into total confusion. For the first two years of their lives they had been as truly loved as any children could be. For the whole of this time Muriel had been totally occupied with them, and then, abruptly, this familiar and stable centre had vanished from their lives. From then on there had been no more cuddles, no large expressive hands to hold them, no loving voice to soothe them. Now, as it might be, conjured from some genie's lamp, this loving presence was returned to them. They didn't, of course, understand this at the time, but what a turmoil of emotion they must have felt.

For me it was different again. To me she was a true stranger, as I was to her. She and I had been apart from the beginning and I don't imagine she ever included me in her fantasies during the years of separation. In this way, unlike the twins, I wasn't loved and then abandoned; I had been on my own from the start. Nevertheless, the dazzling creature in our midst was my unknown mother materialized at last.

I once explained this subtle situation to a friend who said: 'You think you didn't resent her for having left you, but you must have done. Every child feels resentment against its mother for having abandoned it.'

I didn't; possibly because no one ever suggested to me that I'd been abandoned. But I see now that the twins did, and that this vital difference in our earliest beginnings was responsible for the different relationship between them and Muriel and Muriel and me. I see now that from the first day when she appeared on our doorstep there was, between both of the twins and Muriel, an unconscious straining by all three to return to the halcyon beginning when love flowed freely. It was a deeply disturbed state of affairs, understood by no one, and in time it came to trigger off explosions of jealousy, bewilderment and blame.

At the time of this visit Muriel was in London to look for a job. She wanted to go on working. She had plenty of contacts now and considerable confidence. Her health was good. She was not in a hurry; she meant to take her time, to sift through all the possibilities and make a wise decision. There must be no mistakes. If nothing more inviting offered itself she had two strings to fall back on, both of which, at the moment, she was keeping up her sleeve: she could still go to America to raise money for the Italian Red Cross—she had the trunkful of pamphlets and photographs of the Duke with her, all the paraphernalia which had been ready when she fell ill—or she could get in touch with Sir John French who had promised to help her.

Muriel was aware that this was a crucial time in her life. It was of vital importance that she make the right decision. She was now accustomed to living at a distance from Roger, and she knew that to go back to the old way of simply being on hand when he was free to come to her, with nothing to do in between times, would never again be enough for her. She was not the same creature who had left England in the war. She had proved herself the equal of anyone in courage and fortitude; she had played an equal part with men in the horrors and terrors and suffering of war, and she knew that she had grown in interior stature from the experience. She wanted to do something worthwhile, to help people, and she knew that she could do this. She had never understood her own nature and its urgent demands, and she didn't understand it now, but she had proved that she was uniquely capable in certain areas of activity and she was determined to build on this.

She was staying in London at this time with Doris Delevingne. Doris was then only twenty-two—ten years younger than Muriel—but already she had made quite a name for herself in the highest circles for her mad exploits and rich lovers. She was pretty, intelligent and wild; unlike Muriel she was remarkably uninhibited for a strictly brought up young woman of that period, and she openly claimed for herself a total sexual freedom. She was witty, original, outrageous, a marvellous entertainer; women liked her as much as men did. Everyone except for a few aristocratic mothers and their strait-laced friends liked her, and she treated her women friends with great generosity and kindness.

Muriel never told us how she met Doris—they must have tumbled over each other somewhere and Doris, in her open-handed way, must have offered to put Muriel up for a while—nor did she mention the lovers. But she sometimes spoke with nostalgia of the exquisite things in Doris's flat in Park Lane, the sumptuous furnishings, the glass and silver, the clothes, furs, jewels; altogether, the ambience of high-life surrounding her made a deep impression on Muriel, indeed, her time with Doris became, in retrospect, a cameo of excellence.

It seems unlikely that Doris knew of our existence. She would have made a good confidante; with her intelligence and kindness and her nose-thumbing attitude to the conventions she might have given good advice. But when Muriel went to stay with her she had no intention of moving permanently to Barnes, and she may well have told Doris a different tale about herself which later, when her plans so dramatically changed, she felt herself unable to retract. Doris was noted for her honesty with women, and Muriel could never bear to be seen in a bad light; she wasn't able to endure being at a disadvantage. There was also her rooted conviction that if it were

93

ever to be found out that Roger had two families he would be ruined. This had become a mania with her. No doubt Roger had often stressed the need for discretion, but he seems to have allowed himself considerable licence; his friends and business associates had always known of his liaison with Muriel, and all of them deplored it. It was only his first family who were kept in the dark.

Did Muriel really not know that their secret was no secret? Or did she use it like a crutch that she dared not relinquish? Again and again, later, she would explain some action on her part: 'I had no choice,' she would say, 'if it had ever come out it would have ruined Uncle.' Yet it had always been out and he was not ruined.

When the visit with Doris was over they never met again. A few years later she married Viscount Castlerosse, and later still she died of an overdose of barbiturates.

What prompted Muriel to drive out to Barnes? What prompted her to break the rule—no visiting—laid down ten years before? An inner compulsion is seldom a simple matter. She had a strongly masochistic side to her nature and a wider division of brain and heart than most; it was only in some inaccessible part of her pysche that her right hand knew what her left hand was doing. Later she explained the visit by saying that she had decided on the spur of the moment to give herself a little treat. There were no problems to be faced at Barnes. How could there be? Money was lavish and regular, our letters frequent, loving and uncomplaining; those from Roger had always kept her informed of our latest requirements and how he had dealt with them, sometimes adding an affectionate word about 'dear little girls'. Miss Coutts's letters didn't count; she was almost illiterate and only when pressed would she send a few lines to say that she had nothing to report, no worries of any kind.

We can picture Muriel in the car on the return journey into London, her dreams of her own bright future like so many broken toys. She must have felt herself utterly deserted. She had always had a pathological horror of dirt and bad smells and any form of ugliness —war horrors were something else—and now she was plunged into this nightmare. She didn't blame Roger—'Men don't notice things' —she blamed Miss Coutts and Life, which had turned against her.

94

She never told us how she spent that first evening of disillusion.

She seems to have put up no resistance, and I've sometimes wondered why she gave up so easily. People usually do what they want to do. She could, after all, have got rid of Antie Coutts and her belongings, had the house done over and found another housekeeper. She could have sent us away to boarding school—this was to come later—or she could have sacked Antie Coutts, got rid of the house, and herself have started up with us somewhere quite different.

Instead, at a single stroke, she renounced all her dreams of independence. Calling herself Mrs. Perry—which we had always supposed her to be—instead of Miss Perry, she decided to move in at Woodlands Road, into the house which appalled her, and take charge, at the same time keeping on Antie Coutts who was equally repellent to her. And to do this and protect Roger from exposure she must simply disappear from society, disappear out of the life of every friend and acquaintance who was not already in the know. This meant dropping, without explanation, everyone who had come into her life since the beginning of the war. She made one exception only, Mouse McCalmont, who already knew the situation, and it was only after a year or two that she took up this friendship again. All the others were lost to her for ever. 'I had no choice,' she would say, 'I had to think of Uncle.'

It was a desperate solution for someone who would always be in sore need of support and reassurance, a very invitation to the old enemies, loneliness and frustration, and this time, coming when it did, when she was beginning to be comfortable in the new rôle that she had worked so hard to achieve, the rôle of an independent young woman with an admirable public record for war services, and a private record of considerable conquests, the dangers were formidable.

I think there were two subterranean pressures at work in Muriel's decision. She was truly shocked and distressed at our condition, and this hit her in an area that was always delicate: she had never lost her feeling of guilt at having fled soon after I was born. I think she saw this new crossroads in her life as a chance to wipe out the now regretted flight and start all over again. And there was something else, perhaps the strongest pull of all: right from the start she had formed a passion for her 'son Sam'. Although Stella now looked a fright the old alchemy was still there. Muriel wanted to be with her 'son'.

I have said that she was looking for work. She knew this was the sensible course, but I now wonder if it was what she really wanted, if perhaps it was no more than a gesture towards an independence that she knew in her heart she could never achieve. I now wonder if she may even have felt a certain relief as the bonds between herself and Roger and herself and us children tightened their hold upon her destiny.

Yet if this, or something like it, is the truth, it was not what she told herself. She tended to dramatise a situation, and now she told herself that she must sacrifice her own inviting future—her whole life—for the sake of her children. It was her duty as a mother. When she moved in at Woodlands Road a few months later she was firmly established in this attitude.

When Muriel came to live with us in 1922 a certain event had taken place in Roger's life without her knowledge. Towards the end of 1919, in the Grosvenor Chapel in South Audley Street, he had married Netta Aylward. They were still living in Richmond; Joe and Nancy were now grown up but living at home, and Peter had been killed in the war. In this way Roger was the only person involved who knew all the true facts of this complicated situation. For instance, no one in his first family knew of the existence of his second family, although we knew of them; Muriel believed him to have been married to Netta from the beginning; we children didn't know he was our father; Antie had been fed a story of semi-fiction, semi-truth, and scrambled the two together. Roger was the only one who knew all of the truth.

The reasons for this marriage are uncertain, as are the reasons for his not having married Netta long before. Possibly the death of their eldest son, the one who would have gone into Elders & Fyffes, drew them to each other in their grief. Muriel was never to know of the marriage.

When she moved into our household we were sent away until the upheaval was over. Antie took us to the seaside to a rented house. With all of us in her way, Muriel said, she would never get anything done, but her real reason was to get Antie out of the house.

It had been undeclared warfare between these two from the first encounter; Muriel was not only repelled by Antie, she was afraid of her, so much so that she never found the courage to tell her to go.

'Wouldn't you think she'd go of her own accord? Can't she see there's no room for her now? Whose children does she think you all are?'

Antie sat on: she was impossible to uproot. She had no relations and nowhere to go, she said. Did she also drop a hint threatening exposure?

Roger's response to emotional scenes was one of tortoise-like withdrawal. There had always been scenes in his own home between Nancy and her mother and he had built around himself an invisible barrier which made him inaccessible to either party. Nancy once told me that she often longed to put her case to him, to get at him first when he came home from the office in the evenings, and that she never once succeeded. 'I don't think Mother did either,' she said. Now, he slipped out of the war between Muriel and Antie in just the same elusive way.

Dinks dear,

It seems *years* since I saw your dear face & it is poor consolation to hear you sobbing your heart out at the other end of the phone. Buck up, old girl, you are young & beautiful & have a lot of pals who would do anything for you. Don't let a crossgrained old woman spoil your life.

Did he forget that the pals were no longer there to offer encouragement, that she had given them up for his sake?

Except for Antie's bedroom—she had firmly locked the door and taken the key away to the sea with her—Muriel had the house properly cleaned out and the stinking larder with its rotting bananas fumigated. There was not much she could do with Antie's furniture, but several pieces were mended when we came back and the overall effect, with the windows opened and all the fustiness gone, was of a different house. From now on Antie lived almost entirely in her bedroom, and so did Muriel in hers. Antie's door, which had always been left ajar, both day and night, was now implacably shut and she rarely joined us, even for meals. She had a gas ring in her room on which, we already knew, she sometimes made herself scrambled eggs, rummaging for her supplies, butter, bread, milk, eggs and salt, under the bed; she used the floor as her larder. She still made her weekly journey to the bank, always at the same time on the same day, stomping down the stairs, bonneted and shawled, and looking straight ahead. Only now she went alone. When she came back her string bag would be bulging. She would climb the stairs, her face grim and unyielding, and stand outside her door fumbling in the voluminous skirts for her key; when she went out she always locked her door and took the key with her.

What no one knew until two years later when Antie died in her bed was that soon after Muriel took over control of the house and of us Antie had secretly got into touch with a nephew—we didn't know she had one—who worked in a firm of insurance brokers. She explained to him her changed situation and asked his advice: he gave it. At the age of seventy-six she bought an annuity for herself with all the money she had saved in the last nine years, and placed it in the hands of the nephew's firm. I don't remember the sum involved, but it was considerable.

When this became known after her death Muriel was convinced that Antie had deliberately and systematically stolen the money, bit by bit, for her own gain. Even the relief that she felt now that Antie was finally gone didn't soften the blow. She was horrified; this was the kind of conduct that was utterly foreign to her own nature.

'To think that all these years she's been nothing but a common thief,' she kept repeating.

The twins and I were stupefied. Antie a thief! It was impossible. Even now I doubt it was so simple. Antie was a miser through and through, a compulsive hoarder; spending was sinful, saving and austerity were high moral principles. 'You never know when you'll need it' applied to every mortal thing, and most of all to money. On top of that her mad old mind may well have prompted her to husband the money against a mythical situation in which we children as well as herself should be gravely in need of it. She was, after all, the sister of a doctor: she must have witnessed many heart-rending scenes of children suddenly abandoned and penniless; Uncle, the provider, or Muriel, or both of them, might suddenly die leaving us nothing at all.

Muriel kept asking us questions about Antie, hoping to hear something detrimental to her character, but not one of us could find a thing to say against her. She was good, and she had loved us.

'Oh, what's the use of talking to you,' Muriel cried at last, 'I think she's put a spell on you all!'

But this was not until two years later.

When we came back from the sea we found that Muriel had taken over our night nursery and Frances's little room for herself and put us all to sleep in the old day nursery. In her gifted way she had created a charming setting for herself with new curtains, a big new bed with fine linen, shoe racks in the cupboards and a large dressing-table with brushes and powder puffs, the giant bottle of Jicky, a tumble of necklaces in a bowl, and any number of knick-knacks; above all, the room was drenched in her personality. We had never known anything like it. In the chest of drawers there were piles of silk underclothes, camisoles, petticoats, French knickers, all in the most ravishing colours; silk was a revelation to us, and so were kid gloves.

The twins didn't share my absorption in her things; I was the only one of us who was interested in her clothes, in the ceremony of her manicure—our nails were cut with scissors—in her hair brushing, her face creaming, in everything she did. I was endlessly inquisitive, poking about in her drawers and cupboards, fingering everything and asking questions. At first she found this amusing, but after a while it got on her nerves. Soon she was saying, 'For God's sake someone take that child out of the room. I can't stand the way she watches me.'

It was Stella whom she wanted with her: she wanted her 'son'. But Stella wasn't interested in Muriel's personal ritual, and she was bored by bedroom life. Muriel was always saying, 'Where's Stella? Why isn't she here? Send her up to me.' It was soon after Muriel came to live with us that Stella's dazzling smile left her for ever.

Muriel was not used to dealing with children and she felt lost

99

in our highly concentrated little circle. She tried to pretend that Antie was no longer in the house, that she, Muriel, and we three, were alone; we, on our part, could no longer be natural, even among ourselves, in the charged atmosphere. It was impossible to ignore Antie's closed door, knowing that she was behind it. What was she doing in there? What was she plotting? Why had she imprisoned herself? We had never discussed her among ourselves: she had always been there, like our beds or breakfast, and we didn't discuss her now, but I, for one, felt guilty: as her adored child I felt it was I who should now somehow effect her rescue, but instead of doing this I dreaded her reappearance. When she did come out it was mostly to empty her chamber-pot, and the cistern took on a new angry hiss as she pulled the chain. When she saw us by chance she rarely spoke to us any more, and her face had changed: it was puffy and tight and her eyes had gone back into her head. We, too, were now slightly afraid of her; it was impossible not to know that something dreadful was going on.

In this looming atmosphere Helen began to show signs of bad temper. Muriel called her Echo and Shadow, and when she wasn't mocking her she ignored her altogether. I don't think she ever liked Helen, and she was jealous of the twin relationship. Helen held a newspaper to her nose; no one had noticed how short-sighted she was. Soon she was given glasses and this, too, was a subject of mockery. Muriel called her Miss Schoolmarm. 'You'll just have to take them off if you want to look nice.'

Nothing went well. None of us seemed able to respond in a suitable way. Helen had regressed; Stella's bright smile had gone; I was increasingly unwell; Antie brooded witch-like in her lair. There must have been days when Muriel was tempted to throw in her hand and leave us again.

'I'm doing all this for you,' she kept saying, 'and where's your gratitude?'

And then she made a tremendous effort and came to a lot of decisions all at once. We were hooligans, our manners were appalling; how did we expect to take our place—three places—in the world later on if we just sat about the house all day grumbling? Muriel often made these wild appeals to us and we met them in silence.

'You expect to have it all done for you,' she would say.

Well, she would do it. We had already learnt to ride, now we were to be coached in tennis and swimming, learn to play the piano —an upright piano was at once installed in the front room—have elocution lessons to teach us to speak properly, and we were each to be given a bicycle of our own. Furthermore, we were going to school. We were to be launched from the deep end into the sort of life that other privileged children led. We had never mixed with other children and, although we could read and write, we had never done lessons with a qualified or even reasonably intelligent teacher. All this was to be changed, indeed, everything was to be changed and all at once.

It was a generous resolve. Muriel had never been to school, nor could she ride, swim, play the piano or sing, and she had never ridden a bicycle. She was determined to give us the advantages that had never been offered to herself in childhood.

We never knew on whose advice it was that Muriel settled on Putney High School. It was then run by a progressive intellectual called Miss Beard, and on the staff, teaching English, was Viola Garvin, the daughter of J. L. Garvin of *The Observer*. Neither Roger nor Muriel had intellectual friends, but someone must have pointed out to them that this was a very good school. We were to go alone, the three of us, across the common to Barnes Station, catching a train to Putney and walking up the hill; in the afternoons we would reverse the journey to home.

Muriel took us into London to buy tunics and purple blazers. We had become schoolgirls. She got up early every morning to give us eggs and bacon for breakfast—'Eat up now—you can't go off on an empty stomach'—and bundled us out of the house with our satchels like any other mother. We were all fervently acting out our new rôles, and for me it was disastrous.

There was never time to be sick before we set off, so I threw up on the common, on the platform, in the train or on the way up Putney Hill. It was the same every morning. Stella would grab my hand and drag me along.

'You *can't*, there isn't time, we'll be late. Oh, look at her, she's doing it!'

Soon, not unnaturally, the twins were ashamed to be seen with me, so I was bustled out of the house earlier, alone, to catch an earlier train. But I often missed it and they would find me, feigning invisibility, on the station platform.

Nor were matters any better in the classroom. I couldn't do lessons: I seemed unable to see or hear what was going on or to respond in any way.

Release came before half-term. We were playing netball and I fell on the asphalt, gashing one of my knees. We had been brought up never to admit a hurt, so I went to the locker room, peeled off the broken stocking, fragments of which were imbedded in my bleeding knee-cap, and then covered up the mess with a fresh black woollen stocking. In no time I had blood poisoning and spent the rest of the term in bed and on crutches. I never went back.

Stella had also been in trouble. Predictably, none of the teachers had any control over her and at the end of the first term she was asked to leave. She was a bad influence. Her final undoing had been to go out for a walk in the middle of a lesson and return with a dog she'd found wandering. She argued that a lost dog was more important than a lesson and refused to be parted from the stray until its owner had been found. The lesson had been wrecked.

Helen had got on rather better. She was considered educable; she had conformed and tried to work, and Miss Beard suggested that for her own good she should be separated from her twin. She would never work properly, Miss Beard said, while she was under Stella's unruly influence. Miss Beard offered to take her in as a weekly boarder—she already had two others, sisters, whose parents were abroad, as full boarders—to live with herself and go home for weekends.

The twin-ness between them had always been heavily under-scored; now they were to be parted. This was particularly painful for Helen, whose very centre seemed to depend on the duality. Later, when they were grown up and each was married, a curious aspect of the twinship revealed itself: Helen was constantly mis-taken for Stella, but no one ever mistook Stella for Helen. I think the reason for this was that Helen had always wanted to *be* Stella, whereas Stella didn't want to be Helen.

We all three had a passion for Miss Garvin. With her Rossetti looks and her luminous personality she was the most romantic creature we had ever met. Muriel was romantic too, but she was fascinating rather than beautiful, and she was unsatisfactory for adoration. Miss Garvin had a tubercular leg—the knee didn't bend —and this, together with the pallor of her heart-shaped face and great swimming eyes, made her irresistible. Hurrying from one building to another her hair always flew backwards in line with her black gown, and she covered the ground much faster than people with two articulating knees.

It was in the holidays after that first term at Putney High School that an incredible event took place. Miss Beard and Miss Garvin, together, offered to take the three of us to Paris on an educational trip for a week. It was to be them and us, no one else.

Muriel agreed to let us go. We didn't know it at the time, but the dates coincided—or were made to coincide—with one of Roger's trips abroad. Muriel said she couldn't face a week alone in the house with Antie so she would take a little well-earned holiday herself. She, too, would go abroad.

At this time Roger used to call in at Woodlands Road two or three times a week on his way home to Richmond, but this was the first chance they had had to go away together and be properly alone. Muriel didn't say they were going together—she only ever admitted to the yearly visit to Bad Gastein to take the waters—but from now on they had many trips abroad and sometimes Muriel went alone.

She would need some clothes, she said, so she went up to London on a shopping spree, taking Stella with her. Stella must be taught to appreciate clothes, Muriel said. It was typical of her that she saw no incongruity in wanting her 'son' to like pretty clothes. Stella came home looking like someone else in a grown-up's wine-red cloche hat with a dark blue ribbon round it. This was the first of many such expeditions with Stella, and it started a ritual which thereafter was always observed.

Before leaving the house Muriel would take a wine glass from the cupboard in the dining-room, wrap it in a clean handkerchief and put it in her bag. When the serious shopping was done she would buy a bottle of Veuve Clicquot in the Provisions Hall at Barkers. They would then catch a bus to go home and get off it two stops before their proper destination. They would take to the common, find a deserted bench and settle themselves on it. Muriel would then open her bag, take out the wine glass, making a little tablecloth of her handkerchief on the bench between herself and Stella, and place the glass in the centre of it. She would then, with difficulty, pop the champagne cork. They always drank the whole of the bottle, glass for glass, and Muriel would open her heart to Stella, telling her tales of Doris Delevingne and the lost days of luxury in Park Lane, of the Duke of Aosta and his imperious ways, of Pat de Bathe, and of the glittering unknown future that she had given up for our sakes. She never included stories about Roger, but it was here, in a champagne glow on Barnes Common, that she fertilized the ground of extracted promises that were to be so richly fulfilled in her later years.

'You're my only son,' she would say, 'you must never forget that. And it's a son's duty to look after his mother, never to desert her no matter how old she gets. You'll never desert me, will you? You'll always love me and look after me, won't you? You're all I've got, my only son. . . .'

A new school was found for Stella and me. It was a private school called Levana where only French was spoken. It was run by two maiden lady sisters, the Misses Fountain, and was so exclusive as to have only twenty-five pupils, including us, when we went. Two years later, when it closed down, there were thirteen.

Like Helen at Putney we were weekly boarders and went home for weekends when Muriel was there. She cooked delicious meals for us and was happy to see us. She taught us how to eat her favourite dishes, oysters, caviar and asparagus, and how to lay a table for a dinner party. Among papers after her death there was a stand-up menu that Stella had made, decorating it with little drawings of a plate of food, a decanter and a bottle. It reads:

Sole and oister sauce
Roast chicken
Potatoes
Cauliflower
All kinds of fruit

Cheese and biscuits
Chocolate
Rich red wine
Old Smuggler
Soda water

At some later time Muriel has written on it: 'December 1923—Stella Smirke at 13 years old.' Roger had called her Stella Smirke after the famous jockey because of her winning smile. He enjoyed puns. After one of these indulgent weekends Stella wrote:

Darling Mummy,
    Thank you awfully for the Paradise of a time you gave us in the weekend. Every minute was perfect and like a dream. You did everything you could think of to make us happy and you succeeded in the extreme . . .

But from now on Muriel was often away and we sent our letters to Roger's office to be forwarded.

. . . Tomorrow is an eventful day for You Come Home. Write and tell us what time you arrive. Try before we go to bed. Auntie says you may stay on longer if it does you good, but you won't, will you? Because you *promised* you wouldn't!

Most of these absences were almost certainly spent with Roger, but we only knew they were together when they made their yearly trip to Bad Gastein. Roger wrote to Stella from there.

Darling nephew,
    I have just had lunch with your Mummy & I think she is looking much better for her rest & treatment here & she is certainly in a lovely spot. They have given me a bedroom overlooking a most glorious waterfall & as I sit here it is just *roaring* under my window. Farther down the valley it is just a little river rushing on between narrow banks with fields on both sides. I have never seen a more beautiful place & I do so wish you were here to enjoy it. Unfortunately it is raining, the first wet day your Mummy has had so of course she is blaming me for bringing it. Did you get my letter from Hamburg last week? I hope so

as I put two pounds in it for you & Shrimpy to keep you from starving!! Poor child, my heart bleeds for you. Mummy is being starved too. You should have seen her tackle a few bananas I brought with me. The first she has tasted since she left home.

Mummy tells me there are no shops, no motorcars, no buses, no cinemas, in fact no amusements of any kind here, only mountains with snow on the tops & valleys with lots of little and big waterfalls, lots of trees & very few birds. I saw a few horses, but no one riding. No flowers but a few buttercups & forget-me-nots. In fact I wonder what *you* would find to do here. Of course you could *eat*. There is no golf course or tennis, but there is a spring of *warm* water that everybody drinks from. However if it does Mummy good nothing else matters. You might drop Helen a line to say you have heard from me. Give Shrimpy my love. I got her letter & yours & hope you are both well & happy & not too scared by the thunderstorms to play a good game of tennis. Longing to see you all again,

Your old
Uncle

When Muriel was at home she made enormous meals at weekends; the twins were always ravenous. Antie still ate in her bedroom and rarely left it, but the atmosphere in the house was considerably lighter. We would tap at her door to say we were home, but we never went into her room. Sometimes she would silently appear in a doorway and we'd all stop talking, a wave of guilt at her exclusion hitting one in the chest, but it soon passed. We had almost forgotten Antie.

On one of the weekends, in the middle of lunch, I said: 'Mummy, are you divorced?'

Muriel's face was a picture of outrage. 'Certainly not! Well, I like that! *Divorced?* I most certainly am not divorced. Whatever put the idea into your head?'

'Annabel Mann says it sounds as though you are,' I said.

'What on earth have you been saying to her? You'll kindly not discuss me with the girls at school. I've told you before. What *have* you been saying, I should like to know?'

'Annabel's mother's been divorced twice,' I said, 'and she asked

106

me if you were. I said I didn't know, and she said whenever you're not sure they usually are.'

At another weekend lunch I said: 'Mummy, are we common?'

This was much worse. Muriel's face went a burning red, and it was a second or two before she could formulate words.

'Common, indeed! COMMON!' She kept repeating the word. And then she couldn't stay seated any longer. She pushed her chair back and started walking up and down the dining-room behind the twins' chairs. We had never seen her so agitated. And who, she soon wanted to know, had made a suggestion like that?

There were two sisters in my class, Anne and Barbara. Anne was a strong-minded rather sadistic girl who organized both her sister and me. My desk was beside hers. One day she said:

'We're not going to be friends with you any more.'

I asked them what I had done. They wouldn't tell me. I insisted.

'You're something beginning with C,' they said.

There had recently been a wave of cheating throughout the school, or so the elder Miss Fountain had said. I had been filled with admiration of the cheats. How brave, how ingenious they must be. How unlike me. I wanted to cheat but had no idea how to go about it. Did, then, the sisters believe I had been cheating? I asked them. They said no.

'You're common,' they said, 'that's why.'

One of the benefits of our isolated upbringing was that we never heard class talk. Antie was Scottish, and nationalistic pride took the place of the Englishman's worship of class. So I was interested and not in the least distressed to be called common. But Muriel couldn't finish her lunch that day. I watched her and wondered why she was so upset. She went on pacing in the small room.

'Your father came of good yeoman stock,' she kept repeating, 'the backbone of England. Ask anyone. Common, indeed. I've never heard anything like it. I've a good mind to get the Miss Fountains to expel those two.'

In spite of ever-ready correction from me Muriel always referred to the Misses Fountain as the Miss Fountains. She never touched on her own antecedents that day—the whole of her outrage was centred on the slight to Roger's breeding—and her agitation was so great that I failed to notice this interesting omission.

When the school in Wimbledon went bust it was decided that Helen should leave Putney High School and reunite with Stella and me in a new school still to be found. Stella wrote to Roger during the last term in Wimbledon.

Dearest Uncle,   26.2.26

Thank you so much for the things you sent. The chocolate did my heart good to look at and will do it even better to eat. I could almost start a sweet shop! I got a long letter from Mummy yesterday. She was still in Turin and was contemplating going to Vienna. She said she might be back next weekend if she didn't go, but I don't think she will be home somehow—I hope not for her sake.

I was awfully worried because last week when you wrote you had ghastly pains in your arm, and you never told me what was the matter with it and if it was better? I am dreadfully sorry to hear about your leg. Do tell me how it came. Also where you went for the two days. You know how curious I am, and you kindle it so by saying you had been away, and not saying where! Do satisfy my curiosity.

I hear we can't get in to Bendenden House. Helen is still full of Putney High School and will probably make an awful fuss when she leaves. You see, Miss Beard has her firmly and fairly and squarely under her thumb. Poor Helen feels quite nervous of me, I feel sure, after having been warned what a desperate character I am by Miss Beard. She's between the devil and the deep sea because she won't own she's ashamed of me and my 'unpolished' ways, but she really is, goaded on by Miss Beard. I'm beginning to feel I'm an out and out bad 'un, the black sheep of the family, as both Miss Beard and Miss Garvin have that opinion of me.

Auntie C. seems quite worried over us. She sent me three stamped postcards yesterday to send her throughout the week to say we were all right!

All my love, dearest, and I do hope your dear old leg is better.
Yours for ever,
Sam

During the next holidays we went to Bristol to attend the launch-

108

ing of an Elders & Fyffes boat. Helen was unwell and stayed behind with Antie.

We went up by train with Muriel and joined Roger at the Elders & Fyffes Bristol office. We had just been shown in when the telephone rang. Roger answered it. When he put down the receiver he sat for some seconds before speaking. Then he said:

'That was the doctor from Barnes. I'm sorry to say that Auntie Coutts has died in her sleep.'

When Antie failed to appear that morning, Helen, the only other person in the house, had knocked at her door. Failing to get a reply she had bravely opened it and gone in to find Antie dead in her bed. On our lately installed telephone Helen had rung the doctor. Later our cleaning woman came and offered to stay with Helen until we got home. We didn't wait for the launching.

I have no recollection of Antie's funeral.

The same doctor—he had a twin brother who was also a doctor and they made their calls on horseback—now advised that Helen should have her tonsils and adenoids removed. She had already been seriously ill with pleurisy and double pneumonia since Muriel came to live with us, and now was seldom free of colds. We had all had measles and whooping cough but this was the first operation to be performed on one of us.

It took place in a nursing home in Putney. When we went to see Helen the next day she refused to speak to us. This was not because of her throat. She lay in the bed glaring at us in a passion of outrage. She felt betrayed. She had been excluded from the launching party; it was she who had found Antie dead in her bed; she had spent the whole of that awful day with no one but the cleaning woman for company; and now she had been abandoned in this place to undergo, all alone, the alarms and humiliations of an operation.

When Muriel stroked her forehead and spoke to her Helen turned her face away. The matron advised us to leave and come back the next day.

It was the same. Helen again rejected us. We were all upset and bewildered; not one of us understood at the time what was happening, and I, for one, was shocked at this ruthless display of temper. This time Muriel acted.

'The child's not happy here,' she told the matron, 'I'm taking her away *now*. Bring some blankets.'

We bundled her up and took her home in a taxi and Muriel and the twin doctors nursed her in Frances's old room off Muriel's bedroom. But a sense of injustice persisted: I don't think Helen ever lost the feeling that she had been treated shabbily, abandoned for the second time. Throughout her life she longed to be loved by her mother. Irrationally, she saw the incident of the tonsils as an outstanding example of persecution.

The next school was Clovelly-Kepplestone in Eastbourne. It was a large private school and I only caught glimpses of the twins in the distance. They were now welded together again.

In my last school the tone had been one of seedy gentility; this one was more openly snobbish, with great stress laid on what a lady did and didn't do. The headmistress was a formidable old tyrant with an uncanny knowledge of everything that went on in the school. She had quickly sized up our situation and deeply disapproved of Muriel.

'If that Perry woman doesn't give Diana a new tunic next term I'm going to buy her one myself,' she once said.

I heard these interesting snippets of gossip from her adopted granddaughter with whom I shared a room. Another time this girl asked her grandmother—the subject being always in the air—which girl in the school exemplified good breeding. 'The Perry girls,' she was told.

Muriel might have been pleased to hear of this exoneration from the previous label, but I never told her. She was often away at this time, indeed, we seldom saw her. Once we all three spent the holidays with a family in Jersey, and twice the twins went to stay with newly made school friends and I stayed on at the school throughout the long summer holidays with a handful of other girls whose parents were also abroad.

I still couldn't do lessons. I was never naughty or difficult like Stella—I was simply waiting for time to pass until I was grown-up—and I think the teachers didn't know what to do with me. Instead of lessons like history, geography and arithmetic I was allowed extra piano practice and drawing classes. I was only allowed to play games until half time and I still kept vomiting.

I stayed at this school until I was just fifteen and then Muriel decided to take me away and make an actress of me. I never knew what was done to get me in at R.A.D.A. I don't recall auditioning, and I was two years younger than anyone else. I thought I should die of joy. My elder sisters were still at school and I had left it. We had also left Woodlands Road. Roger had bought the house in Castelnau, Barnes, and while we were homeless Muriel and I lived in a furnished service flat at Kensington Palace Mansions opposite the Gardens. Roger wrote to Stella.

Sam darling,   22.11.27

My conscience keeps putting its foot up & kicking me hard for not writing to you, but forgive me dear child as many days I find it difficult to hold my pen & again many days I am too busy to write personal letters. Anyway today I took your Mummy out for a snack of lunch & am now feeling able to sit up & talk & write to you. The new home at Castelnau is going to suit you all. Shrimpy is on top of her form. She swanks about Kensington shopping for your Mummy & never counts the change. She goes out to buy bread & butter & forgets the butter. She buys six eggs & arrives home with five. She went to tea with a chum yesterday & returned to the flat for *dinner* about *nine* o'clock. By that time your Mummy was in bed. Anyways she's full of beans & your Mummy is full of houses & wallpapers & carpets & curtains. Congrats to you & Helen, specially to Helen, for getting through in French, it was a real good effort on her part as she hasn't had your chances.

Bless you darling. All my love,

Unks

I was so full of beans I could neither eat nor sleep. When we were in Paris with Miss Beard and Miss Garvin I had discovered the trick of putting my finger down my throat in the lavatory and effortlessly throwing up. By keeping myself more or less permanently empty I had removed the fear of throwing up in public. I had felt triumphantly secure. Now, my sudden freedom of movement, coupled with the heady excitements at R.A.D.A., kept my stomach in a state of perpetual agitation, and I had gone back to my former practice. My childhood headaches had come back.

Gower Street was my ideal with its dingy drabness; I hated the expensive formality of our rented flat in Kensington. As soon as I could get away I meant to live in a bedsitting-room with a gas ring, in an area like Gower Street, among other people struggling for their ideals.

At R.A.D.A. I was paralysed with shyness and the fear of retching in front of everyone, and at the same time I was rapturously happy. I talked my head off. I was still very small and so much the youngest that I was petted and teased and fed on cream buns at teatime and generally treated like some child who had been left there for the day instead of a serious student. When I wasn't at R.A.D.A. I wandered about London day-dreaming. I was so happy I sometimes forgot how ill I felt. I had no idea what acting entailed.

Back at the flat I practised make-up and smoking, showed Muriel how to fence and made her hear my lines. But the draught was too strong. One evening I started crying and couldn't stop.

At the end of the first term Muriel took me away from R.A.D.A. and sent me back to the school in Eastbourne.

Chapter Eight

ON THE day we were to move into the house at Castelnau we found that the previous owner had sneaked in and spitefully cut off all the electric light flexes; he had cut them off flush with the walls and ceilings. Muriel said it was an omen. 'He's put a curse on the house.' Later she said, 'There was a curse on the house from the start.'

The twins came home at Christmas for the last time. They had left school; they were now seventeen and they had both been prefects; even Stella had learnt to conform. And they had grown away from me. They had their own friends now, their own interests, and at home they were even more withdrawn than they had been at Woodlands Road.

Muriel collapsed as soon as we were in. It was not only the move that had been too much for her; every part of her world was drawing to a crisis. Roger's health was deteriorating fast. He had already had two strokes; Muriel was with him both times, once in Austria and the second time outside a restaurant on the pavement in London. And there was more than this. Shortly before we left Woodlands Road Muriel had found herself pregnant again. She had gone to a gynaecologist, faked certain symptoms and asked him to perform a curettage. When she came round from the anaesthetic he was standing at the foot of the bed.

'You lied to me,' he had said, 'don't ever come to me again.'

To add to these traumatic experiences she found, when the twins came home, that Stella, her adored 'son', was hostile and uncommunicative; she had friends of her own in London now and wanted to be with them instead of always at home. In Muriel's already overwrought state this was the last straw; she was consumed with jealousy.

113

She had been secretly drinking for some time, but only spasmodically. Now, with the weakening of her central controls, she was unable to stop herself. She never discussed Roger's failing health; she belonged to a generation of women who were incapable of discussion, besides, she would not have liked to expose her inner thoughts. She kept all her terrors to herself and, having no outlet, they formed a canker, an accumulation of power from the destructive impulses. When she went into a change of personality caused by drink it was this baser side of her nature which took over.

Very occasionally one of her pre-war women friends came to lunch or dinner. Muriel wanted to show off her pretty house and also, perhaps, her children. It was always a disaster. Before the guest arrived Muriel would have worked herself up into a frenzy of nerves, moving the furniture, changing the tablecloth, wearing herself out with agitation. There was no pleasure in it. When the guest arrived she would be drunk, incapable of conversation. Sometimes she fell over. It was pitiful, but we three sat stonily regarding her with cold incomprehension. Once Mrs. McCalmont came to lunch. She was a very old lady now, and it was the last time we were to see her. Because Muriel really cared for her good opinion it was the biggest fiasco of all.

Mrs. McCalmont was late and by the time she came Muriel could no longer talk coherently, nor could she eat. She sat at the table, her head bent forward, the tears running down her face. Looking back, I am surprised that Mrs. McCalmont made no move to break up this painful scene. For over fifty years she had been a gay widow in the most sophisticated London society: she was now an imperious old lady whose invitation to an exclusive luncheon read more like a command, and she had a reputation for the racy phrase. She could have sent us from the room and tried to comfort or scold Muriel, or she could simply have left the house, seeing that conversation with her old friend was out of the question. She did neither. Perhaps she had sent her chauffeur away to get his lunch somewhere. Mouse McCalmont sat silently at our table and ate her lunch —and so did we—pretending that nothing was amiss. She didn't try to make conversation with us, and as soon as lunch was over she left. Coffee wasn't offered.

We somehow stumbled through the Christmas holidays and then

Helen went to a finishing school in Paris and Stella, who had refused to go with her, went daily to a school in Victoria to do a course in dispensing, a resolution so farcical that I have forgotten how it came about. Helen only stayed in Paris for one term and then chose to do a secretarial course at Pitman's. I went back to the school in Eastbourne.

Just over a year later the twins ran away. But before that happened the possibility came about of quite a different twist in Muriel's destiny.

When I arrived home for the holidays the first thing I noticed was a motor car in our garage. It was, it transpired, a present from a Major Deed. He lived in South America and had come to England to buy polo ponies. He was rich, a bachelor and, as well as ponies, he was hoping to take back with him a wife. He had asked Muriel to marry him.

I questioned the twins. 'Will he really marry her?'

'Of course he won't,' they said.

Deed-o was a stocky, rather coarse-grained man of about fifty with a bushy moustache. He had no small talk—or any other sort—and was ill at ease in our drawing-room. The car stayed in the garage since Muriel couldn't drive, but she decided to take a course of dancing lessons at the Empress Rooms in Kensington. Not wanting to go alone, and since Stella hated dancing, she took me with her to *thé dansantes*.

Deed-o had taken a house in Wimbledon and exercised his ponies on the common before breakfast. Muriel wanted him to see me riding—he had confided to her that he was ill-at-ease with children and she hoped our passion for horses might tip the scales—and asked him to take me with him one morning. He sent his chauffeur to pick me up. He put me on a pony and I followed him. We never exchanged a word. Then he took me back to his house and put in front of me a plate piled high with eggs, sausages, kidneys, mushrooms and tomatoes which sent me flying to the bathroom. A few weeks later he went back to South America alone and Muriel sold the car. She never told us how she met him.

When the twins ran away they didn't tell me where they were going—I was too easily tricked into giving away secrets—but I knew. In Sussex there was a private art school run by the woman who had taught art at the school in Eastbourne. She had now left Eastbourne and set up her own small establishment. It was called an art school but really it was a place of refuge for girls like ourselves who were in trouble at home. Only two or three unwitting parents paid fees, and the other girls, the penniless ones, did the work in the house and garden to earn their keep until their private problems were sorted out. It was this art mistress who had uncovered our illegitimacy during the twins' last term at school; she had also pointed out to them that they would come of age at eighteen. They were now eighteen: no one could force them to go home.

I didn't know all this then. The twins hadn't told me. Particularly I didn't know about the vital legal point, and nor did Muriel. Soon after they'd gone she went to a solicitor and came back so crushed that she could hardly speak. She was stunned. Earlier that morning, before setting out, she had felt confident, a force to be reckoned with.

'If they think they can just walk out like that, after all I've done for them . . . Where's their gratitude, I should like to know. At least the law doesn't allow a mother's children to desert her like that before they're twenty-one. I'll have them *brought* back.'

There had been more of the same, but when she came back she was a changed woman. There were no histrionics or tears. She was suffering. I could feel it, and I kept asking her what the solicitor had said.

Of course she couldn't tell me because that would have meant telling me about herself and Roger. She said that sometimes children couldn't be forcibly brought home after they were eighteen. I didn't press her. I dismissed this rocky statement as one of her usual muddles. I saw her as incapable of taking in a rational argument or statement of fact. It happened all the time. Obviously this time she had made a muddle of whatever the solicitor had said to her, but a muddle on the right side: the twins couldn't be brought home against their will.

I also didn't know until much later that Helen had written to Roger from the country asking him to see her privately. She had journeyed to London and presented herself in Bow Street. Roger took her out to tea. Sitting opposite him she gathered together all her courage.

'Are you our father?' she said.

116

He didn't answer for some seconds. Then: 'You must ask your mother,' he replied.

He had sworn Muriel to secrecy.

My dear girl,   31 Bow Street, W.C.2
                                                            4.1.29

The twins have behaved abominably to you & you can certainly speak plainly to them, or to anybody else who speaks for them. If they talk of money you can certainly tell them there's nothing doing. It is high time they were told that all you have & that's not much is in the form of an annuity & that when you die, & they are certainly trying their best to kill you, your money dies too & then they will have to work or starve.

You have spent your life thinking of them & have done more for them than any other mother that I have met has done for hers & if I were you I would be very frank with them & let them know the facts.

I am sorry for you & realise what a rotten time you have had & are having.

Yours
Roger

21.1.29   31 Bow Street
Darling,   W.C.2

You sounded all wrong on the telephone today & each time you spoke I had four men in my room very intent on business. Don't for heaven's sake let things get on your nerves & make you miserable. You only make yourself ill & me wretched. I thought you had fixed on letting things rip & wait & see what the twins would do eventually. You are doing & have done all you can for them & more than any other modern mother that I know. Forget about it a bit & don't for God's sake turn on me. If you & I don't pull together what on earth will happen. Pull yourself together & I will call in the morning. Don't *talk* of flu or you will get it.

Really I am as sick as you are & I am so sorry for you too, but we must keep a hold on ourselves.

Your old
Chug

117

Soon after the twins were gone it was found that Roger had cancer of the tongue. He was to be treated with radium needles in a nursing home next door to his home in Richmond.

It was at this time that Muriel felt haunted at night and begged me to pull my mattress into her room. She was now terrified of losing me as well as the twins, so she took me away from the school in Eastbourne—it was too near to the art school where the twins were living—and sent me as a boarder to a secondary school in Essex. At the same time, out of fear that the twins might somehow abduct me, she made a secret arrangement with the headmistress to send on to herself, unopened, any letters addressed to me which didn't have a large X in the bottom right-hand corner of the envelope. The ones marked X which reached me were, of course, from herself, and once there was one from Roger.

I didn't tumble to this for some weeks—I assumed that the twins kept losing my address each time I sent it—but when at last I did I asked the headmistress for an explanation. She was a dried up little woman who looked like a parrot with bald eyes. She said she was glad I'd found out, that she hadn't wanted to do it in the first place, and would I now make some other arrangement with my mother. She also said she couldn't understand why I kept changing schools, but that if I went on like this I should find myself at the end of my school years precisely as I was now—knowing nothing. What she didn't tell me was that the twins had arrived at the school one Sunday morning soon after I went there to take me out—and to give me cigarettes to smuggle back in—and that she had turned them away at the door.

At half-term I went home for the weekend, challenged Muriel with her duplicity, and refused to go back to the school. Nothing would make me, I said. In the end Muriel promised to rescind the letter arrangement and agreed, if I went back, that I should leave at the end of the term. In fact, I stayed there for two more terms. I never managed to carry out my threats in the way that Stella did.

While I was away at school Helen went up to London one day to be interviewed for a secretarial job, and then took the bus to Richmond.

Metcalfe's London Hydro (Ltd.)
Richmond Hill,
Surrey.

Dearest,

Helen called and left me some flowers, bluebells & violets etc. that Stella had sent up to me with a sweet note. Helen left a note but no address on it. You might let them know that I am not up to letter writing, but I am getting better & was very touched by both their letters.

My pulse & heart are good & they say with a rest after the things they have put me through during the last ten days I should be wise to give the whole thing a real chance.

Take care of yourself, dear. I had caviare & asparagus for lunch, a whiskey & soda & am now smoking a cigar. My love to you.

Roger

Roger was not the only one to receive flowers. Although the twins had left home for good they did everything they could to persuade Muriel that they had done this only to lead their own lives, not to abandon her.

My darling Mummie,

Here are a few lovely Spring flowers for you from the garden. We have little yellow crocuses too, but they are difficult to pick.

How are you, darling? And funny old Di? Please give her my love and tell her to write to me. Yes, darling, I would like you very much to send me (or to save for me if inconvenient to send at the moment) all my books and music. Would you ask Di to send me sometime *this week* the books I unwillingly lent her to cheer her up at her school. Could I possibly have my desk, dear? It would be most frightfully useful as I have a room of my own, you see.

Your loving
Stella

I have already said that the twins' feelings towards Muriel were different from my own: mine were violent—why did she never wipe away the tears, but let them run endlessly down her cheeks?—and

119

I often dreamed of killing her. Stella had loved her and still did and always would, and Helen wanted to be loved by her. This pattern was to remain unchanged for many years to come. On her side Muriel's jealous passion for Stella continued, and so did her absence of affection for Helen. Towards me I think her feelings fluctuated: sometimes she seemed to hate me, and sometimes she was drawn towards me; I was a 'funny little thing', a better listener than Stella was, and I was the only one left to her. The twins were just as devoted to Roger as I was.

My dear one,

I had to laugh just now. Your letter arrived just now & never a tongue had licked the glue, that is it was absolutely open for a lot of gossiping nurses & other folk to read. Last week Helen did the same thing after marking her envelope Private & Personal. Then when she called with Stella's flowers & left them at my *house* she left a note without even an envelope to enclose it, so you can imagine what a chatter is going on below stairs. Don't for goodness sake mention it to any of them. Just leave them guessing. It is part of Helen's deep laid scheme to *find out*. I am steadily getting better, but my poor old tongue is very sore still. Everybody is very nice to me & very attentive. Wadd himself is perhaps the exception, he is casual. I am sleeping well however which is half the battle. Keep Helen away if you can. Now I'm done. I can't stick it out of my chair for very long. Take care of your dear self.

Your
Chug

Darling,

Stella is indeed the limit. You are right about her glorious future and what we have spent to get it. I wish you could see me now. The doctors have just gone & left my neck in a straight waistcoat which I must wear for 5 hours out of every 24 for the next nine or ten days. No pain or sensation to come from it & you may be sure that I am going through with it. Don't worry dear my worst trouble today was neuritis. Every day I get it rather badly about four p.m. in fingers & arms & steadily through

the day I throw up lumps of mucous. I'm a cheery soul I am,
ain't I? All my love, dear heart,

Chug

There was no telephone in his room, so for weeks he wrote to
her every day, always ending with words of concern about her own
health. There was never any question of her going to Richmond to
see him; Richmond was forbidden territory.

. . . I am taking great care of myself & would like to see signs in
your letters that you are doing the same. Do, there's a dear thing.

. . . Take *care* of yourself darling.

. . . I can quite imagine you sitting up & contemplating selling
everything. We have struck a bad patch both of us & can only
pray for a streak of something better. I wonder of we two which
is really the worst. I fancy you could give me a stone & lick me easy.

. . . There is no news for you, darling, except that I am slowly
mending. I am worrying about you more than myself. Take care
of yourself & don't worry about *any* of your very curious women
friends.

. . . I am not allowed to speak or *smoke*. Entirely on slops through
a rubber tube. Quite a dinky pair of nurses both night & day.
I am really top hole. If only I could believe that you are.

. . . I hope you will take care of yourself. That is everything.

Muriel was always ill in the holidays. She would ask me to
massage her swollen ankles and her aching temples. I hardly ever
saw her drinking, but I don't think she was ever quite sober. She
was, of course, rent in two over Roger's illness and the loss of Stella,
but she never talked to me about either of them. Instead she would
say that Life had gone against her, that children were nothing but a
heartbreak, showing no gratitude.

After the twins left I shut myself off from feeling. This had
become necessary. When the full current of her misery was turned
upon me I felt as though I were drowning. After a while, I found
that my barrier of un-feeling was not enough; it was necessary that
I should hate her. I told myself that I hated her for the change that

had come about in the twins: not only had Stella's smile vanished, her whole nature had been wrenched about, leaving her pessimistic, harsh, calculating and rigidly on the defensive. Helen's personality had quite stopped developing. This was how I reasoned and I blamed Muriel for every part of it. The simple truth is I was afraid of her; I was afraid of being pulled right into her whirlpool of despair and drowning in it.

I could see no possible reason for such despair. Why did she never enjoy herself? To me she seemed never to make the smallest effort. We lived together at this time, she and I, like strangers. I knew nothing about her and little enough about myself. Looking back, I cannot believe that had she confided in me, told me the truth about herself—and me—I should not have been kinder. Certainly I would have been deeply interested and proud to be involved. I once tried to explain to a friend the poignancy of this lost opportunity. My friend said: 'No doubt you would have liked to know the full story, but what about your sisters? Surely Muriel's decision was the wiser one, and certainly the more unselfish?'

A year later, when I was seventeen, I wrote some childish verses about Stella which I give now to show the anxiety I felt about her.

> A very gorgeous girl indeed
> My sister Stella looks,
> Equalled alone, in face and form,
> In quite the greatest books.
>
> A dashing girl my sister is
> As anyone can tell,
> Made up of stars and sugar plums
> And other things as well.
>
> Seductive, proud, assertive, gay,
> 'Tis fatal to be charmed,
> You'll groan with thirst, and ache for rest—
> In every way be harmed.
>
> The thing to do is stay apart
> And watch the others roast,
> No need to suffer tortures with
> Tonight's unlucky host.

For Stella's laced her heart up tight
—So sad it is to see—
No one knows why or what she wills,
And least of all does she.

One morning I went into the drawing-room to find Helen standing there with Muriel. I had not heard the front door bell. They must have been there for some time because Helen was well into some argument and barely gave me a glance.

It was a good while since I had seen her; nor had I heard from either of them. Almost everything about her was unfamiliar, but she still stood in the same way: hugely tall, she stood very straight, feet slightly apart, on the defensive like a human goal-post. She was wearing clothes I'd never seen before and there was a feeling about her of having just come from other company, from people I didn't know. She made me feel childish and left behind.

'We want Diana,' she said, 'I've come to get her.'

I couldn't believe my ears. Neither of them looked at me when she said this. They were confronting each other in the middle of the room, and although I was so close to them I didn't really exist.

'Well, you're not going to have her!' Muriel slammed back. 'She's all I've got left and I'm not going to give her up!'

It was one of the rare times I ever saw her angry. She was like some animal at bay.

There was a terrible scene. Helen remained icy throughout, and they both seemed unable to move from where they stood. The tension they had generated, and the fact that although I was standing so close I was still invisible to them, made it impossible for me to speak. It ended in Helen's defeat. I was under age. Nothing could alter that.

'We'll win in the end,' she said prophetically, 'you'll see. One day she'll walk out just like we did.'

And then she left the house.

I can still see Muriel's face as the front door slammed. She didn't look at me because I wasn't important. The violent things that had just been said were only incidentally about me. Even I knew that. They were about something much deeper and far more terrible than the question of whether I lived here or there.

I was badly shocked. I hated her, or so I believed, but somehow not quite like this. I wasn't shocked by the words that had been used—I believed that nothing was unsayable—but I was shocked by her vulnerability: at this moment she seemed almost annihilated.

And there was something else. Helen had never been caught up emotionally with Muriel in the way that Stella and I always seemed to be. It was therefore unseemly that she should have been the one to do the stabbing: only the totally involved could stab each other with honour. That day, perhaps for the first time, I had an inkling of what it must be like to be our enemy: one against three.

Chapter Nine

ON THE day that I went back to school for the last time Muriel put me in a taxi with my luggage, told the driver which station to go to, and then turned and went slowly up the front steps of the house to stand in the open doorway, watching, as the taxi drove off, her right arm raised in a gesture of farewell, only the tips of the fingers weakly moving. She looked mad, like a poor demented creature from whom the life force had been siphoned off; her face was ugly from all the internal weeping, and, of course, tears were now running unchecked from her eyes. She wasn't looking at me: with the ruthless concentration of the lonely, she was seeing herself being left yet again; those expressive eyes were fixed upon the world in general with such accusation that they seemed incapable of seeing.

When the taxi turned into the main road and she was lost to me—it was a semi-detached house with a little drive shared by the two houses—I knew as surely as if I was still there to see it that she would go on standing in the doorway, looney-like, until the mere fact of standing so long would make her stagger. She would then retreat into the house, slowly closing the door behind her, and in the drawing-room she would sink into the nearest armchair, folding herself over double, and stay like that, motionless and only half-conscious, for several hours.

She was alone: Roger was in the nursing home; I was gone until the summer holidays; the twins were gone for good. Solitude had always been her greatest danger. She had no hobbies or interests of any kind, and now, apart from writing and posting a daily letter to Roger while he was still in the nursing home and unable to speak to her, she had nothing whatever to do for weeks and weeks, and no prospect of anyone, apart from the cleaning woman, coming to see her. Inevitably she would drink; it was the only way she knew of to blur the edges of this nightmare of emptiness.

At some earlier time she had been a patient of an Italian doctor called Castellani. He had two nursing homes—one in Harley Street and one in Putney—and a flourishing practice among well-to-do women who drank too much. He would diagnose nervous exhaustion and put them into one of his homes to dry out, and it was said that his favourite patients passed through the waiting-room, after a consultation, with lipstick smudges on their faces.

Muriel had already been in both of his homes. So far she had always managed to judge the moment to reach for the telephone; her instinct for self-preservation had always come to her rescue. This time it was the same. I had been back at school for about a month when she managed to ring up Castellani and was taken into his nursing home in Putney.

In June she was back in Castelnau with renewed courage. She was now on the wagon and, as always upon recovery, ready for adventure. She paid an unannounced call on Roger. She knew this was forbidden, but in certain moods she liked to stir up a little trouble. After all, why shouldn't she go to see him? She told herself that if anyone else was there she would simply brazen it out. In the event, he was alone. He wrote to her the next day.

Dinks dear,   9 June 1929
   Oh, what a surprise! Today I am wonky a bit. I am up & dressed but no guts to do anything. Can hardly see or hold my pen. I had my bath this morning all O.K. but I am now feeling all out. Not much of a day anyway, but I had thought of going out again. It is now 4.30 p.m. & I haven't got a kick in me. Slow but sure. I wish you were looking better.
                              Your old
                                 Chug

Dearest one,   12 June 1929
   I have no fresh news except just constant but very slow progress. My legs are safer, but only just. I am having slight massage morning and night, so now you know all about me. I have got a splendid pulse. Now I wonder how about you? How

126

are you. I have no doubt jolly miserable & just living behind your shutters. This however we can't help but oh the pity of it.

Well, darling, I have had my usual chat to you. Bless you always,

Your
Chug

At the end of June he came out of the nursing home and went down to Southsea alone. Originally, Muriel had planned to go to Bad Gastein with him to take the waters and be back again before I came home for the summer holidays. But Roger had been too ill. Now they hoped that the sea air would make him stronger. It was impossible to plan further ahead.

2 July 1929   Queen's Hotel,
                                                     Southsea

Sweetheart,
    I thought I was never coming to the end of my Barnes budget. What with you and the Bank manager. Firstly this is nowhere near Brighton. There is no reason why you shouldn't come on your own to this very pub, book on your own & trust to luck. Joe left yesterday morning & wires me he will be back to supper tonight. Perhaps he will bring me some news of the family. I am stronger on my pins & in the head already but the weather is atrocious, dull, cold & showery. Helen seems quite fond of you. Stella is a strange thing. I have a barber coming now after a struggle. I didn't get one yesterday. The valet chap I have has weird hours when he is available but he is just what I wanted. So if only you were here all would be well.

Your own
Chug

4 July 1929   Queen's Hotel,
                                                     Southsea

Dearest,
    It is a quarter to one & I am still in my bedroom loafing. My doctor blew in, tried my pulse, heart etc., chatted about Southsea in general & blew out again. My valet came & rubbed my legs, helped me with my bath. Everything passed off well & I am

seriously thinking of trying a bath chair after lunch. It is brighter today. Joe came down to dinner last night & went up again this morning. He tells me he has offered to motor the family down on Saturday for the weekend. Whether it will come off I don't know, but he himself will come I know. I don't suppose any of them will stay over Monday. The Royal Pier is under the same management & it is on the front here, so why don't you come down this week some time on your own. We could surely fix up to meet here, or at your pub. My jolly old bath chair stunt would come in trumps. I am safer on my tootsies but I find it is slow work.

All my love, dear
Your
Chug

Muriel shut up the house and took the train to Southsea. She booked a room on her own at the Royal Pier Hotel.

Sunday night
10 to 9 p.m.
Darling, The whole crowd have just gone in two motors. I am all alone. My man is due about 9.15 & should finish at 9.30. If you hunger for a kiss as much as I do, just come.

Your own
Chug

This was the last note he was ever to write her. When my school broke up I went down to Southsea to join Muriel, and in September Roger died.

Muriel had had no direct dealings with Roger's doctors, so when he died she assumed it was from heart failure following a stroke— the third—which he had had in his bathroom at the Queen's a few days earlier.

Joe Ackerley gives a different account. Referring to the spasms of pain which his father had suffered over so many years he writes, 'His jumps were "neuritis" only by courtesy; he was suffering from a syphilis contracted in Egypt in his guardsman's days . . .' To this is added a footnote: 'I am uncertain of this. It is in my head, but I don't recall how it got there. Perhaps Dr. Wadd inserted it, but I can't substantiate it. The disease may have been contracted later.' Joe goes on to say that the syphilis was '. . . incompletely eradicated [in Egypt] and now in its tertiary stage. I myself learnt this from the doctors only after he died of it.'

Muriel never knew that he died of syphilis, just as, even more mercifully, she never knew that he was unmarried when he met her.

At the time of his death I still believed him to be Uncle, the unofficial head of our family, the one who had always paid the bills and had the final say. I had never questioned Muriel's devotion to him—it was the one constant in her shifting moods—and if, later in Vienna, she had told me that he was *her* father—and our grandfather—I would hardly have been surprised. Even now, looking back, the way she always talked about him, and her behaviour with him whenever I was present, still conjure up a picture of a woman with a much-loved father. He was the most important person in her life, the one who came first. So when he died I couldn't understand how it was that she didn't plunge into justifiable mourning. Here, surely, was a proper cause for grief, instead of the usual miasma of unspecified despair. But she didn't do this. She didn't even drink. She was worried about money, and where it would come from now, but this was something else.

I now think that she didn't break down because she had already, and for some time, reached the limit of despair. You can't go further down than bottom. In a way, her mechanism for suffering was blunted. Her love for Roger and his for her represented the sole deep relationship of her life; she had loved him with all that was best in her nature, indeed, her darker side might have belonged to another woman for all its effect upon their union. In this way she had no sense of guilt or conflict. She felt guilty about us, her illegitimate children, but not about Roger. And she was used to being apart from him: the association had been structured on absence. Now that he was finally gone their secret orchard was still intact. For the rest of her life her face always softened at the mention of his name, and she never criticized him. First and last he was her hero.

The recent discovery that his father had a mistress and other children had amused and surprised Joe Ackerley. Self-absorbed by nature, he was not in the least disturbed by this unexpected disclosure; it was no concern of his and he dismissed it from his mind. He was a writer; he was literary editor of *The Listener*; in those Southsea days he was head over heels in love with Albert. All in all, he had plenty to occupy his mind. His talk with Nancy about their father's goings-on had gone in one ear and out of the other. Nancy, too, was taken up with her own problems. Neither of them had given another thought to the implications of the long association.

It was not until Joe, as his father's executor, came upon an envelope at Elders & Fyffes addressed to himself and marked 'Only in the case of my death' that his eyes were opened to the truth. Inside the envelope were two letters.

(1920)   My dear lad,

Seeing you this morning, a grown man, with every sign of a great intelligence and a kindly nature towards human frailties, I think I ought to leave you a line to explain one or two things in my past which it is inevitable you will have to consider in case anything happens to me in the near future. I shan't leave much money behind me, not being built that way, but I don't think there will be any debts worth mentioning. Since I came to man's estate I have provided for my sisters and wish them to have one thousand pounds clear. My will leaves everything to Mother, but you can arrange things for me in these matters I write of, as since I made my will I have arranged an agreement with Elders & Fyffes that in case of my death during the next ten years she will get £1500 a year for the remainder of that period. If I don't die she ought to be all right. Now for the 'secret orchard' part of my story. For many years I had a mistress and she presented me with twin girls ten years ago and another girl eight years ago. The children are alive and are very sweet things and very dear to me. They know me only as Uncle Bodger, but I want them to have the proceeds of my Life Insurance of £2000 (fully paid up and now worth £2500) in the Caledonian Insurance Coy; the policy being with any private papers in the safe here. I would also like £500 paid to their mother. She still keeps her maiden name and doesn't live with the children. You will now realize why I didn't keep a car!! I am not going to make any excuses, old man. I have done my duty towards everybody as far as my nature would allow and I hope people generally will be kind to my memory. All my men pals know of my second family and of their mother, so you won't find it difficult to get on their track.

Your old dad

(1927)   Dear Lad,
I opened the envelope enclosing this other document just now to refresh my memory. Seven years have passed since I wrote it and seven years of expensive education for the three girls etc. etc. It means that my estate has dwindled almost to vanishing point and my latest effort viz. buying a house in Castelnau for them has about put finishing touches. The position today is: Two policies of £500 each, Harry Wadd owes me £514, and my fully paid policy worth £2765 in pawn with my bank against an overdraft. Mother is entitled to draw about £3000 a year if I die before 1930 and after that probably E. & F. will carry on a pension for her in reward for my long service. At any rate I hope so. Muriel *must* have the £2000 policy. I have always promised her that and she has certainly loved me for all these years and when you see her and her decorations for work done during the war, OBE, Italian Victoria Cross etc. etc., and you see the girls and hear of their love for me, you will see that all that can be done is done for her. You met her lunching with me last year, and you and Nancy met the children years ago at the Trocadero with old Miss Coutts.

Your old Dad

It was a shock, indeed. Without a word of preparation there was to be virtually no more money for anyone: William Whiteley, the Universal Provider, as Roger liked to call himself, had shut up shop. Grave as this was, there were even more disturbing elements: the Ackerley family life, and Roger himself, were now spotlighted for fraud. Joe writes: 'It was the kind of shock that people must receive when some old friend, who has just spent with them an apparently normal evening, goes home and puts his head in the gas-oven. The shock, after the shock of death, is the shock to complacency, to self-confidence: the old friend was a stranger after all, and where

131

lay the fault in communication? My relationship with my father was in ruins; I had never known him at all.'

He goes on to say, 'We had never been brought up to think of money, it was always there and as much as we wanted, and if it occurred to me at all that my mother's share of these lean savings looked somewhat thin . . . the thought did not affect what I considered my bounden duty, indeed my instant consent, to the old chap's wishes. They must be honoured, of course, and the office would naturally provide for my mother . . . I was interviewed by his partner, now sole head of the firm, Arthur Stockley. He at once laid down the law, in the firmest, even harshest manner. He clearly disliked and disapproved of my father's mistress, and had no intention of letting her into any spoils, or of submitting to the sentimental blackmail, as he regarded it, of my father's blithe and unbusinesslike assumptions. He was perfectly clear as to what Elders & Fyffes were prepared to do to help my mother—and what they were not prepared to do. They would provide her with a pension, perhaps £500 a year, subject to revision at the end of ten years, but only on condition that my father's wishes with regard to his mistress were entirely ignored. If I handed over to her the insurance policy of £2000, my mother, as far as they were concerned, would get nothing.

'Even now I don't see what else I could have done in face of this ultimatum but acquiesce . . . my duty, I had no doubt of it, was to her; I regretfully dishonoured my father's posthumous wishes. This dilemma in which I had been put I communicated to my father's mistress in her Castelnau house; of that interview I now recall nothing whatever, but my notebook tells me that I undertook to pay her youngest daughter's school bill.

'I never saw (Muriel) again and had no further part in the life of her family, my three half-sisters, until many years had passed. Indeed it would be true to say that I gave them all scarcely another thought. Reasons, good or bad, can easily be marshalled: excepting for the youngest girl, whom I had met only once and quite recently, they were strangers to me; they were a secret, my father's secret, kept from me for over twenty years, and a secret which I had already decided to hide from my mother; they did not yet know of my relationship with them; I felt no interest or curiosity about them;

I was leading a homosexual life, totally indifferent to girls, my own sister was worry enough with her disastrous affairs and her frequent jealous warfare with my mother. I had certainly no welcome in my heart for any more sisters; they were of an age to fend for themselves, as I would now have to fend for myself and my family; the house in Castelnau belonged to them, a considerable asset, while our own house in Richmond was rented.

'During these transactions Stockley said to me, "By the way, your father's desk is now your property. If you take my advice, you will let me have it burnt with all its contents." I said, "All right." . . . What the desk contained I have no idea; my father kept no papers at home; if he had any at all they must have been in it . . .'

Muriel's letters must have been in it, too.

I was back at school when Joe went to our house to tell her there was no money for her, but she never told me of his visit. Her attitude to money was admirably sane for someone of her temperament and lack of education: she was quite unmercenary; her jewels were beads; and her furs never went beyond a collar or a stole, although clothes were one of her greatest pleasures. She knew that Roger, always so generous, was often worried about the endless demands on his pocket, particularly in the last years. I don't think he ever gave her large sums; she sent him all the bills. She hated doing this and always kept some back, although she knew he would never reproach her. She was shy of asking for money; in the early days she had pressed him to make a settlement on the twins and me, never on herself.

Much later she told me it was a mercy that Roger had died when he did. Elders & Fyffes were near ruin. It was Roger, the Banana King, with his flamboyant personality and nerve, who was largely responsible for the fantastic growth of the business in the early days, and it was also he who had brought the firm to its later perilous condition. He was only sixty-five when he died, but he had been old and ill for some time; he was out of touch with a changing world and his huge extravagance and unbusinesslike behaviour had proved disastrous. Muriel told me that had he lived he would have been almost penniless; Arthur Stockley would not have allowed him to return and his pension would have been greatly reduced: the money simply wasn't there, indeed, it was not until years later that the business got properly back on its feet again.

In Southsea Muriel had said that she had sixty pounds in the bank, and she had taken some notes from Roger's wallet as well as the tickets for Vienna. When I came home at Christmas she had sold the grand piano. Like Joe I never thought about money; my allowance was still half a crown a week because Muriel said, openly, that if she gave me more she knew I would leave her. That Christmas she grumbled, as usual, about my lack of money sense, and, as usual, I took no notice. She talked about selling the house, and had, presumably, already raised money on it, but I barely listened. She made all the arrangements for our trip to Vienna, and neither of us looked ahead beyond that. I think we were both waiting for something to happen, for something or someone to point in a certain direction. And I was waiting to be grown-up. Muriel had said she wouldn't give me a training of any sort, since I was bound to leave her if I could earn my own living. The twins had done this and she wasn't going to be caught the same way twice. Now that I had left school we were simply to go on living together. 'Like other people do,' she said. I had already tried to apprentice myself to a temporary cook we once had at Castelnau, and Muriel had stopped it. 'You'll only upset her and she'll leave.' Domestic by nature, I was sorry about this, but I wasn't too concerned about training for a job since I never saw myself in a context of work, only of love. I knew that as soon as I gained control of my own life I should fall in love time after time. I thought of nothing else and, in the meantime, and fairly obediently, I was waiting for an opportunity to start.

In Vienna Muriel stayed in bed. She gave me money to buy bottles of brandy for herself and Hanzi—she felt guilty about having them sent up from the restaurant—but she wasn't drowning herself in drink. She seemed peaceful, almost happy, just lying there, and I don't recall that she ever left the hotel—we were there for a week—or showed the smallest interest in the city outside.

In her gossips with the chambermaid she learnt that on Saturday nights in our hotel there was dancing in the restaurant. So far we had eaten all our meals in her room.

'We might go down on Saturday,' she said, 'it might be amusing.'

When she said this I felt my insides contract. I still had no clothes for evening. If we went down I would have to wear a woollen day dress and lace-up walking shoes. I explained this.

'Don't be so silly,' Muriel said, 'when you're young it doesn't matter what you wear. It's youth that counts. When you're older you'll understand this.'

'But I'm not older,' I said with stubborn logic.

'No, but you will be, and then you'll see. You shouldn't put up obstacles. You must learn to enjoy yourself while you can. You know you like dancing—well, now's your chance.'

It was a large, expensive hotel. I'd had plenty of opportunity to study the other visitors in the entrance hall and on the wide staircase. It was the most sophisticated setting I'd ever been in, and I found it alarming. Everything about me seemed to be wrong: I was fair, flat as a boy, and my eyes were moony and blue; the women in the hotel were busty and short, vivacious, with hot, dark eyes that were full of movement. The men's eyes were even hotter: I had passed several men, alone, on the staircase, and each time I did this I had received a hard, sexually assessing stare. I wanted, above all, to be noticed, but, at the same time, I was fearful of responding unsuitably. When these bouncy little Viennese ladies received the long, stripping look, did they hold the stare or turn away? I had seen several men with Erik von Stroheim shaved heads and tree-trunk necks who made my head reel when our eyes met. I longed to be thirty.

Muriel and I went down to the restaurant on Saturday night. She was wearing a dark evening dress and pointed slippers with *diamanté* buckles; her arms and shoulders were incredibly white and smooth, and tonight she had no blemishing bruises. Her skin was so soft that the merest touch produced a black unsightly mark which later turned to yellowy green. She was in the best of spirits after her long rest. When we went into the restaurant several heads turned and stayed turned.

It happened that as we stood waiting to be led to a table the orchestra stopped playing and the couples on the floor started to go back to the tables. The restaurant was packed. It was like a brilliant scene in a movie. I knew this because I had been to the movies surprisingly often, particularly from Woodlands Road. Muriel

135

would suddenly say, 'You can all go to the cinema in Putney this afternoon if you like.' Then, sometimes, this prized treat would be rescinded at the last moment and with no explanation. 'I don't want any fuss but you won't be going to the cinema this afternoon.' It never occurred to us that Roger was coming to see her, or had just cancelled the arrangement. In this way the scene that I was about to take part in was vicariously known to me.

It was during the lull, with no music, and conversation suspended on the way back to the tables, that the *maître d'hôtel* came forward. He indicated an empty table on the far side of the room and motioned us to follow him across the nearly deserted dance floor. Muriel set off, with me behind her, reluctant to expose myself in this glittering array of naked shoulders, jewels, silks and satins, gleaming white shirt fronts and a sprinkling of uniforms. In a moment of quiet, before conversation among the diners had got going again, I reached the edge of the dance floor and my sturdy shoe went down upon the parquet—crash. Out of panic I hesitated, but the next foot was bound to follow, and it did—crash. And the next and the next. I tried to hunch my weight up in the air, to tread on tiptoe, without appearing to do so. All to no avail. I went crash-crash-crash across the entire width of the dance floor, now totally deserted except for myself. It was, to date, the greatest public humiliation of my life.

Muriel studied the menu and told me what certain dishes were in English. I didn't respond. She knew my moods as well as I knew hers, and she knew, now, that I was choked with shame. She took no notice.

Restaurants and bed were the two settings in which she was happiest and at her best. She brought quality to a restaurant; with her confident air of enjoyment and her striking Kay Francis looks she was the sort of patron that high-class restaurants welcomed. She was quite at home with menus, no matter how huge; she would never attempt to order in French or German, but she had eaten in so many restaurants with Roger that she seldom had to ask for translation.

'We'll order *á la carte*,' she said, 'I expect the dinner's good, but it's nicer to choose.'

Still ignoring my sulky silence she ordered for both of us, and half a bottle of champagne for herself.

'Uncle was always trying to get me to drink champagne,' she said, 'and I never really liked it, but I think I feel like it tonight.'

This Muriel was a totally different woman from the Woodlands Road and Castelnau Muriel; I had only seen this Muriel once before, in Harrogate. When the band started up again she watched with lively interest as the couples took to the floor, and picked out the best-dressed women and followed them with her eyes.

'You see that little woman in green,' she said, 'she'll be French. They have a different kind of chic from the Viennese. You can always tell.'

She watched the women. I watched the men.

'You see that old woman in grey dancing with the fair young man,' she said. 'He'll be the resident gigolo. He's danced with a different woman every time. They always have one in the big hotels. He asks anyone who's alone and they give him something at the end. I expect he'll come over to us. It might be amusing.'

He did. Arrived at our table, he gave a stiff little bow. Would either of us like to dance, he said in English, addressing Muriel.

'Go on,' she said to me, 'have a dance. You know you want to.'

I gave her a murderous look and shook my head. Muriel smiled up at the young man conspiratorially.

'She thinks her shoes aren't right,' she said in her purring voice.

She danced with him twice and I watched them, noting with spiteful pleasure that the gigolo was simply doing what he was paid to do, moving sedately round the floor without enjoyment or conversation. He wasn't holding Muriel closely to him, amorously, like some of the other couples, and he never once looked into her eyes with the ardent gaze that had never yet come my way.

The evening went on. Muriel's spirits remained the same, and so did mine. I tried hard to recover and failed, and nothing occurred outside myself to shift the leaden weight in my stomach. When the orchestra leader announced the last dance I was glad; we could leave after it. But, suddenly, out of nowhere, the gigolo was back at our table. He seized hold of my hand and pulled me to my feet. I was going to dance with him, he said, he wouldn't take no for an answer.

I went out on to the floor, turned round, and before I could open my mouth to speak, we were off, clipped closely body to body. For the first time that evening he was really dancing, and he was doing it with me. He whirled and twirled me among the staid couples, and they made room for us. The thought shot through my mind that what he was really doing was celebrating the end of a boring evening, but I didn't care. I forgot my dreadful shoes and all my other miseries: I was giddy with joy. We didn't speak. Once, he held me away from him and laughed in my face, and then his arm brought me back so that we fitted right the way down like jam spread. When it was all over the lights went out for a second and, in the darkness, he planted a little kiss on the side of my neck.

After a week in Vienna we went up into the mountains to Semmering. Muriel was to go on a diet and take the waters in a luxe hotel. We were still unpacking when various white-coated people came in to discuss with her the treatments and diet they recommended. She was to have daily massage, special baths, colonic irrigation, some electrical treatment for her ankles, regular dosings of the famous waters, and a particular diet. I, too, was to be given a diet to fatten me up.

This daily routine with its semi-nursing—a sort of nanny system for grown-up people—suited Muriel admirably. This was a very comfortable hotel with large, bright, verandahed bedrooms overlooking a vast snowy scene of exceptional beauty. It was entirely surrounded by white, peaked mountains, in a lunar world of stillness.

On that first morning, in pyjamas, I sat on Muriel's balcony under the blazing sun, surrounded by snow, and drank scalding hot chocolate topped with cream. This was my first experience of sun and snow and I thought it perfection. After breakfast Muriel bought me a blue and white woollen cap from one of the shops in the hotel, and I put it on and went out for an exploratory walk while she gave herself up to her new routine. We were to meet for lunch.

I had already noticed that in this hotel, like the one in Vienna, there were no children or young people of my own age. When I mentioned this to Muriel she said that both hotels were too expensive for families. In the vestibule that morning visitors who were not staying behind for treatments were shouting to each other about arrangements for the morning. Outside the hotel was a small hotel bus to take them to some prearranged spot, and horse-drawn sleighs, ordered from the hall porter the night before, were lined up waiting. I was the only one to be going out on foot.

I left the hotel and struck off along a snow-covered track which disappeared in the distance round the curve of a mountain as though over the edge of the world. My feet gave a soft scrunch on the snow, and the air was pure and exhilarating. There was no sign of habitation in front of me, and not a soul in sight.

When I reached the curve I looked back; the hotel was a speck in the distance. I went on, round the curve, to find myself in a greater white wilderness of mountains, my track proceeding into infinity.

Solitary walks had never been my favourite occupation, but when I left the hotel, pleased with my new cap and caught up in the beauty of the scene, I'd felt adventurous and happy enough to go trudging off into this ravishing setting. Now, alone, in the snowy vastness, I was suddenly filled with unspecified fears. The stillness and the space were like my life, empty, loveless and with no change in sight. If I ran away now, over the next range of mountains, I should come to another one, and yet another. My life was the same. There was no possibility in sight that I should ever be united with civilization.

That morning I took the longest walk of my life so far. From the moment I'd become frightened I'd had difficulty in breathing; my lungs were perpetually full, so that I couldn't take in more air. I thought I was going to choke, and my head throbbed.

I got back, as arranged, at lunchtime. Muriel had enjoyed her morning of massage and a bath in health-giving water. We went down to the restaurant and I couldn't eat my special lunch. Muriel said I'd walked too far. I still couldn't breathe properly and I couldn't swallow food. I didn't try to explain this because I didn't understand it, just as I didn't understand why I still felt frightened. Something had happened to my nervous system; I often had moods of throbbing emotion, but this was different. I was on the edge of hysteria, but I was far too inhibited to cry out or scream.

I couldn't sleep that night and the next day the whole of my face was swollen. The white coats were consulted and reassuringly told us that high altitudes affected people in curious ways; in a day or two, they said, all would be well. But they were wrong. I got steadily

139

worse, and after the first week—we had booked for a fortnight—we left and went back to Vienna.

This must have been a real disappointment for Muriel, but she never reproached me. She was kind throughout the whole ordeal and thought up treats to distract me. Twice we went for sleigh rides, sitting side by side under heavy strong smelling fur rugs, the bells of the horse's harness merrily tinkling as we slid over the icy tracks. But it was no good. I couldn't sleep, and I couldn't eat because my throat had swollen. My skin seemed to have serpents wriggling under the top layer and I couldn't stop twitching. My face stayed puffed and I lived on hot chocolate. The food in this hotel was the most delicious I'd ever seen, in fact, many years later, during the privations of the second war it was the memory of these temptingly presented dishes at Semmering, all uneaten by me, that returned to tease me.

We spent another week in Vienna and then we went home. I remember nothing at all of the journey, and hardly anything of the next few months at Castelnau. The Muriel who loved to travel, if only from one hotel to another, was left behind in Austria. Some people are stricken again with asthma when they return to a scene of asthmatic memory; Muriel succumbed at once to her Castelnau self. We lived from day to day in a vacuum; nothing had been decided; neither of us seemed to have a future of any sort.

Early that summer, when I was still seventeen, the twins sent me a one-way ticket to Sussex to join them, and a one pound note for expenses. I could do housework to earn my keep, they said; Helen had learned to cook and Stella worked in the garden. I wouldn't be eighteen and officially of age until April of next year, but they rightly judged that Muriel wouldn't go to law to get me back for so short a time.

I left without telling her. I knew that if she collapsed, as she surely would, I should be done for. I may have written a note, but I don't remember doing so. Unlike the twins I meant never to return or to see her again: I meant to sponge her from my life for ever. I believed that only by total and permanent severance, both physically and in my mind, from her vampire life of self-destruction, would I be able to save myself. At the time I didn't realize that history was repeating itself. Soon after I was born she had behaved in much the same way that I was now doing, barricading herself against feeling, obeying, instead, the same blind instinct to flee.

I packed a small bag and walked out of the house.

Chapter Ten

Muriel now had no one. She collapsed, and Castellani took her into his nursing home for the last time.

This breakdown was worse than any of the previous ones. Muriel was in the home for weeks. And she recovered. Once the downward plunge was arrested her tenacity to life and her extraordinary courage returned, as it always did, and she brushed her hair and tended her nails, and told herself that she had just suffered a particularly bad bout of the dysentery that had nearly killed her in the war.

It was on a morning in July 1930, as she waited for her breakfast to be brought up—she was recovered now and would have to leave the home in a day or so—that she saw something in the paper that made her suddenly alert. She had been idly looking down the Deaths column when she saw a familiar name: Scott-Hewitt. A Mrs. Nora Emily Scott-Hewitt, wife of Lt.-Colonel Alfred Scott-Hewitt, D.S.O., O.B.E., had died at an address in Cornwall.

Greatly wondering, Muriel ate her breakfast, and then wrote a letter of condolence to the widower, adding: 'Are you *my* Scottie?'

Muriel's Scottie had come into her life in Italy during the war. On a certain cold and rainy day, after a full day's march for the troops, they had all stopped for the night, under orders, on the outskirts of a little village. As they approached the village she had already noticed some British soldiers. She fixed up a billet for her driver, and then set about looking for somewhere for herself to spend the night. She found a disused farm out-building a little apart from an empty farm house. This would do her nicely. Too tired to bother with food, she had just arranged herself as best she could, alone, when there was a tap at the door.

Standing outside, a torch in his hand, was a British officer. He introduced himself and from the pockets of his greatcoat drew out a cooked chicken and a bottle of wine. He had seen her, he said, taking her things in, and had gone back into the village to see what he could find in the way of provisions. He now offered to share his dinner with her in her billet. What could be nicer? Later they parted and she never saw him again.

A reply came to Muriel's letter. He was her Scottie. He told her that his wife had tragically taken her own life, leaving him with a seventeen-year-old boy. They had rented a cottage for the holidays in Cornwall and were still there. He asked Muriel to come and stay with them, to help them both to reorganize themselves after the shock of his wife's death.

Muriel had always believed in omens. This was an omen: a good omen. The child in her, the part of her which refused to come away from never-never land, found omens irresistible: also premonitions. She was always amazed by coincidence and often gave occurrences little shoves into the realm of premonition. Thus, it was not enough that on that July morning she should discover that an old acquaintance of a few hours, encountered some twelve years before, was now in trouble at the precise moment that she herself didn't know where to turn: it was both omen and premonition.

'When I woke up that morning I knew something was going to happen,' she would say later, 'I had a premonition.'

Muriel packed a bag and took the train to Cornwall.

She had to change trains to get to the little country station and this meant a long wait; it was dark and raining when she reached it, much the sort of evening as on that first encounter in Italy. This was another omen. There was no taxi, but the house she wanted, she was told, was near. Never a walker, Muriel nevertheless walked, carrying her case.

After one or two false alarms—the dark always confused her, and she was, in any case, one of those people who contrive to get lost on a straight road—she found the house and started up the path to the front door. There was a light on in the uncurtained room on the right, so, instead of knocking on the door, she tiptoed towards the light. She looked in.

In the middle of an uninviting room lit by one oil lamp there was a long trestle table with no tablecloth but, scattered over it in disorder, the remains of countless snacks; dirty plates, knives and glasses, empty beer bottles, packets of biscuits, empty cans and crusts of bread and, in the middle of this mess, seated at the table in a little clearing which he had achieved by the simple method of pushing things away, was a dishevelled youth, his head upon his arms on the table, fast asleep.

One glance was enough to size up the situation: no one had civilized the cottage and the boy was hungry and desolate. This was the kind of crisis that Muriel understood. She knocked at the door.

Alfred Scott-Hewitt was a soldier through and through, the persona of the gruff, inarticulate British army officer, with a twinkle in his blue eyes. He was born in 1876 in Mackay, Queensland, one of six children, three boys, three girls. His father was a sugar planter. The children were all still young when the family returned to England, and after his schooling Alfred joined the army. Serving with the Queen's Own Royal West Kent Regiment he spent several years in India after the Boer War, also in Ceylon and Singapore. He was retired now and living on his pension. His wife had been a melancholic, a sad, ill lady who would set off alone on a purging pilgrimage and end up on some bishop's doorstep, distraught and sick. Alfred had fetched her back from several of these distressing flights. She further persecuted herself with the belief that her olive skin was due to mixed blood, an idea which she found insupportable.

All in all, it had been a sad little family. Alfred was a lonely, possibly frightened man—hence the gruff exterior—who had insulated himself against distresses. Towards his son, Desmond, their only child, he behaved with strict militarism, treating him in much the same way that he did his dog, which he was fond of but treated roughly, since any other way would have seemed unmanly; when he allowed himself the indulgence of an occasional caress he would follow this up by harshly shoving the dog away from him. It was a conventional story, as was the fact that within the limits of his income he was inclined to drink too much. Unlike Muriel he didn't suffer a change of personality when in drink; simply, he was a bit of an old soak.

Muriel brought order and comfort into the cottage, and she was kind to Desmond and cooked him nourishing meals. At the end of

144

the holidays he went back to school for his last term, and the lease of the cottage expired. The crisis was over.

Alfred was unwilling to return to his home, with or without Muriel, and she, certainly, had no wish to go back to Castelnau, to the house in which she had never known a moment's happiness. Together they moved to a small house on Dartmoor where, for the sake of appearance, Alfred's unmarried sister joined them. A few months later Alfred and Muriel were married in the local church in the village of Manaton, and Alfred's sister went home.

It was only after I was well into this quest for Muriel's past that it came to me for the first time that in order to get married she must have filled in a form giving details of her birth and parentage. What would she put? Since obtaining her wartime passport—which she had mutilated in order to preserve those secrets—nothing like this had been necessary. I had forgotten that in this one respect, her marriage, she would be forced to make these declarations.

With some excitement I wrote to the encumbent at Manaton church and waited. Was I about to learn the truth at last? When the answer came the details were not extensive. Muriel had described herself as a Widow, and for Name and Surname, Rank and Profession of Father, she had declared: Henry John Foster, Artist.

This was, indeed, a surprise. Was this the painter 'stepbrother'? Was Henry John Foster really her father? Was he even a real person or simply a made-up name, the only alternative to putting Unknown? In vain I looked him up in various catalogues of English artists; nor does his name appear in any museum or art gallery in Clifton or Bristol. The witnesses to the marriage were Alfred's unmarried sister and a cousin, neither of whom would have had cause to question Muriel's entries in the register. Was this the reason, a safeguard against inquisitive eyes, why even Stella was not invited to the wedding?

The news that they were married came to me through Stella who was always in fitful correspondence with Muriel. In her reply to Muriel's letter Stella told her that I, too, had got married, a few weeks earlier, in the registry office in Hampstead. Neither Muriel nor I wrote to congratulate the other, and neither daughters, sisters nor mother attended either of the weddings.

Muriel was now a married woman with the duties of a wife. This radical change in her situation had come about within a few months. It was a union formed in desperation between middle-aged strangers, whose only similarity was loneliness. Even their war experiences were not easily shared: as a professional soldier Alfred's interest lay in strategy and weapons, while Muriel's knowledge was empirical. She had always felt lost in the country; I doubt she had ever taken a walk for pleasure in the whole of her life. At Bad Gastein with Roger she had complained of 'no shops, no motor cars, no buses, no cinemas, in fact no amusement of any kind'. Now she was living in a cottage in the wilds of Dartmoor, and not just for a few days, drinking the waters for her health; Alfred expected them to live there for the rest of their lives, just the two of them. They were not well off; Alfred had only his pension, and Muriel had her furniture and the money that would come from the sale of the house at Castelnau, but no income. They would have to be careful.

Alfred was a born countryman; he loved the moor with its unrelenting moods and stern beauty. He went for regular walks in the morning and afternoon, rain or shine, leaving and returning at precisely the same time every day. He gave himself jobs in the house, coal scuttles, knife sharpening and so on, and carried them out to a timetable. He had always led a regular life and saw no reason to do otherwise now. He liked to lunch at one o'clock, have tea at four-thirty and dine at seven-thirty. He couldn't understand unpunc-tuality—Muriel was always late—and had never heard of a woman staying in bed unless she was gravely ill.

Muriel was urban: weather and the changing seasons meant nothing to her. She would have liked to look out of a window on to a garden permanently filled with flowers, but as soon as a bud appeared she picked it and brought it into the house. She liked all new-born animals but soon tired of them; it was their helplessness and the drama of birth that appealed to her. She hated domesticity and most of all she hated anything that happened, or needed to be done, regularly, and, like a gipsy, she hated to stay long in one place.

Now that the crisis was long over she was lonelier than ever. Alfred seemed to have no friends, not even far away friends, nor did he appear ever to have had any. He was on pleasant terms with his three sisters, who all led interesting lives, but not on close terms. He seemed not to need friends. He was never bored; he was, in fact, very content with his new life. He was proud of Muriel's war record, and I think he felt a certain pride in having married a good looking and unusual woman. They sometimes drove to Bovey Tracy and had drinks in one of the hotels there. They got to know the landlord and his wife, and sometimes stayed on after closing time and joined them in their private quarters. Seen among the other women in Bovey Tracy Muriel had an air of some distinction, and this gave Alfred a pleasant sense of ownership. She was still an attractive woman, and after all, women were famous complainers.

Desmond went into the army when he left school and eventually was stationed in India, where he stayed for the next five years. Alfred and Muriel were alone. Each autumn Muriel wrote to Stella to say that she dreaded another cold, wet winter on Dartmoor; there was no 'life' in the country, she said, she might as well be living on the moon. There was nothing to do. She felt trapped, unable to escape.

It was inevitable that she should fret herself ill. They had been living in this way for three years when the local doctor agreed that the cold and the general strain of life on Dartmoor was affecting her heart. Doctors had always said whatever she wanted them to say.

In a stifled sort of way Alfred was an affectionate man, or rather, he often seemed on the brink of affection. He knew that Muriel missed her daughters; he had none himself. When she suggested that they buy a house near London that was big enough to provide a home for Desmond, the twins and me, he generously agreed. He hadn't yet met the twins or me.

It happened at this time that we were all three at loose ends, or about to be. My marriage was over, Stella was out of work, and Helen was coming to the end of a temporary job. Of the three of us Helen was the only one who was genuinely fitted for employment. She was a good secretary, hard working and reliable; she had passed out of Pitman's third in her year. She took temporary jobs, saved up, and then spent her savings in the south of France, usually taking Stella with her. Stella, quite simply, conned herself into comfortable employment and never stayed anywhere long. I did much the same, but in a more menial way; until I got married I had managed to keep going as a waitress, cinema attendant, house parlourmaid and so on. I now meant to teach myself to type.

I had been married to a writer who was more than thirty years older than me. He had said, 'Use me as a stepping stone,' and I had done this. He had been my teacher, the first person to take trouble with me; he had endorsed my most fervent views, and with infinite patience persuaded me that although I was the most ignorant young woman he'd ever known I wasn't stupid. This was a revelation. We had lived together for over three years. We had spent several months in Italy and France, mostly staying with his friends, and with his encouragement I'd written a novel. Eventually I'd torn it up, but I was now determined to be a writer.

During all this adventurous time I was never well. I was tall now —I had shot up to five foot eight—and I weighed under seven stone. I still couldn't eat as other people did and I still vomited. I realized that this was due to psychological disturbance but this knowledge, in itself, didn't make me well. Just as one term at R.A.D.A.—which had been a paradise—had knocked me over, now, the marvel of being loved, meeting famous people, and generally living the sort of life that I had dreamed of, had the same effect on me. I took sleeping pills at night and drank too much at parties; I had appalling swings of mood that I couldn't control. I had left my husband because I believed—and so did he—that if I went on like this I should soon be dead.

During all this time I hadn't seen the twins and we rarely wrote to each other. This was from indolence and not from lack of affection or concern; each of us worried incessantly about the other two. Stella, always in touch with Muriel, was helping her to find a house near London, and Muriel begged her to use her influence with Helen and me to look on it as our home.

Eventually they settled in Weybridge, Surrey, and we all three joined them there. Still shocked from the failure of my marriage I was grateful for somewhere to go, and at the same time painfully aware that I was stepping backwards. The twins were already there when I arrived. I was glad to see them and quickly slipped under their dominance. I was less childish than I had been when I joined them in Sussex five years ago, but only a little less; maturity was still a long way away.

Living at closest proximity to a man is a habit not easily come by at forty-one. Until she married, Muriel had never regularly shared her bed, and she had never before had to look at the same man day after day after day. In Weybridge she was seldom alone with Alfred except at night, but predictably the arrangement was not a success. As always, Muriel's whole system rebelled against the ordinary tasks of day-to-day life, the regularity of meals, the ordering, preparing, cooking and clearing away. With every fibre of her being she resented her rôle of home-maker: she felt like an unpaid servant; like someone who was only an unpaid servant.

Everyone in this ill-assorted household was acting out a part for which he or she was singularly ill equipped. Not one of the members of this *soi-disant* family—Desmond came home on leave twice during this period—had had any experience of family life; Alfred's first marriage had been stricken by the abnormality of mental illness; Muriel had never before been married, and the four younger members were none of them very young any more, nor were they easy or especially considerate. The twins and I used Stella's bedroom as our private sitting-room and kept ourselves apart from the others as much as possible; we played tennis—there was a large garden with a tennis court—and went for walks together and I started another novel. Alfred retired into himself, took his dog for short military turns along the pavements, and sometimes dug in the garden; he was polite to us—and I hope we were to him—and it was impossible to tell what he thought about his new household. Perhaps he didn't know.

As soon as I had learnt to type I got a job with a film company in London. I shared a room with Helen, who was also working now, and we both went down to Weybridge for weekends. Stella stayed on there. She had bought a loom and wove lengths of tweed, and after a while two French boys came to stay and she taught them English. This meant more cooking for Muriel.

For two or three years she struggled on in this way and then they sold the house and bought the Lincoln Arms. This was the pub in Weybridge to which Alfred and Muriel drove each evening and sometimes before lunch as well. It was a pleasant little pub, badly situated at the end of a blind, empty road; it was on the river, invisible from the main road. It had failed with several successive owners, but there was a legend that an ex-naval commander had once made a go of it. It was now hoped that an ex-army officer would prove an equal draw. What they didn't take into account was that when they promoted themselves to owners the pub lost its only two regular customers.

Shortly before the move I left them for good. I refused to set foot in the Lincoln. I knew that if I did I should be pressed into service behind the bar, and that one emergency after another would keep me there. This would never be expected of the twins, but it would be of me. The twins both had exquisitely narrow helpless hands that couldn't tie up a parcel or mend a stocking; no menial task was ever expected of them. It had always been I who, willingly enough, did their emergency washing, ironing and mending. Stella, in particular, did up her clothes with safety pins until I sewed on a button, and it was I who cut the canary's nails and gave the dog a bath when it fouled its bottom. I enjoyed my superior handiness, but I was not prepared to wash glasses behind the bar.

I would have severed myself from them even if they had not moved. Muriel and I were natural enemies; our views on every subject were diametrically opposite, and I was violently intolerant at that time, harsh and unyielding in my judgement. I saw her as bitter, destructive, pessimistic and totally wrong headed in every respect, and I hated all these qualities with a passionate loathing. I couldn't shrug them off as the twins seemed to do. I believed that life was for loving; that love was all that really mattered, and Muriel seemed to me to epitomize the negation of love.

But I couldn't get her out of my mind; I was obsessed by her. She pounded about in my head, making no sense. For instance, why was this be-medalled one-time quartermaster and organizer incapable of running a small household without endless muddles, complaints and physical breakdown? Why had she dedicated herself to misery? Why? Why had she resolutely turned her face against enjoyment? And why did she insist on making me feel guilty? It was, above all, this corroding guilt that now made me hate her even more viciously than I had before. Like some eastern beggar, blind, with suppurating stumps instead of legs, she relentlessly exposed her suffering condition as the price of my own independence. I was determined to fight free of her, to banish her from my life for ever.

I no longer remember my last weekend in Weybridge; no doubt

hard things were said, most of them by me. Some weeks later the move to the Lincoln Arms took place and Stella went with them, but she was not to be there for long. She answered an advertisement in *The Times* and went off to Budapest as a governess and, as soon as she had established herself, following their custom, Helen went out to join her. Alfred and Muriel were once more alone together.

Chapter Eleven

The 1914 war had come at just the right moment for Muriel and the second war was to do the same. By then—this was some two years after I had finally gone—the Lincoln Arms had failed and Alfred and Muriel were faced with the alternative of bankruptcy or selling out. This situation had been looming for months. A new life, of one sort or another, was inevitable, but Muriel kept putting it off. The prospect of a humdrum domestic existence for just herself and Alfred in a small house, still to be found, was insupportable to her. As so often in her life, she was waiting for something to happen. And something did happen: war.

Soon after the twins and I had gone to Weybridge we had run into an old school friend, now married, who was living a few miles away in Addlestone. This was Peggie Bradbury, now Paterson, who had been head girl at Clovelly-Kepplestone. At school she had been an energetic joky girl, and now she was an attractive, rather wild, married woman, the wife of a tall, good-looking man who, it turned out, had once been a casual friend of Joe Ackerley's. The twins were delighted at this encounter—they were the same age as Peggie—and from then on the four of them met a good deal, motor racing at Brooklands, pub crawling and sometimes going up to London for a night out.

Peggie was pretty in a cream and roses way, and good natured, generous and not very serious. The wildness came out when she drank. She had had an unhappy home life; her father had been her refuge, and when she was fourteen he died. In her despair she had started drinking soon after this and used to smuggle half-bottles of whisky into her locker at school. She was never found out. Now she sometimes became violent and tried to jump out of a window or a moving car. This alarming instability matched oddly with her normal behaviour which, like her face, was carefree. She seemed too immature to be married; she laughed a lot and had strong legs and lunged about making mistakes. She really must improve, she would say, winking.

Dick Paterson joined the navy on the outbreak of war and was called up at once, leaving Peggie alone in Addlestone. She had nothing to do. The twins were no longer there and she had made no other friends in the area. She was lonely, unsuited to solitude. She had already met Muriel at the Lincoln, and now she called in there increasingly often for company. Soon the two women were deep in plans.

Muriel had seen her chance of escape: she would put the clock back and take a motor canteen to France. Like an old war horse she was pawing at the ground. Alfred had always been proud of her first-war record, and now, not entirely reluctant to get away himself, he put no obstacle in her way. His unmarried sister was living in a house at Boar's Hill near Oxford. She was not well off and she had taken in a lodger. It was decided that Alfred should replace the lodger and sister and brother should pool their resources.

The Lincoln Arms was sold—at a loss—Alfred went off to live with his sister, and Muriel and Peggie went ahead with their plans. They were soon joined by a friend of Peggie's, Cynthia Elliot.

I can only give the barest outline of Muriel's life in the second war and after it. I had parted from her in a spirit of deepest hostility, and our estrangement was to last, almost without let-up, until six months before she died. Added to this, my own memories of the war years are more clouded than those of any other period of my life. I had married for the second time in June 1939 and after my husband joined up I worked in various dreary clerical jobs, mostly in London. Any news I had of Muriel came second-hand through one or other of the twins. They, too, had removed themselves from her as soon as they could manage it but, as before, they did so only physically. They each had a deep feeling of family ties which, for one reason or another, was something which had failed to stamp itself on me. As always, they kept in touch with Muriel.

In Budapest they had been frantically watching, with the rest of the world, as peace receded. Helen was engaged to a millionaire, a

Hungarian. He had been Stella's friend, but as soon as Helen arrived he quickly transferred his affections to her. They planned to marry and start a new life in America, but he was not in a position to leave the country until he had wound up his business affairs. Shortly before war was declared he sent Helen ahead of himself to the south of France—where he had money—to await him there, but he left his own exit too late and they were separated, unmarried, for the next six years. Stella, who had stayed behind, got herself on to the last transport out of Budapest and made her way to Cairo.

In England Muriel and her small party were coping with red tape, filling in forms, presenting themselves for a medical examination and waiting for orders. Things had changed since 1914. Muriel had expected to go off with her little band as private volunteers, only loosely attached to the Red Cross, making her own decisions and generally charming her way through officialdom. But this war was different. Nevertheless, she must have used the old familiar tactics to get herself passed fit by a doctor. She was not fit, nor had she been fit for many years. For a long time she had been drinking heavily and continuously; her heart was bad and her legs were chronically swollen. Only her courage was unimpaired.

They arrived in France with their motor canteen at the end of April 1940, and two months later they were taken prisoner by the Germans.

They had gone out as a voluntary unit under the auspices of the British Committee for the French Red Cross, but from the start nothing had gone right. Within days of their arrival in France the Germans took Amiens and reached the sea at Abbeville. Muriel and her party made their way to Nancy, there to attach themselves to the 3rd French Army, but when they got there they found the whole area evacuated. There was no one to give orders, and no one to issue the necessary identification cards which they needed before proceeding further. In any case, to where should they proceed? Without identification cards they went south for two days and at Luxeil joined a French Red Cross convoy which was on its way to the French hopital at Bussang, a village about fifty kilometres due east. There they stayed until 22 June when the Germans entered and took the village.

They were prisoners of war. The official report of their progress reads: '. . . Three weeks later they were removed to Mulhouse where they remained for four or five days and afterwards to Cernay (Sennheim) where they stayed a few weeks. They were then sent to Freiburg, where they were imprisoned in the civil gaol for 5 days. On their release they were taken to Villengen, Stalag Vc where they remained until early in September. From there they were removed to Heilbronn Stalag Vb, where they spent over 5 months.'

The twins and I were shocked to learn that Muriel was now a prisoner of war. We knew no details but wrote to each other obsessively—our letters took weeks to arrive—to say so. Through the Red Cross in Cairo Stella quickly organized parcels for Muriel and applied for her repatriation. Alfred did the same from England. In France Helen somehow arranged for parcels to be sent to Muriel from America, and I pestered the Commissioner of Police, a Dr. Methven, who happened to live in Weybridge, for news of her whereabouts. I could not get her out of my mind, but I had closed my heart against her and I was not going to open it easily. From now on I sent her a letter and cigarettes from time to time, but I did it with a poor grace, and it seems that fate took a hand in the delivery of these letters: only one of them ever reached her.

It was October before Stella received the first card from Muriel.

14 October 1940. Darling, two cards together from you Sept. 17 & 21. It was grand. I read them several times a day. I am looking forward to my first parcel but it has not yet arrived. Darling of you to do it. I shall be allowed to send two letters & 4 cards a month now, but they take a long time. Please keep writing to me. I feel like a fly between two frames of glass, but I am happy about you my sweet. Another card following this. All my love & thoughts, Mother.

On 13 February, 1941, they were moved to the Internierten Lager, Leibenau. Here, two months later they received a letter from Berlin stating that their repatriation had been agreed on by both the German and British Governments. On September 26 they left the internment camp to join the first transport of repatriated British wounded. First they went to Bad Sulza, Stalag 1Xc, and from there into France, to Rouen, where they stayed for some ten days awaiting the repatriation transport. It never materialized. The scheme had fallen through and they were brought back into Germany with some of the wounded to the British Surgical Hospital at Obermassfeld, Thuringen, where they remained, nursing the wounded, for the next seven and a half months.

An orthopaedic surgeon later told me that the arrival of the three women at this prison hospital was the best therapy that the wounded men could have had. There were no other women. 'Just to see them in the wards made all the difference,' he said, 'and they were very useful, too. We got very fond of them.'

28.1.42 Darling Stella, Write me as often as poss. You would hate the cold here, 15 below zero & I work in an annexe & it is cold crossing the road just in cap & overall. Your coat is with me night & day, on my bed at night & to & fro to work. I am relieved you are in a warm place. P. is very well, C. also—she is working in the operating theatre. Love, Mother.

It was during this period of the three women's internment at the hospital that the greatest concentration of air bombing over Germany took place, by the Americans in the daytime and the British at night. Many severely wounded airmen were taken to the Surgical Hospital at Obermassfeld.

30.1.42 My darling Stella, After 6 long months I got a letter from you & a lovely parcel ten days ago. I was crazy with joy, as I had been thinking something had happened to you or I was forgotten. I wrote to American Embassy to enquire. The sight of those cigs made the German Guards jump miles high & I was able to repay some of my debts to our English officers that had helped me. Nighties & warm things were a Godsend. I've given up asking Alfred for things, somehow nothing turns up. I didn't write letters last month. It looked so hopeless as nobody had written to me. Very busy in the hospital here. We have all the severely wounded, but they are a grand crowd & I have made many friends. It's a great experience for one's nursing. We are the only 3—with 450 men & officers, otherwise orderlies nursing. On the other hand life is a great strain. One letter from Helen in four months. Tonight we read a Play to the Blind. My dearest love, darling, and thanks, Mother.

31.3.42 My own darling Stella, Such a long time since your writing. Can't think why it takes so long. Do you write often? that's the thing. Letters are the only thing to keep one going. Still living in hopes of getting home but God knows when. We have been here just on 6 months. Awful. Winters so cold & snow for months. This hospital is over-crowded 450 with staff. Hope you like the photo I am enclosing, orderlies & Drs & us three, like bags of flower, taken in the open when it was freezing. I had a letter from Di the day before my birthday—wasn't it nice of her remembering—tickled to death! I was presented with a bottle of home wine made from raisins and sugar fermented. I live on potatoes and swedes. I have fearful tussles with my restless temperament—& just kick myself at times. All my love sweet Stella. M.

10 Sept. 1942. Stella darling, Such a *lovely lovely* parcel arrived from you today & only two months coming. Darling if you only knew the thrill I get to receive a parcel. Especially from you. I dreamt of you the other night—that I was saying goodbye, never to see you again, and trying my hardest not to show it—as I did when I said goodbye to you when you left the Lincoln that morning nearly 3 years ago. It seems to have been since you have grown up always goodbyes & farewells. Anyhow I have had a great deal of happiness from you when you were children. You were so sweet & I did spoil you, not that you could agree that I was spoiling you all really. I have no regrets darling, for you have all turned up trumps, so you see I am very proud of you. Take great care of yourself and don't overdo things. I do long to see you looking your old lovely self & *unspoilt*. Life is pretty mouldy at present for we are in punishment—the last 5 weeks we are not allowed to sleep in our rooms, but 80 packed together in the Canteen. Reprisals etc. I miss the Hospital work so much. All my love, M.

Part of the hospital staff at Obermassfeld had been dispersed and Muriel, Peggie and Cynthia had been moved back to the camp at Liebenau.

24 November 1942. My darling Stella, No letters from you for so long & life is very heavy, bitterly cold & damp & heating almost

nil. So you can imagine me. I wear your tweed coat by day &
nights on my bed. I am so short of warm garments to put on.
A transport left here for Palestine but I could not get on it as I
am on the Military List and not a Civil Person & I have to wait
for the wounded. We are very over-crowded here, prisoners
arriving daily. What it all means nobody knows. You would be
amused to see our collection undressing at night. I must live
long enough to enjoy a little luxury once again otherwise I will
be darned annoyed. No parcels arriving for me. Darling you
won't get this in time to bring you my love for Xmas but you
know you are always with me. Be a good girl my sweet Stella. No
news of Diana, she never writes, hard hearted Hannah. Have a
good time but be sensible & don't overdo things. If I had got to
Palestine, too wonderful. M.

6 December 1942. No news of transport. Will it ever come.
I shall be white haired and toothless soon. In our fourth year
now. I love my photo & look at it every night but it makes me
homesick. Please, darling, take great care of your health. All my
love, sweetheart, M.

In January Muriel was offered repatriation. The official report
reads: 'A special case was made in the case of Mrs. Scott-Hewitt
and, owing to ill-health, her name was permitted to be included
with those on the list for the first transport via Lisbon for England,
which left this camp 18 January 1943. Mrs. Paterson's and Miss
Elliot's names were refused on the grounds that they were military
prisoners and Mrs. Scott-Hewitt then decided not to go without
them.'

1 January 1943. Sweetheart, A very happy New Year & all that
you could wish for yourself, darling. I have been thinking of you
today & drank a silent health for yours & Helen's happiness. My
third daughter I never hear from so I can only hope she is safe &
well. Darling, your lovely parcel of cigs & food arrived the day
before Xmas, was it not wonderful? I can never tell you the
excitement a parcel from you & Helen means. Well, darling, some
of our people have got to Palestine. I was down to go this week
but the transport is going to England. I know you will understand

that I could not accept & leave the other two behind. 32 going—they are wild with excitement. I would not have enjoyed my liberty, so don't think that I am depressed. All my love, darling Stella, Mummie.

Loyalty alone would have prevented Muriel from leaving Peggie and Cynthia, but there was another reason why going home to England was unacceptable to her. Although she was unwell she had no intention at that time of stepping aside from the war. Had she managed to get to Palestine she would have rested for a while and then, by hook or crook, plunged back into some active war zone.

28 April 1943. Stella darling, It's so miserable getting no news of you & Helen. I hope all is well with you both. Nothing from Helen for months. Only those poor devils who have been prisoners can know the nervous strain of being shut up & getting no news. A good thing it's not you, darling, you'd go crazy. I had a card from——in Cairo. She was staying in a lovely Hotel & having beautiful food. I wish people wouldn't talk of food in letters. We speak when lights are out of things we would like to eat until someone shouts 'Shut up, I can't bear it!' Darling, if I ever do get away & have to wait at Lisbon I shall do my hardest to get to you for a bit. Keep that under yr hat. I am banking on your help, sweetheart. All my love, Mother.

27 July. Sammy darling, Just a line to send you my love & thoughts. Our nerves are all very razzled & everybody is ready to fly at each other's throats for no reason. They are getting up a show here & I am in the same room as the producer & it's Hell at times. Peggie also in the room. She, by the way, looks marvellous in health & looks, but not so in temper. On the other hand I am considered an asset in Placcidity. I am not too fit. The heat is tropical. My day starts at 6.30 a.m. and goes on until I go to bed. All my love, take care of your dear self, M.

The three women were at last repatriated in September. Muriel wrote from Lisbon.

5 October. Stella darling, I did think I would get a friendly greeting from you. I sent you a cable of my release. Helen wired

me but not my Stella. I have been laid up with my heart after a long journey & 6 days in trains & not allowed to fly yet. Also stuck with very little money & no clothes. Peggie & C. have left so I am alone here, my third week. I collapsed completely after the journey, was very worn out before. I had lunch with your friends —— from Cairo. They were very kind, offered to lend me money which I did not accept, but gave me a very handsome handbag, she said a present for Stella's mother. I may leave in a week. All my love sweet, Mother.

There was no question of Muriel getting back into the war or of joining Stella in Cairo.

At Boar's Hill Alfred and his sister had been leading the sedentary wartime life of two elderly people. They welcomed Muriel back and she stayed with them for several weeks recuperating. But this could not go on, nor could Alfred afford to support her in a separate establishment. She went to London and lived there by herself in a bedsitting-room in Sussex Gardens, doing poorly-paid Red Cross work in the tube stations and canteens. In between times she went back to Boar's Hill for short visits. It was not a glorious return, and she was unhappy and lonely and in poor health, but she stuck it out doggedly for the rest of the war. Eventually she received the 1939–45 Service Medal, bringing her wartime decorations up to eight.

Just before the war ended Stella, the maverick, became engaged. Helen and I had often wondered what sort of man would manage either to slip a bridle over her head or perhaps out-brigand her. We had never considered a simple answer. We had thought her unconventional, and we were wrong. She married—at St. George's, Hanover Square, where Roger had married Netta—a regular soldier, a romantic with a loving heart, and her hitherto piratical spirit responded with instant recognition to the most conventional life with him. Badly wounded, he had to leave the army and eventually became a gentleman farmer. He had been brought up in an atmosphere of feudal values which he accepted without question. For the next twenty-two years he adored Stella, and then he died. They lived in the country and gradually, as conditions after the war made it possible, surrounded themselves with dogs and horses and pursued a calendar of sport, and Stella found an outlet for her tenderer feelings in local organizations for the luckless and the old. She was generous and extravagant; like Roger she preferred to give rather than receive and, again like Roger, she had her protégés: when interviewing servants she tended to take on the more hopeless applicant, out of pity, rather than the more efficient. She became a gardener.

Muriel's love for Stella had always been poisoned by jealousy. She had probably never considered that Stella would one day belong to someone else. The shock was severe. Stella's husband was a man of deep simplicity, a good man, and these qualities proclaimed themselves with extraordinary clarity to strangers as well as to the people who knew him. He was much loved. I have said that Muriel was always amazed by goodness, and now it took her a while to get used to this unfailing source; she looked for traps and found none, and slowly, as the years went by, she came to accept the truth. Even the most rabid jealousy requires some fertilization in order to flourish, and Stella and her husband attached Muriel to their lives with such tact and generosity that she hadn't a leg to stand on. When Stella was first married her husband was comfortably off, and later he inherited a great deal of money. From the first they sent Muriel to the best doctors and paid the bills and in a hundred ways made her life more comfortable. But the Stella of her dreams was now no more than a ghost of the past.

Muriel could not settle. She must, she said, find work. She was nearly fifty-five and in chronically poor health. She was not happy in England, nor had she ever been; apart from her apotheosis in Italy all her best times with Roger had been abroad. She often said that she never had any luck in England; the climate had never suited her; she felt tethered, trapped and misunderstood.

She offered her services to organizations that cared for servicemen abroad, but no one would take her on. She was unskilled and no longer young. At last, in desperation, she approached the Church Army, and they agreed to try her out. She was to be hostess to soldiers and their families for rest periods in a leave centre in Hamburg.

This was a new venture for Muriel and it proved remarkably successful. For the next five or six years, mostly in Austria, she worked in Church Army centres, helping to organize the food, mothering young men, listening to wives' problems and generally making life pleasant for everybody. She was not in Hamburg for long; she moved to a centre in the mountains in Austria, and later to an even more beautiful location on the island of Nordeney. The pay was small but the life was healthy and not arduous; mostly the men were non-commissioned ranks, but occasionally officers turned up for a spell of leave. Later, one of the Church Army Sisters who had worked with Muriel told me, 'She liked the officer type . . . brigadiers and such like. Once we had three brigadiers off the train at the same time. She enjoyed that! She always minded about her hair.' This Sister also told me that she had always assumed Muriel to be a widow, alone in the world; she never talked about her private life, and not one of her co-workers knew that she had daughters and a husband. This was the way she had wanted it. She had rejected her true centre so long ago that now little of it remained, and she must have found here, where no personal background was looked for in anyone, that she could live at last in a measure of tranquillity.

The last two Church Army centres in which she was housed were situated in exquisite locations among pine forests and snowy slopes. In spring and summer there were wild flowers everywhere, and Muriel particularly enjoyed taking picnics to the men in a horse-drawn sleigh. Her only worry was her health.

Stella darling. I was very happy to get your letter & to know you are both well. We had a very sad week, the King's death! & the same night an A.T.S. girl suddenly produced a son at 2 a.m. No one had a clue she was with child. She tried to walk out in the snow & could not & it was born on the stairs & no one to look after her. Then a doctor came & took them to an American Hospital 2 hrs away, but the mother died a few hours after. I was going to take the baby to a British hospital in Hanover. It meant 3 days there & back. I just couldn't make it, which grieved me, as my leg has given me a lot of trouble & pain. It's the old trouble from the circulation, the blood doesn't get through. I am having treatment for it. We have had 13 days of constant snow & it is now 6 ft. so the children cannot get out & it's pretty nerve racking. I could scream myself with the noise.

Thank you very much for the coffee & the shrimps—but please don't bother to send anything. I can manage quite well. The coffee was addressed to Germany, I am in Austria. I think Helen's Xmas present of chocs must be in Germany too. I cannot get over this girl's unhappy death. So many of us would have helped her—and the child with no parents—but I shall do my best to try to get it adopted. I never go out now, as I have to keep my leg up whenever I can. I think health is the most wonderful thing. God bless, Mummie.

The death of this pregnant girl and the plight of the new-born baby must have stirred unbearable memories in Muriel that were now long dormant. She would have seen herself in the young girl's place, incapable of giving up her secret, totally swallowed up in her isolation from everyone else in the world. Muriel's heart would have overflowed with sadness.

From time to time she came home on leave and stayed at Boar's Hill and with Stella and her husband. Stella sent her to still more doctors in London and did what she could to make her happy, but these visits were strained and sometimes painful. Like colonials back in the Old Country Muriel was out of touch; she felt unneeded and in the way, and she could not always subdue her jealousy. The stability in both Stella's and Alfred's lives seemed to her to be directed at herself like an accusation. She mistook content for complacency and viewed it with contempt.

Stella darling, Thank you so much for your nice Xmas card. I didn't know you were getting me a stove, as you thought it impossible. It might have induced me to stay in England. I never could stick the cold. Everything congeals inside me. I developed chilblains on my unfortunate feet. Lots of snow here & I have an easier time this year, lovely & warm, also a present of an electric hot water bottle which I don't really need here. They all think it's a miracle that I'm still here. All love to you both, M.

Stella darling, Two letters from Helen & one from you together. I've had a few ups & downs. The doctor isn't satisfied, he says I'm a problem. I cannot walk properly in spite of rest, so I had a beastly minor op on my spine. They stick needles in & draw off a specimen of fluid—3 needles jammed in. I never want to have it again. It isn't really my leg, it's my hip doesn't work—what a muddle life is. I never thought all this nonsense would happen to me. If only I can get fit for the journey to U.K. Love sweet Stella, M.

My darling Stella, That lovely parcel arrived so sweet and thoughtful as always. But I feel you have given me your own lovely shawl. The nurses say I look like a queen in it. I start my tests tomorrow week. If there is anything they will send me to Hamburg Hospital. But I have decided I won't have an op. again. I've had one big one & couldn't face another. Do write as often as you can. It's the only thing to look forward to. They won't start X-raying until I am stronger in case I start bleeding. A surgeon came yesterday to examine me. He is determined to find out everything. I'm so grateful I've got you who will understand everything. No, darling, don't think of coming out. I am in a safe place & well looked after & everything is up to date. But I am still weak. I have had a bad summer really. Life seems such a muddle to me. All my love sweet Stella, M.

Muriel was iller than she knew. As soon as she was strong enough to travel Stella flew out in August 1951 and brought her back to England for good.

She spent some time in a nursing home and then joined Alfred at Boar's Hill. Earlier that year Alfred's sister had died. He was now looking after himself and was glad of Muriel's company, but she had never liked the house; it was not her own and she felt out of place there. Stella and her husband decided to establish Muriel—with Alfred—in a little house in Graham Terrace in London. They arranged a deed of covenant in her name and explained to her that with a home and an income of her own she would now be financially secure for the rest of her life. She was to have no more worries.

Stella redecorated the new house, choosing carpets and curtains in Muriel's favourite colours; she got Muriel's own furniture out of store and took infinite trouble with all the fittings. It was a labour of love; it meant a great deal to Stella to be in a position to give her mother this charming house and a worry-free old age. When all was done she engaged a daily woman and filled the house with flowers.

Muriel came up to London to see her new home. Stella took her to lunch in a restaurant and then together they drove to Graham Terrace. For weeks Stella had been labouring with workmen and late deliveries and now at last the stage was set. As she put the key in the door she had the same thrill as at a first night in the theatre. Muriel followed her in.

They went from room to room in silence, Muriel peering into corners and opening cupboards. But she made no comment. And then, the tour of inspection over, they stood face to face in the drawing-room. Muriel said: 'How on earth shall I get the dustbin up into the street?'

She had never been able to bend with the wind. Now she saw herself as an object of charity. Everywhere she looked her eyes met with details of Stella's thoughtfulness: gladioli and carnations were Muriel's favourite flowers, so there was a huge vase of each in the room in which she was standing; a box of her favourite chocolates was over there on a table; upstairs in her bedroom she had noticed a bottle of mineral water and an ashtray and matches by the bed—Stella did not smoke, Muriel did. And the Stella who had done all this, who was now looking at her awaiting a word of recognition, was not Muriel's 'son' Sam, it was the now established married Stella who no longer had need of her mother. Muriel's pride reeled.

With Alfred and his old dog she moved in.

The dog was the first to go, and after a few years Alfred became unexpectedly ill and died rather suddenly. Muriel was stunned, and, as sometimes happens to people who have side-stepped the violence of their true self, outraged that he had left her.

Shortly before Christmas in 1959 she went into hospital for a series of tests. On the day that she came out Stella rang me. The result of the tests was inoperable cancer.

Chapter Twelve

WHEN STELLA told me that Muriel had only six months to live I had lately come to the end of two years' treatment by hypnosis and was feeling, in a way, more perilous than at any time during this painful period. That is to say, with all my defences stripped away I never knew from one moment to the next what was going to happen to me; I would find myself suddenly shaking all over, or in tears, or, worst of all, with the feeling that I was about to utterly dissolve in some mysterious fashion yet to be demonstrated. I never knew when this unrelated panic would overcome me. On the other hand, I knew with absolute conviction that as time went on and I steadied, my life would no longer be conducted from behind a wall of nerves. I no longer vomited or took pills of any sort; I ate normally and had put on over a stone in weight; my figure now went in and out and even the shape of my legs had changed.

There had never been a time in my life when I had not felt smothered, in some curious way, by an incubus from which I couldn't extricate myself. I couldn't get outside it. I always felt ill, and also vaguely frightened, often very frightened, about nothing in particular. This irrational fear had often puzzled me. I believed myself to have been born with a singularly happy temperament; making friends had never been a difficulty, on the contrary, I had always found people absorbingly interesting; I was incurably optimistic. Why, then, was I desperate? I never thought about killing myself, but I couldn't conceive how anyone managed to live their life through to its natural conclusion, the sheer weight of unhappiness being what it was. I had known for a long time that I couldn't right myself, that I needed help, but I hadn't known where to find it.

I was nearly forty when a friend told me of a doctor who treated by hypnosis. After five minutes in his room I knew that at last I had found the man who could help me, and it was this conviction, which never wavered, that had carried me through the ordeal of the next two years. I was not an easy patient: I couldn't talk about myself. Instead of taking the official chair for the patient, placed at the side of the doctor's desk, I used to make for a chair on the far side of the large room and we talked across the space. China tea was always brought in and we drank it before I lay on the couch. I was there for exactly an hour once a week and the time flew. We talked about his family and his other patients—nameless—because it was part of the therapy. It was also part of the therapy that I should talk about myself, but I couldn't do this and he never pressed me. But he told me more than once that other patients were often violent, screaming, sobbing, hitting the couch and generally throwing themselves about. This was clearly an invitation to do the same, but impoliteness on such a scale was impossible for me. Antie's little girls knew how to behave. Alone at home it was a different matter; as time went on I re-learnt how to cry, but I couldn't even tell him this.

I had been going for nearly a year when, seated on a bus that was curling round Hyde Park Corner, something happened to me. Suddenly, without warning or preliminaries, I was miraculously freed from the constricting interior fetters beneath which I had spent the whole of my life. I had stepped outside them. It was like suddenly standing naked and joyful in warm sunlight. This condition lasted for two or three seconds only, and then I was back within the fetters. But this didn't matter. I knew that the time was coming when I should be out in that clear brightness for good: that that was what feeling well was like. It was a revelation. When I told the doctor about this experience he said, 'You're going to be one of my great successes!' He had often told me that when the treatment was over I should never again, no matter what the circumstances of my future life, sink back into the black pit from which he was helping me to escape.

And so it has proved. After two years he knew fewer details about my life than any casual friend. But he seemed to know me, and he made me well. He gave me a second life.

He was a young man, thirty-six when I went to him, small, with

clever, nearly black eyes in a white unlined face, and the smile of a
healthy boy. He was self reliant and experimental. When he married
his tall wife he had fifty pounds in the bank, and her wardrobe
consisted of two jerseys and two skirts. He was brilliant and very
likeable.

When the treatment was over I went to see him and told him
that I meant to sit with my mother through the next six months.
He was not pleased.

'You don't have to, you know,' he said.

But in this he was wrong. I did have to.

Muriel and I had only met briefly once or twice since Stella's
wedding just after the war, and then only when we had to. I was
living in Sloane Street at this time, about fifteen minutes walk
from Muriel's house, but I never went to see her. Since Alfred's
death a companion had been living with her, a woman whom they
had got to know in Devonshire. At that time this woman and her
husband had been proprietors of a hotel in Bovey Tracy. The
husband had died, his death more or less coinciding with Alfred's
death, leaving the two widows alone, and Muriel had written to her
friend offering a home in exchange for housekeeping and light
cooking duties. Since her arrival Muriel's health had deteriorated
rapidly.

The companion was highly organized and seemed fond of Muriel,
but I always found her a rather sinister figure. Muriel had now been
in Graham Terrace for some years and had lost interest in the house,
also the garden, which Stella had planted for her with loving care.
Knowing that Muriel picked every flower at once Stella had put in
heavily scented, old-fashioned roses, Albertine and Ena Harkness,
Zephyrine Drouaut and Madame Hardy. And she had arranged for
a gardener to go in twice a year, in spring and autumn, to do the
heavy work. But from the start Muriel never went into the garden,
and Alfred, whose horticultural interest lay in tidy edges and dead-
heading, was not inspired to labour alone.

In the house, too, everything was shabby and sterile; the handle
of a broken ornament still lay within the bowl awaiting glue; the
stuffing of the chairs lolloped; Alfred's old dog had peed all over
the carpets; anything of value had been sold long ago. Some houses
gain from fadedness; the life in here, you feel, has been so rich in

incident, emotional and intellectual, that time or available cash spent on tidying or smartening up could only be at the expense of the greater riches. Muriel's house was not like this, it had simply deteriorated. It was tidy, too tidy—the companion saw to that—with no books or papers lying about; there were no books in the house, no newly received postcards stuck up on the mantelpiece; there was nothing to suggest contact with the world outside. In spite of the flowers that came every week from a florist—Muriel had always said she couldn't live without flowers and Stella had placed an order with a florist—in here you felt enclosed in psychological mustiness. It was a lair. Muriel's own atmosphere, which she created wherever she went, was even thicker here than it had been in Castelnau. Added to this, the companion threw off quite an atmosphere of her own. She had been an alcoholic and had stopped drinking purely by the force of her own will power, which now made itself felt as something under immense pressure straining for release. This heroic achievement of teetotalism was not easy for Muriel to accept, and on mischievous days she would tempt her friend: 'Just one little glass won't do you any harm . . .' But to no avail. This stoical woman had been nurse, cook, housekeeper and companion to Muriel since Alfred died, but it was an uneasy association; Muriel resented her deep dependence on her friend.

After Muriel's death, in a gesture of gratitude to this companion, Stella and her husband gave her the free use of the house for the next six months to give her time to reassemble her life. When she finally left she secretly took away with her the tied-up bundle of Roger's letters. When she herself died a few years later—she was burnt to death in her bed—her grown-up son sent the letters to Stella. Neither Muriel's nor Roger's names appear in any of them, so the son must have known whose letters they were, and that his mother had taken them, possibly with notions of future blackmail. She once wrote to Stella asking for a hundred pounds, and Stella, not knowing about the letters, sent it. Like Roger before her, she was a good touch.

In appearance Muriel had changed. She was now smaller, thinner and round shouldered; she no longer wore a corset because any constriction hurt her, and her legs were puffy from a heart condition and vein disorders. Her face had coarsened and her strong dark hair was now pepper-and-salt with white, though just as thick. She had lost all pleasure in clothes and wore loose old-lady things for comfort. Only her hands, ineradicably elegant, gave a hint of former times, although her nails were no longer immaculate. She still marked in her eyebrows with a black pencil. Her eyebrows had always been one of her secret shames; they were thin and scattered untidily. We had never seen her pencil them in, but the lines were always there. At night when she cleaned her face, she did so above and below the precious lines, leaving them undisturbed.

At first I went to sit with her in the morning or the afternoon, but when she got worse I spent most of the day there, only leaving like an office worker for a lunch hour. Sometimes the companion would offer me a sandwich and a cup of coffee, but I always made an excuse. I felt her to be slightly mad and also vindictive, and I was still not firm enough in myself to be able to sit in the kitchen with her and swallow food.

The first time I went to see Muriel I had stood on the doorstep for some time, unable to put my finger on the doorbell. I had felt panic welling up inside, the old familiar panic that I had been learning to subdue. It was one thing, in her absence, to tell myself I was no longer afraid of her; it was quite another thing to be voluntarily about to step into her presence, and I was not at all sure that I could do it. Was the doctor right, after all? He had said that I didn't have to.

What I had not reckoned on was an amazing truth which I understood on the instant of seeing Muriel again: she was more afraid of me than I was of her. It seemed an impossibility, the purest folly, a concept that had never crossed my mind. Yet it was so, and my terrors vanished. On this first visit I stood looking at her as she grappled for composure, a sick and pathetic old woman, and felt nothing but compassion. After that it was simple. We quickly became accustomed to the other's new self: I had not come to persecute her, and she was not going to shower me with guilt.

She seemed not to know that she was dying. She never asked me why I had come back into her life, and she never once talked about death. I have no idea if she believed in an after life or not. Nor did she know she had cancer. In spite of her aversion to reality I had decided to answer truthfully any questions she might put to me.

If she asked me if she was dying, I reasoned, it would be because she wanted to approach in a mature fashion the last experience of life: death. And if I told her the truth and she found it too much for her she would magic it away and be as before. But she asked no questions.

She had become totally self absorbed like an unenquiring child. She was glad to see me but she never asked me about myself, the details of my life, or what I had done during the long years of our estrangement. This was not out of tact or delicacy but simply because only matters directly concerning herself came into her head. She had forgotten Helen as though she had never existed.

After the war Helen had settled in Los Angeles, and then, after the failure of her marriage to the Hungarian, in New York. Soon after she got to New York she formed another romantic attachment which lasted a few years, but it was not a happy affair.

Helen had a business-like kind of brain; unlike Stella and me she was good with figures and had a shrewd commercial eye. She was interested in advertising and money matters in general. You could imagine her running an agency, or being some big-shot's personal representative. She wore rather tailored clothes and had a flair for guessing the next turn in women's fashion. With her secretarial training behind her and her special eye she might have made a good career in business. She sometimes talked of taking a course in business management, but the initial dynamo to get her started was lacking and it came to nothing. Her heart was not in it.

She had never broken free of the twin-ship. As time went on she took to spending three months of every year with Stella and her husband in England, and the other nine months came to be periods that she simply filled in, back in New York, before taking her place once more at Stella's side. She seemed very American to us, and she told us that she had tried to be American; she had tried to be all sorts of people both real and invented. She often talked in this dissociated way. She would say did we think a certain attitude of mind suited her. She was still without a real identity and kept trying out, as it were, different shapes and sizes. She never complained or said she was unhappy, and her enthusiasm and capacity for enjoyment were still those of a child. But there was something dismaying, even alarming, in her formlessness.

Once, alone with Stella, I said, 'I think Helen may kill herself.' Stella replied, 'So do I.' We were both shocked by this brief conversation. At the time it took place we were sitting side by side in Stella's car in a traffic jam outside Oxford. Neither of us could explain why we felt so vividly that Helen had no future. Exactly a year later she wrote to tell us that her right foot had become paralysed. It was the beginning of lateral sclerosis. For the next two years she consulted doctors in America, Switzerland, Germany, France and England, and finally, when she could no longer manage alone, Stella and her husband took her in to live with them, to be nursed in their house, for the last three and a half years of her life. Helen had come full circle; she was now in the only place she had ever wanted to be: with her twin.

She became a different person, fulfilled, rather beautiful, euphorically happy. First from a sofa and then from her bed she was the focal centre of Stella's household. Stella, who had never found it easy to accept the inevitable, now rearranged her life and took the most devoted and imaginative care of her twin. A specially designed extension was built on to the house so that she could be wheeled into the garden and generally mix more easily with visitors. Her room, from which she held court, was filled with exotic plants, ornamental birds in large cages—Stella had aviaries in the garden—and eastern rugs and drapings; instead of a sick room it was like entering Aladdin's cave. Until now Helen had never found it easy to make friends, but the cheerful dying gave affirmation to the health of the living, and visitors now spent happy hours sitting with her in her fairy-tale setting telling her their secrets. Helen's own happiness was reflected in her face; she was radiant.

During these anguished years Muriel closed her mind to the gravity of Helen's condition. She neither asked after her nor sent messages, and up until the day she died Helen waited in vain for a word of love.

I have never fully understood Muriel's attitude at this time. She had always been jealous that Helen was Stella's twin, and when Helen finally moved into Stella's house she was very jealous indeed. Was she not also ill, all alone in Graham Terrace? But this hardly seems to explain such prolonged and deliberate cruelty. On the day that Helen died Stella got someone to telephone the news to Muriel.

Later, the companion told us that Muriel was intractable and cross throughout the day, refusing to eat. And from that day she never mentioned Helen again.

Muriel had persistently refused to go into hospital or to have nurses. For the first few weeks after she was bedridden, the companion gave her blanket baths and attended to her bedpans. From the first I had made it clear that I would sit with her unstintingly but under no circumstances would I nurse her. As it turned out, this arrangement worked well. With me she was as good as gold—'I've got my baby back'—always glad to see me and often believed me to be there when I was not. To cheer her up the companion would say, 'Diana will be here at two', and Muriel would contradict her, 'She's been here all the morning, sitting in the window, reading.'

She liked me to read aloud; we read *Oliver Twist*, *The Warden*, *A Christmas Carol*—at Christmas—*The Custom of the Country*, two Raymond Chandler's and a Margery Allingham. When she dozed off I went on reading, and when she came back, from dozing or from that other drugged state that seemed so far away, she always asked me to fill in the bits she'd missed. She was like a child with its nanny, knowing it wouldn't be scolded, and relieved to find nanny still sitting there.

Sometimes the pain was excruciating, and when the drugs were increased she suffered in a different way that seemed hardly any better. When she was drugged she was mostly in a sleep that wasn't like sleep, not even nightmare sleep or real unconsciousness. Once, I arrived in the morning when she was coming out of this state; she was in great distress, waving her arms about trying to shield her face.

'Get her out of here,' she was muttering thickly, 'I won't have her in here. Shut the cupboards . . . lock them . . . and the door . . . Get her out . . .'

I tried to comfort her. What was the matter, I asked her. I tried to take her hands, but she kept putting them up in front of her face. I told her she was coming out of a bad dream and she kept repeating that it wasn't a dream. It took a long time to make any sense of what she was saying.

During the night, it seemed, the Mother Superior from the convent in Trieste had been standing at the foot of the bed looking down at her. This was the nun who had told Muriel she would cry on leaving the convent in the first war. I couldn't understand why she was unwelcome now.

'But weren't you pleased to see her?' I said. 'You always said she was a wonderful woman.'

'I won't have her in here,' Muriel kept muttering, 'she's not to come here . . .'

'Did she speak or did she just stand there? I wish she'd come back while I'm here,' I said.

'It's not a joke,' Muriel said. 'I won't have it. I'll lock the door tonight. I'll bolt the windows.'

She claimed that the Mother Superior came two nights running and simply stood at the end of her bed looking at her. I was curious to know what had passed between them, all those years ago, that now made the Mother Superior someone to be feared.

'Did she try to convert you when you were weak and ill? Did you tell her about Uncle and us? Did she think you were flirting with the Duke?'

But she wouldn't tell me, and I had the distinct impression that I was asking the wrong questions.

The first temporary nurse was brought into the house when Muriel was too ill to notice, and after that they came and went as the weeks slowly passed. Sometimes Muriel took a fancy to one of these nurses, but on the whole she was hostile with them; she saw them as enemies, counting her drinks and watching the level in the bottle. She was now allowed to drink what she liked, but drinking had never been a pleasure to her, and a drink taken openly, in company, was a disturbance of the norm.

On the day that she went into a coma Stella was in London and had gone to see her. I had stayed at home that morning knowing Stella to be there. The doctor arrived.

'I have something in the car I could give her,' he said, 'to ease her on her way. That is, if you would like me to do this. She would not come out of the coma.'

Stella and I both knew that Muriel would die any day now. For several weeks she had had day and night nurses and been in great distress; mostly she was barely conscious, and when the drugs wore off she was in terrible pain. In this way she was never free from pain or distress, or from both of these states simultaneously.

'No,' Stella said, 'and I know my sister would agree with me.'

I did agree, and I have often thought about it since. How did we justify the withholding of permanent release to someone in this desperate situation which, it seemed, could only get worse? We didn't try to justify it. Stella couldn't bring herself to end Muriel's life, and had I been there I would have felt the same, although I question if I would today. As it turned out, she lived for another three weeks during which time she had a remission, no more pain—it simply vanished—and consequently no more drugs. During those last three weeks it could almost be said that she enjoyed herself.

Our days were different now. She was still like a child, but now she was a playful child. She liked me to peel a pear for her and feed her with it although she could have fed herself. She took a renewed interest in her flowers and wanted her hair brushed several times a day. She enjoyed the opening of Stella's constant stream of presents and their surprise contents, like so many Christmas stockings.

'Stella's been very good to me,' she said dreamily, one day, 'she's always looked after me. She was so lovely as a child, so loving and generous . . .'

In these last months Muriel's love for Stella had subtly changed. She seemed not to mind her absence. It was my company that she now enjoyed, in the comfort and security of Stella's unceasing generosity. The fact that Stella was seldom able to come to London worked in Muriel's favour. The hoydenish, intractable Stella of Muriel's memory no longer existed, but Stella the loved one who would never desert her mother, now talked with her nightly on the telephone and was evident in every aspect of Muriel's fading life. Stella had become the chariot in which she rested.

Two days before she died Muriel suddenly said to me: 'Why did you hate me so?'

We looked at each other. This was perhaps the first intimate question she had ever asked me. I was sitting close to the bed. She was relaxed and at peace, the expression on her shrunken face gentle and trusting, and it came to me with a shock that I had never before seen her like this, exposed and unafraid: for the first time she had opened the door to her true self and was bidding me enter. The thought came to me that this was the way she would have looked at Roger after they made love, and I felt a wave of gratitude for this unique moment between us. I bunched myself up in the chair. Now that she had asked me this searching question I urgently wanted to tell her, to make her see. But how was I to do this? How to explain, in a word or two, turbulence on such a deep level? Besides, there was the drink. Without the drink everything would have been different, but this was something that she had never been able to admit to, and now it was too late. We gazed at each other as she waited for my answer.

'You were so—untrue,' I said slowly.

It was a feeble answer, but I couldn't think of a better one, and as soon as I started to speak I knew I had lost her. Her face changed at once. The door snapped shut; the defences were up.

'But it wasn't my fault!' she cried. 'What else could I have done? I wanted to tell you but he wouldn't let me. He wouldn't let me!'

I should have known she would misunderstand, yet for one glorious second anything had seemed possible. I patted her hand reassuringly. We were back to square one. I was glad I hadn't brought up the drink.

'It doesn't matter now,' I said. 'It's all long over.'

Later that day I said: 'If you could have your life over again what would you like to have done with it?'

She was not greatly interested. Her eyes moved about as she considered. 'I don't know,' she said vaguely, 'I suppose I would have liked just to be married to Uncle.'

This was so lacking in self knowledge that I said nothing. We were silent for a while and then an idea took hold of her. She brightened and moved her head to one side coquettishly.

'If I could have my life over again,' she said, 'I think I should be . . . a prostitute.'

She was lying there, quite small now, dying, a foolish old woman. I looked at her. Where had all the power gone? It had simply ceased to be; the machinery no longer worked. But the power had been there. With the smallest turn of the screw she might have organized some notable change in the world. Now only the foolishness remained. In a way, she had always been foolish; her lack of intellectual fibre, of mental muscle, was not only due to lack of education, it was a vital flaw in her make-up, and it was this flaw, this incapacity to use her mind, that had finally tipped the scales.

'Of course I'd be very choosy,' she went on in the same skittish tone, 'I wouldn't take anyone . . .'

At two o'clock on the morning of 5 May, 1960, the nurse advised me to go home to get some sleep. Muriel had been unconscious for the last twenty-four hours. 'She'll be all right now for the rest of the night,' the nurse said.

'How can you tell?'

'I don't really know,' the nurse said, 'you get a feeling. I'll ring you if there's any change.'

Just after six she telephoned. 'If you want to see your mother alive you should come now.'

It was too early for taxis. I walked. It was a beautiful pale morning, the streets deserted. So the hour had finally come, the hour when Muriel would be released and Stella and I would enter a state of life that had always seemed unimaginable to us: a state of life in which there was no longer an area in the mind that never slept, an area that kept bursting at the seams with the pressure of her unhappiness, that was always shot through with the guilt-ridden thought, What will the next crisis demand of me? There would be no more of this: an era was ending.

In Cadogan Square the daffodils and tulips were less gaudy at this hour than they would be in the stronger light of noon. As I hurried along a cat scuttled guiltily across the lawn and leapt on to the trunk of a flowering cherry tree; I heard its claws unite with the bark. I wished there had been more joy in Muriel's life, less weeping. The waste of so much precious emotion over the years was like a crime. How could she have allowed it to happen? These thoughts were not new to me, but today, at the ending of it all, they came with exasperating poignancy. She had spent the whole of her life in battles against bogies. Yet even in the days of hating I had known she could not help herself. A psychical blight had settled early in the secret years and done its cruel work. The dice had been loaded from the start.

I was light-headed from lack of sleep. Although Muriel had been off drugs for the last three weeks the whole of the house still reeked of hovering death. I wondered if now, at this instant, she knew she was dying, and if she was frightened. I didn't run but I walked as fast as I could. I got to the house ten minutes too late. She had not known; her heart had simply stopped.

She was cremated at Golders Green Crematorium, and neither Stella nor I went. There was a small chapel attached to Stella's house in the country; here, she said, she would arrange a special service for herself alone. But I can give no explanation of my own callous behaviour, indeed, the thought of it now amazes me. I held views about funerals—barbarous customs, when you're dead you're dead—but I must have known that had Muriel ever thought about it she would not have shared this view. I am at a loss to explain how it came about, how I could be so heartless as to withhold from her this last small act of common decency, but I did. This decision was not in any way a demonstration on my part, of that I am sure. It was barely a decision. The important thing had already happened: Muriel was gone. Gone for ever. The cremation of her body was the merest formality, of no real significance. This is how I saw it, blinkered, thinking only in my head, and now, too late, I wish that I had gone.

Postscript

SOME YEARS before she died Muriel had asked Stella to see that her ashes were scattered at sea. This was not because she had any feeling for the sea—it always made her ill—but simply because Roger had died at Southsea. Muriel wanted her ashes scattered as near as possible to the Queen's Hotel, and Stella was determined to carry out her wishes.

On the telephone we discussed how to do it. It seemed unlikely that pleasure boats, rowing or motor, would be available in May, and I couldn't remember the coastline of Southsea, how far the pier reached out into the sea, even if there was a pier. We decided to take the ashes to Southsea by train, together, and to do the best that we could when we got there.

We met at the station on a brilliantly sunny day at noon. Stella and I were not used to each other as grown-up people. Our chosen ways of life were so different that although I sometimes went to stay for short visits we rarely met, and when we did we were never alone. For the last six months we had talked constantly over the telephone, between us directing the unhappy course of events at Graham Terrace, but during that time we had seldom come face to face. This meeting, then, had a double significance: we were to scatter Muriel's ashes and also spend some hours uniquely alone together.

It was typical that I should arrive first, in plenty of time, and that Stella should saunter along the platform as the guard was banging the doors shut. Tall and rangey, she was better looking than Muriel had ever been, more strictly handsome, and her stylishness was different: she looked very expensive. We caught sight of each other at the same instant and a thread of conspiracy passed between us: an excursion like this, just the two of us, was a bit of a lark; we were

179

young again, playing truant. We had thought we were meeting simply to do a duty, but something unexpected had changed the quality of our outing; neither of us had foreseen this leap of pleasure at the sight of the other and, for a moment, we were confused.

I had already found an empty carriage. We got into it. Stella had the urn containing the ashes, now wrapped in tissue paper, at the bottom of a bucket-shaped leather bag. I had brought a small basket with sandwiches and a sizeable flask of cherry brandy—given by Stella at Christmas—for a picnic on the train. We put the basket and the bucket-bag on the luggage rack and settled down facing each other. After a few seconds the train pulled out of the station.

We kept looking at each other, smiling foolishly. There was, between us, a shyness and a jealously critical third eye, ready to seize on any betrayal of early memory. Somewhere mixed up in the fashionable woman opposite me was my childhood sister.

'We'd better take a look at it,' I said at last.

I got the bucket-bag down from the rack, took out the heavy tissue paper parcel from the bottom, unwrapped it and held the dark urn in my hands. I studied it. This was the first crematorium urn I had seen. It was the colour of stale chocolate, about six inches high, without handles, and it was cold to the touch.

'Well,' I said, 'there we are.'

Stella and I looked at each other in silence. We had stopped smiling. Neither of us could find words to express the enormity of the thing. It was inconceivable that inside this object in my hand there was a little grey powder, and that that pinch of powder was all that remained of the figure who had affected both our lives so deeply. I ran my finger round the top of the urn.

'It's sealed. It doesn't open,' I said. 'There won't be any scattering.'

'We'll just drop it in the sea then,' Stella said, 'that'll be the same.'

I wrapped up the urn in the paper, put it back in the bucket-bag and put the bag back on the rack. I sat down again, but it was no good. I couldn't sit still.

'Let's have lunch,' I said.

I got up again and brought down my basket from the rack. I

took out two glasses and filled them with the lovely red liquid from the flask. I handed a glass to Stella and held up my own.

'We'll drink to her,' Stella said, and as she said this our eyes went up to the rack.

We took a long pull at the cherry brandy and put our glasses on the ledge below the window. I undid the packet of sandwiches.

The train rattled along. The sun was illuminating the countryside in purist pale gold, but even Stella, the country lover, only managed to look out of the window from time to time. We kept watching each other uneasily. We might have been waiting for a bomb to go off. At last I said: 'I can't stand it up there.'

I took the bucket-bag down and placed it on the seat beside Stella.

'It's silly,' I said, 'when one knows it's not the real ashes. And even if it were . . . Anyway, it's just an amalgam of—well, of quantities of other ashes.'

At Southsea we inquired about trains going back, and then we got into a taxi and told the driver to take us to the sea.

There was a pier: its end, well out into the sea, was roofed over and its sides were constructed of sheet glass, furthermore, the entrance to it was padlocked. It was useless for our purpose.

The tide was half-way up the deserted shingle beach, and the waves were regular and gentle. It was a perfect spring day at the seaside, and there wasn't a boat in sight.

'We've got plenty of time,' Stella said, 'we'll go down on to the beach and sit down and work out what to do.'

It was while we were making our way towards the beach that we saw a sort of mini-pier that the proper pier had masked from our view. It was really a boat-landing, not stretching out to sea as far as one would have wished, but its end was in deepish water. And it was accessible.

'Supposing,' I said, 'we dropped it over the end and then the tide went out and left it stranded on the beach . . .'

'I don't think it will,' Stella said firmly, 'and, anyway, there's nowhere else. Look for yourself.'

As we walked the length of the boat-landing the air got fresher. We reached the end and looked about us. We felt very conspicuous. What would a watching person, a policeman, perhaps, imagine we were up to?

'Let's get it over quickly,' Stella said.

I took the parcel out of the bag, peeled off the paper and held out the urn. 'I think she would like you to be the one to actually do it,' I said.

Stella took the urn and held it in her hands. We both looked round again. There seemed to be nobody about.

'Hurry up,' I said, and then, as Stella went on holding it, 'Oh, give it to me!'

I took it from her and held my arm out straight—it seemed unsuitable to throw—and then I opened my hand.

The heavy urn fell in a straight line down into the sea. It hit the water and went down and down and the water closed over it. Stella and I gazed transfixed at the spot where it had disappeared, and then, suddenly, with a great *whoosh*, it came up from the deep, high up into the air in front of us, almost at face level.

My heart thumped. We watched, aghast. It seemed to be suspended in the air at its highest peak, mocking us, and then it plunged once more, barely disappeared, and then settled itself with absolute resolution to ride the surface, perkily bobbing on the ocean swell. I was the first to speak.

'We've got to go.'

But we didn't go, entirely.

'It's silly to come all this way and not enjoy the sea,' Stella said, 'we'll lie on the beach in the sun for a bit. We've done our best. It'll get washed out to sea. After all, that's what she wanted.'

We walked quite a long way past the real pier before finding a way down on to the shingle. I was never a lover of beach life, nor of sun bathing, but to Stella it was a perpetual craving. She now lay full length on her back and gave herself up to the sunbather's holy torpor.

We must have been there for half an hour, not speaking. I was sitting up, picking up stones and dropping them, bored and uncomfortable. I looked out to sea. And then I saw it.

'Look!' I cried. 'Just open your eyes and look!'

Just a few yards out to sea, coming sideways towards us, drifting merrily on the current, was Muriel's urn. In a few seconds it would be directly in front of us.

'She's doing it on purpose!' I yelled.

182

We rushed down to the water's edge and stood waiting for the confrontation, and when it came I swear the urn was halted in its course for several seconds before it floated on. I grabbed hold of Stella's arm.

'This time we've really got to go,' I said.

We scrambled up the shingle, heading in the direction of the station. We didn't look back.